MUNCHING ON THE SUN

A NOVEL

mark paul oleksiw

Book design by Caroline Teagle Johnson

ISBN: 978-1-775-11112-2 (paperback)
978-1-775-11113-9 (eBook)

MUNCHING ON THE SUN

To those whose words and beliefs inspire,
Lukas is truly your creation.

chapter one

Professor Phillip Solterre reclined back in his leather office chair. Paper of various lengths and colors littered his undersized desk. It was easy to imagine childlike elves had run rampant across his office, tossing paper planes. In the quiet clutter, the aging teacher stared at the clock atop his office door's frame. It was 1 a.m. According to the smattering of fellow teachers who viewed it, the season finale production of *Frankenstein* had gone well. His thirty-five years of experience made him cynical, though. Recalling every missed line and cue, he wondered how many more performances he could tolerate. There was so much more knowledge he could share with them, all past success and failures, representing lessons learned. *They should have practiced more.* His will to achieve perfection used to be enough. Now fatigue and the years, marked by each wrinkle in his skin and ache in his bones, made him pray for survival. Retirement would call for him in a year.

Perched compellingly upon the rightmost corner of his desk was the picture of his wife and two daughters taken during simpler times. Back then his wife would listen to him venting his frustrations until he could speak no more. With a soft, calm voice, she would remind him that the goal was not perfection but to get the best performance out of each student. Nurturing their love of the theater was his reward. As he reached across his desk and stroked her two-dimensional cheek, his heart grew heavy. He wondered what she was thinking tonight, if at all. It had been over a year since, with great heartbreak, he decided to place her. A vulgar disease had chipped away at her mind. It simultaneously ate his soul for nourishment.

Echoes of a distant voice soon overpowered the silence around him. Professor Solterre could tell the voice was coming from the supposedly empty theater. *Drunken students vandalizing school property again*, he thought. Not the first time someone had wandered into the theater with ill intent on their mind. He reached for the phone on his desk, knowing the three-digit direct line to campus security by heart. *Damn fools.* They would show up, decide not to deal with it, and eventually call the police. More paperwork would result. Just what he needed. He managed a dozen or so would be actors and actresses for the last few months. Young, arrogant, and blessed with enormous promise—if he could handle these divas, he could handle a bunch of drunks.

Feet aching in his black Rockport shoes, he made his way out of his office. He felt he had been on his feet forever. The top button of his dress shirt was open. The tie he wore hung dejectedly to one side, swaying with each step. He pulled up his trousers, adjusted his small silver-rimmed glasses, and strode down the corridor to the theater audience entrance. The closer he got, the clearer the voice became, until it seemed to pull him forward. Opening the door, he saw one figure pacing the stage as he spoke, in and out of the faint spotlight cast by the one emergency light. Sliding along the back row of chairs, cloaked by the darkness, he gazed upon the performance acted out on the stage below.

"I was benevolent and good; misery made me a fiend. Make me happy, and I shall again be virtuous."

The young man kneeled upon the stage as if digesting the very words he uttered. His hair, murky brown with an amber hint, appeared uncombed. His eyes were as colorless as the shadows. The red streaks on his face glistened under the one stuttering light. Resting on the knees of torn jeans, his hands clenched tightly, almost as though they were choking a pebble. A youthful face defiantly rose to face the empty seats.

"This is my final performance, my friends. Love is all I asked. I offered my love protection. Freedom from fear. Sacrificing my soul, I was betrayed. Not by her but my ego. Yes, betrayed by my wants and desires. I see that now. In the teardrops that fell before me, I saw the reflection of the truth. All I need now is not applause, just the quiet surrender to my sin. And to be slaughtered for forgiveness."

The young man looked up, his face staring into the distance. The room filled with applause only he could hear. As the blood dripped from his damaged cheek, his face winced in pain. The tired somber eyes searched the emptiness of the theater for acknowledgment of his honesty. With humbleness, he rose to his feet and bowed before the infinite quiet.

From his perch high up above, Professor Solterre became lost in both time and space. The actor on stage bore little resemblance to anyone in his cast. The first lines uttered were from the play he directed. The remaining dialogue came from a place he had never visited. The performance went beyond any acting displayed within his class. "Quite a performance, dear sir." The professor applauded, assuming he had just witnessed an audition. "Were you hoping to audition for a part? Perhaps next year?"

"No, I am not here to audition. Far from it."

"You could have fooled me. My own actors could not have said those lines with more conviction."

"I have fooled many people, I suppose. Maybe it is true that I am a pretty good actor." He laughed, and a trickle of blood slid to his top lip. His hand quickly swiped it aside, streaking the skin beneath his nose further.

"Ah, well you asked for forgiveness. Many have mistaken my theater for a church before. None at quite so late an hour."

"I know there are two chapels on campus. I don't think I could mistake this for one. I'm not that drunk. But, um, is not God the ultimate director?"

"Speak for yourself, young man. I am quite the director in my right." Professor Solterre enjoyed the repartee. "I also have a pittance of a budget, unlike the man upstairs."

"The Lord had to work with many divas in his day, even with his unlimited resources. It can't be so easy." A hint of laughter followed.

"I was not referring to the Lord about the budget. I was referring to the Dean." The older man laughed at his attempt at academia humor while shaking his head like a gleeful child.

The young actor did not respond. He swayed slightly and toppled forward before balancing himself. To the professor's horror, grim reality stepped out from the curtain of reason to make its presence known. The blood on the young man's face was quite real, made visible as the actor stepped from shadows and into the light. Before he could react further, the young man slumped to his knees again, his sobs echoing through the theater.

"Dear God," the professor muttered to himself as he emerged from the dimness of the back row to search for the nearest aisle. "Young man! Young man! I am going to call an ambulance."

The young man ignored the words or seemed to initially. Just as suddenly, his head lifted and his squinting eyes searched the theater for the source of the voice. When he saw Professor Solterre coming down the aisle, he extended his hands together before pleading. "I beg you. Please don't call an ambulance. I'm fine."

"You're bleeding."

"I know. Don't call anyone. I didn't come here to hurt you. I promise. I never meant anyone any harm. I'm fine, just a cut." The words came in spurts. "I got dizzy from a fall. I'm fine now."

The professor reached the edge of the stage, within a few feet of the teary-eyed young man. Still a boy in so many ways. "Your face. Were you in a fight? Were you attacked? Perhaps after drinking?" Trying to gain command of the room, he paced to and fro at the bottom of the stage.

"I've been drinking. We could have quite a debate over whether too much or not enough. A tumble was my reward tonight. Karma. A roll down a staircase while chasing a ghost." The young man chuckled, rolling his eyes at the words he just uttered.

"Chasing a ghost! Young men still chase ghosts, I see."

"So you understand?"

"Ghosts in mini-skirts, blouses, tight jeans, what have you."

Slowly, the young man rose, looking at the older man below him. "How did you know? I mean, the part about a girl?"

The older man laughed. "Drunkenness. Bruises. Blood. Talking to oneself. Must be a girl at the center of it."

By now the young man had reached the far end of the stage. His eyes roamed the theater as he turned back, a look of awe mingled with fear on his face. "I understand if you want to call campus security. It's quite late. I shouldn't be here, troubling you after midnight."

"It is late indeed. But you have done me no harm, and I did enjoy your monolog. Please come back to my office so I can get you something to drink and clean you up."

"Maybe I should just leave."

"And chase more ghosts? Ricochet down more stairs and get into more trouble? Please come with me." The professor's voice grew forceful. Nodding, the young man slowly walked to where the older one stood. Professor Solterre extended his hand to the young man, who took it and leaped off the stage, stumbling slightly into a chair in the front row.

"Last time an actor came off the stage so wounded, a president had been shot."

The young man smiled at Professor Solterre. "I didn't think you were so old as to have been there."

Without another word, Professor Solterre led the way back to his office. The young man staggered and stumbled at times, exorcising the demons he ingested with each step. Pushing open his office door, the professor motioned for his guest to sit in the large leather chair behind the desk.

"Would you like something to drink? Something without alcohol in it?"

"Yes," said the young man, pointing to the remnants of coffee, now quite cold and stale, on a dormant burner.

Professor Solterre walked past the coffee pot to a small fridge, pulling out a carton of milk, which he poured into a Styrofoam cup nearby. "Here you go, young man. Milk is better for you."

The young man slurped the milk. His eyes closed, savoring the taste. Upon opening them, a wet cloth appeared before him. "Please," continued the professor, "clean up your face."

"Thanks."

"So, you came in here not wanting to audition. But you know the lines."

"My story is quite long. It wouldn't interest you."

"Well, the line from the play I know. The second verse you recited was something I have never heard of before. Another play?"

"No, sir, it wasn't a quote from any play. Umm . . . it's just me."

"You."

"Yes, I don't think I even remember what I said."

"Well, it was about forgiveness and sin. Love. All the themes are common amongst many works. I just assumed it was from one."

"Maybe. My own, I guess."

Professor Solterre took off his glasses and looked at them before easing them back into place. As he was doing so, the young man reached into his pocket and pulled out a card from his wallet, sliding it across the table.

"Lukas Wunand. Faculty of Business?"

"Yes, sir. That is my name."

"Why are you showing me this? I'm not going to report you. I do not need to know your name."

"Ghosts don't have identification cards. I wanted you to have proof I exist. I can imagine you would not have an easy time explaining my appearance tonight. Especially someone from the business school wandering on your stage and rambling at a crazy hour."

Professor Solterre grinned and extended his hand toward Lukas. "It is my pleasure to meet you. My name is Professor Phillip Solterre."

"The honor is mine, sir. I should be leaving. I must be keeping you from your wife." Lukas pointed to the picture at the corner of the desk.

"My wife lives in a hospital. She has Alzheimer's. It's at the point now where she does not even recognize me." Lukas had slowly risen from his seat, but the professor's words pushed him back down.

"I don't know what to say, sir. I feel for you." Lukas looked around the room, biting his lip.

"You seem very upset, young man. Why?"

"It's wrong. So wrong. To be apart from someone you love.

Someone who does not know you anymore."

"There is no rhyme nor reason for it. Such is life. I am learning to live with it."

Lukas leaned back into the chair with his eyes closed. "Maybe in some ways I wish it was because you had done something wrong. It would explain why you must suffer. You don't seem like someone who deserves it."

"Why, that sounds positively horrible!" Professor Solterre rounded his desk as Lukas opened his eyes to the ceiling. "You seem to think everything has to have cause and effect."

"I never used to think that. Quite the opposite. I've been wrong all these years. I know that for sure now. Her dad was right."

"Right about what?"

"Everything is logical. It happens for a reason. It's pure math. Nothing more."

"I may have been wrong about you, after all, young man. Perhaps I thought you wandered in here looking for a church. The math department is where you need be. Even the physics department."

Lukas swung his head down to face the professor. The cold cloth felt good against his face. The professor reached over to Lukas, taking the cloth away from his face gently to examine the purplish-blue hue on his cheek. "Looks like you just scraped it. You won't need stitches. A bloody mess, however, you will live." He handed Lukas back the cloth and pulled up a nearby rolling chair to sit. "Why are you so cynical? I would guess you're barely twenty. Performing on a stage, all by yourself, after midnight and a business school student on top of it!"

Lukas smirked. "Now, you needn't wonder why I drink." When there was no reaction, he said, "Seriously, sir, I knew I was never alone."

"You knew I was there?"

"Of course. The audience is as much an actor performing as the person on stage. If you can enjoy my performance, I can enjoy yours as well."

"I do not believe anyone ever has accused me of being an actor."

"We all are. We all are." Lukas's head nodded. Each bob of his head seemed to weigh heavier on him. "I am just so tired of my role."

"Son, we just put on *Frankenstein* here for forty-five nights and a handful of day performances. The actors who played the leads grew tired, too. They knew the audience, some who had seen the play for the first time, depended on them." He paused and looked over to Lukas, whose attention was fully in his grasp. "Dependent on them to expose the beauty of the work they were creating on stage."

"The work is just words on paper . . ."

"No. I must interject. The work is a living thing given life, each one different, with every actor's interpretation. What I have learned in my many years—no two performances are ever the same. Sure, I may crave for it, but there is comfort in the mystery of what will happen on any given night."

As he straightened up in the oversized chair, Lukas's shoulders stiffened. He was lost inside its girth; it formed to the physique of the professor. His eyes turned again to the family photo. "Your wife is quite beautiful. It is a shame. I mean, what I said earlier, don't pay attention to it. I'm just bitter. I shouldn't be. It's my fault, no one else."

"Young Lukas, what could lead you here tonight? I remember you mentioning some sin and the need for redemption. Can this sin be so grave as to make you suffer so in self-pity?"

"I'm not expecting you to understand. Tobin—a former friend of mine—was right. The sun is not meant to be eaten by mere mortals."

"I'm sorry. I do not follow."

"When a man dies at your hands, when you create death, love becomes a ghost."

"Create death? Someone died because of you."

"Worse. I caused a man to die."

Professor Solterre's lips practically burst as he choked back the air, smothering the gasp he longed to let escape. Within the dark bowels of Lukas's eyes, a faint light reflected back. He rose up from his desk as Lukas watched, fingers clenching the chair's arms. Walking with purpose to the door, the professor closed it gently. Upon the professor's return, Lukas relaxed back into his seat.

"Lukas, the night is young. Your audience awaits." He reached forward to pat Lukas reassuringly on the back of his hand. "Your tale does not begin or end in one moment or with one act, I suspect. I want to hear about the full play."

chapter two

"Fawn. Umm, Fawn something something, I think. Give me a sec."

"Dude, are you sure about that answer? A lot is riding on it. You know that by now. Don't you?"

Tobin Preston stared patiently down at young Stephen. He cupped both his hands around Stephen's ears and lowered his head to meet him at eye level. Stephen's eyes started to tear ever so slowly, not from the sheer force gripping his ears but from the gravity of the situation. Tobin slowly bent down, never letting his eyes or his fingers stray from his prey.

Speaking softly and menacingly so only Stephen could hear, Tobin said, "Don't look around for help. This is a biggie, and you have to get this on your own or else no points." In a loud growl, he snarled across the room so everyone else could hear. "No help, guys, I am fricken serious. He needs to answer without any assistance."

Stephen sat on the edge of the antique second-hand couch with his fingers caressing the decades-old worn fabric. His right hand found an opening, and he slowly began playing with the stuffing hidden within. As he tried to summon the answer, he stroked it across his fingertip. Suddenly, Tobin's right hand let go of Stephen's ear, instead reaching for an oversized shot glass.

The smell of cheap vodka floated through the air as he brought it carefully to Stephen's face. Soon enough, the shot glass was nudged gently under Stephen's nose, and the smell alone broke his concentration.

With trembling lips, Stephen looked up at Tobin. "Shit, Tobin. Please repeat the question. Please. I want to be sure."

Tobin smiled back with the full confidence of a battle won. Fear now was evident and present in Stephen. Whether the answer was right or not was no longer relevant. Tobin looked across the room at the assembled partygoers. Most had grown silent as the evening progressed. The game itself, a longstanding business faculty tradition, had taken its toll on some. Drunken students sat or lay scattered here and there across the room. Some asleep on the couches, some on the floor. It was indeed a typical Friday night.

The music, which had been playing in the background, suddenly became quiet. The gravity of the situation became evident to all in the room, whether playing or not. Partygoers nibbling on chips and corn puffs in the kitchen crossed the threshold into the living room. Since the vast majority did not participate, this was truly a spectator sport.

Tobin laughed and called out, "Kyle, what was the question again?"

A short curly-haired young man stepped forward, a colorless, label-free bottle swinging in his hand. "The question is —who is the girl that Otter was supposed to meet for a date at Emily Dickinson College?"

Tobin nodded toward Kyle and quickly turned again to Stephen. "Answer now and remember, if you get it wrong, you have to down two shots, back to back."

As one hand dug into the couch and the other shook nervously, Stephen took a deep breath. He forced a smile and opened his mouth.

"Fawn Leibowitz."

Those following the proceedings erupted in either applause or a chorus of boos, depending on whose side they were on. Out of the ruckus of the voices, a shrill whistle broke through. Kyle took his role as arbitrator seriously and demanded silence as he took center stage. "Guys, listen up. That was a two-point question. Ram's team now has twenty-one for the win. Game over."

The tall physique of Ram sprang from a nearby chair. Before his knee injury in college tryouts, Ram had captained his high school football team. Ram was now a fourth-year student in the faculty and had earned the reward of captaining a team during these festivities. His smiling face illuminated his curly black hair and olive complexion. His last team pick in this Friday night ritual, or sort of ritual, had come through for him and put his team over the top. His knee almost buckled as he leaped out of the hard steel chair. He did not mind his knee failing him again— even grimacing in pain on the floor, he would still be a winner.

Tobin looked across the room incredulously as a wall of humanity rushed toward Stephen, who was gently bouncing up and down as the throng of well-wishers reached out to bump fists with him. For a first-year student, this was pure gold.

No longer able to contain the rage that rang like a bell up from his toes to the top of his head, Tobin took two steps forward and grabbed Kyle's pale brown T-shirt at the neckline. Kyle stumbled into Tobin's chest, raising his head up as hot air spewed from Tobin's nostrils. "Who said that was a two-point question? I did not hear you say it. Totally unfair, you asshole! You never said two points."

Kyle pulled himself out of Tobin's grasp and looked at him sternly, his index finger pointing into Tobin's now contorting face. "You know the rules. What I say goes, and I called it right before I read the question."

"You're just jealous because you had to be the ref. Now you're screwing me over. I have to lose to that fat slob over there? No way. This game is not over." He motioned over to Ram, who was celebrating with his oversized arms around the waist of a younger second-year student. For the moment, Ram was oblivious to the commotion Tobin was creating as his lips claimed the victory like a Roman general.

Kyle did not back down. "It is over. You lost." Kyle smiled at him and blew him a kiss as he pushed by Tobin toward the kitchen. Waiting for Kyle to take a few steps, Tobin reached for the shot glass of vodka and tossed it right into Kyle's back. He stood laughing, waiting for Kyle to turn. Kyle, however, continued into the kitchen seemingly oblivious to the desecration that had just taken place. The laughter retreating, Tobin's eyebrows pressed toward the bridge of his nose as though holding his breath. Suddenly, Kyle came racing out of the kitchen and, in two strides, leaped into the air, striking Tobin in the chest and driving him backward onto a small steel chair. With a piercing shriek of twisted metal, the chair collapsed and the two combatants fell to the ground. Bowls of chips, nachos, and cheesies trembled and shook before finally toppling to the floor where the piling of body upon body created a symphony of crunches. Bystanders, whether on one of the two competing teams or not, quickly took sides and joined in the fracas. Some in anger, some in pure rapture and drunkenness, reveling in the sheer chaos of the moment. Lamps on end tables wriggled slowly and teasingly, brushed by people deflecting into them. As was the case with most typical college brawls, within minutes, no one was even aware what caused the fight. It did not take long before the first crash of glass drifted across the room. Those not directly involved in the flourishing anarchy stood in an imaginary perimeter around the combatants.

. . .

Rosemary Cooper raced in from the kitchen in absolute horror. Rosemary's parents had wanted her to have both independence and security of being proximate to school, so they'd rented this old Victorian house for her. She shared the home with two other girls who contributed what they could to the monthly operating expenditures and did most of the cooking and cleaning. Not that there was much cooking that went on in a university student's kitchen. The garbage overflowed with the remains of cheap chicken wings and discarded pizza boxes. More often than not a leftover Hawaiian pizza would survive the week before also ending up in the garbage. All other permutations and combinations of flavors barely survived even the following day. Hawaiian pizza always seemed like the right choice at the time.

Rosemary doubted the sanity of letting her fellow students use her home for their party. She knew the "game" was a clever ruse for a night of drinking and debauchery, but she gave in to her sense of duty to her fellow student body and would now be paying a stiff price. After three years of studies, solid marks, and the admiration of her parents, it would all come crashing down. She would lose the one thing she valued more than anything else: her parents' trust.

She could feel the tears slowly amassing at the borders of her green eyes. Whimpering softly, she covered her narrow lips with her hand as she witnessed the escalating violence, body after body nudging past her—some to watch, others to partake. Unable even to summon a scream, she turned back to the kitchen and looked through the arched frame to the dining room. The dining table had been replaced and moved to make space for beanbag chairs, study desks, and a bookshelf. She could make out two solitary figures sitting in the beanbag chair. A girl with long flowing, curled-brown hair, a black turtleneck, and faded jeans was nestled comfortably in the arms of a male. In an instant Rosemary recognized his face, her heart pulsated, and her mind swelled with wave after wave of hope. It was Lukas.

If anyone could stop the calamity, she surmised, it would be him.

Lukas Wunand, like Rosemary, was beginning his last year of his undergraduate degree in the business faculty. Of average height and build, he had thick brown hair and a handsome, child-like face. His shoulders were broad and supported his long arms. His hands were delicate while his fingers extended majestically— they could easily pass for those of a concert pianist. It was none of these features that drew the curious into the world of Lukas Wunand, however. Beneath the dusky brows and long lashes were the small slits that housed the most bottomless charcoal-colored eyes. Within those eyes swam a mystery. His eyes were the black hole that led to his soul, or so the girls in the faculty believed. Many were willing to take the journey and get close enough to be trapped within, but Lukas would not let anyone get so close. His persona wore invisible sunglasses that reflected light back upon those who dared to gaze. Peripheral to the fortress built around him was a boy of integrity and reliability. A friend of Lukas's felt protected. You could seek shelter within his walls. However, no one dared to enter the basement.

Seeing how peaceful Lukas looked, Rosemary hesitated to wake him. Realizing she had no choice, she got down on both her knees before him as gently as she could. Slowly leaning forward, she cautiously extended her hand to his knee. As she looked up at him, she was met with a broad smile and Lukas's dark eyes watching her. Rosemary took immediate comfort in his gaze as he tilted his head, observing her moves.

"Lukas, they're going to tear this house apart. My parents will kill me." She spoke quickly and breathlessly.

As he sat up, Lukas's right hand tightened his grip on the girl in his lap. He looked beyond her to the chaos ensuing in the background. With a knowing nod, his lips pursed tightly. "Let me guess: the game got out of hand."

"Yes. Do something. I should never have let them convince me." As she was about to continue her rant, his left hand calmly extended over her lips and his eyes fixed upon hers.

"Rosie, relax. It will all work out. Trust me. This is nothing." He could sense her anxiety and continued in a voice barely above a whisper. "Who is it? Tobin?"

"Yes, of course, Tobin. It's always him. It started with him and Kyle. Now Ram and everyone else is involved. They're going to break everything. They already broke a vase."

"Well, if Ram loses it, more than a vase will be broken. Wait here." As he spoke, he extricated his hand from the girl's waist and placed her shoulders and head delicately down. Much to the bewilderment of Rosemary, he managed to accomplish this feat without waking her.

Lukas marched through the kitchen and penetrated the living area with authority. He stood still for an instant as his head swiveled around, surveying the calamity. He seemed to catch the eyes of Tobin, who was entwined in a loveless embrace with Kyle. With a wink of his left eye, Lukas smiled at Tobin, who smiled back and winked in reply. It was the quiet communication of an alliance forming to end the warfare. Only Lukas had such power.

Tobin broke the chaos of the sounds echoing haphazardly around the room. "Everyone stop! I'll let Lukas decide."

Looking up, Kyle released Tobin from his grip. In the background, Ram's voice exploded like thunder in a glass jar. "I'm good with that." Soon the mayhem and destruction that spun out of control within the living room had ended. At the epicenter of the devastation stood Lukas, his face unsmiling and severe as he listened to what had transpired from Kyle.

"So, if I am to summarize. The issue is not whether Stephen got the question right or wrong. The issue is whether or not it was a two-point question."

Kyle protested instantly. "I made damn clear it was a two-pointer. You know the rules, Lukas. For a first year, it's always two points. Shit. It's your rule. You came up with that one."

Lukas grinned briefly in acknowledgment. Such was his legend that as a first year, he had instituted a rule change. His serious glare quickly returned with a broad smile as he looked directly at Tobin. "Tobin, since it's my rule at the heart of this matter, I have a solution to determine who wins the game."

Tobin laughed, stopping abruptly as he realized his misstep. "I'm listening, Lukas. I was there when you made the rule, so it only fits that you should be the final judge."

Ram shook his head. It was obvious he sensed the conspiracy knocking on his door, ready to steal victory from him, but it was useless to protest. He finally succumbed. "I trust you, Lukas. Whatever you say goes."

Lukas nodded in thanks. "So here is how we will resolve this mess. There will be one more question asked and answered."

Stephen protested immediately. "Not another question."

Before he could protest further, Lukas interjected. "You won't be responding, Stephen. It will be me. If I get it right, you win; if I get it wrong, they win." There was a gasp that swept across the room as the last word came out of Lukas's mouth.

Kyle trotted over to pick up the questions now strewn throughout the room. While reaching to assemble them and choose one,

Lukas grabbed his shoulder. "No need, Kyle. Tobin can pick whatever question he wants. He needs to write down the answer and give it to you." Ram shook his head slowly in defeat as Tobin winked at him. Tobin wandered over to the only bookshelf in the room. Studying each title, he grinned as he pulled one out and found a page to his liking. Within seconds, Tobin had scribbled a question down with an answer and shoved it into Kyle's hands for him to read. Kyle looked at the question, back at Tobin and at the question again. He looked up at Lukas as if hoping Lukas would change his mind.

The fear in Kyle's eyes was obvious. "Ask the question." He then looked across the room. "If I mess it up, it's my fault." His head circled the room, and as it rotated by Tobin's smiling face, he smiled back faster than a flash of a camera.

Kyle took the paper in his hand and extended in front of his face as he read it aloud.

What are the last two lines of the poem "The Raven" by Edgar Allen Poe?

As yelps of both protests and delight filled the room, Ram burst out, "Seriously, Tobin. The question is bullshit. Aren't we business students? How is he supposed to know such shit?"

Unable to stifle his joy, Tobin moved toward Lukas, a skip in his step. "Hint. The last word is 'Nevermore.' You know like no one can beat me, nevermore." He laughed at the ludicrous joke he made, then turned to Ram, who stood with a clenched fist and lips pressed tight. "Look, Ram. No one ever said certain things were off limits or not. You agreed. I chose the question, and Lukas must answer."

In the ruckus over the question, no one noticed Lukas standing silently with his head bowed forward. If anyone did, they would assume that Lukas was acting sorrowful in defeat, a rook in the grand design of the game Tobin had played brilliantly to the end.

Relieved that the house had been spared, Rosemary stood in the far corner of the room and studied her friend from afar. The young girl who had slept so soundly within the bosom of Lukas sidled up beside Rosemary. She now recognized the girl as a first-year student named Kirsten.

Kirsten leaned over to Rosemary and whispered. It wasn't as if anyone would hear anyway. "Is Lukas in cahoots with Tobin? Is that what just happened?" She seemed visibly perturbed that the older boy she had spent time with would be party to such a scheme, let alone orchestrate this unjust ending.

Rosemary smiled while she stared intently at Lukas for one more second before turning to the young student. "How long have you known Lukas?"

"Just met him tonight. We were talking on the couch over there about life and stuff. I must have fallen asleep. He seemed like such a nice guy."

Rosemary laughed and gently patted the girl's shoulder. "Don't assume anything with Lukas. Watch and observe," she said as her eyes moved back to the center of the room. The girl shrugged her shoulders, and her eyes fixed on Lukas, his head still bent down as he swayed like a pendulum.

"Poor guy. He looks totally confused," she said.

On one side Rosemary's mouth rose toward her cheek. She repeated, "*Observe.*"

Kyle looked at his watch and finally spoke to Lukas. "Look, Lukas, you can just quit. One line is fine. If you get just one, that is okay."

Tobin protested halfheartedly. "Oh, for Christ's sake. I gave him a word already. Now he needs to say only one line. Why don't I go to the store and get some Pablum for the poor baby?"

He showed his teeth to the audience expecting laughter but got little. Lowering his head to catch Lukas's eye, he placed a hand on his shoulder before stepping back like a conductor about to accept applause.

Hands in his jean pockets, Lukas lifted his head, his teeth biting down hard on his lower lip, and rocked back and forth nervously. The audience was silent as he slowly parted his lips to speak.

"A couple of words seem to ring a bell." He took a heavy breath and stepped forward, closing his eyes. Then just as quickly, his small eyes opened wide, and their blackness filled his face. The coals were stoked, and the room was bright with the flame that instantly appeared around his body. He rotated around, circling the room and casting a personal glance at each who dared to look at him. In a heavy English accent, the words oozed out like blood from an open wound.

"And my soul from out that shadow that lies floating on the floor
Shall be lifted—nevermore!"

Like some great actor uttering the closing verse of a play, he closed his eyes again to breathe in all of the air, leaving each patron of his performance suffocating in their desire for more.

Unsure what they had just witnessed, the room remained silent. Tobin stood stunned off to the side, glaring at Lukas. "You fricken asshole. You screwed me over. You set me up," he yelled at Lukas with his hands clenched in rage. "How the hell did you know that?"

Realizing what had just occurred, the crowd roared with delight. Ram ran across to Lukas and hugged him tightly. Stephen leaped up from his seat and patted Lukas on the back. Tobin took a threatening step toward Lukas as Lukas broke free of the congratulatory embraces, watching Tobin advance on him. Arms wide, Lukas looked into his eyes and, with a sly grin, said, "You know you still love me, don't you?" He wrapped his arms around Tobin and pulled him in tight to whisper in his ear. "You know they won fair and square the first time, right?"

Tobin whispered back, "I guess so. Shit. I cannot stay mad at you."

"Okay, so stop the crazy crap, Tobin. Ram could have killed you." Lukas put his hands on Tobin's shoulders and then extended his left palm to meet Tobin's. The two friends shook hands; the ceasefire was now official.

From what seemed like miles away, Rosemary looked on proudly. Her instincts were right. Lukas had saved her. She watched knowing she had witnessed a skilled lion tamer at the top of his game and wondered when the time would come when he would meet the one hungry beast that he could not cast a spell over. She looked down at the floor as her last thought weighed heavily on her.

Kirsten poked Rosemary gently in her ribs, trying to get her attention. She waited for Rosemary to turn and catch her eyes. "He is pretty special, isn't he?"

"Yeah. Lukas does have a way about him. There is something special there."

"Does he have a girlfriend? I mean, you seem to be a close friend." She paused, seeming to realize that she might have intruded on something.

"Don't worry, he and I are just good friends."

"I didn't mean anything. I like him, and I just wouldn't want to mow your lawn, so to speak."

Rosemary laughed politely. Her smile, though, flattened into a touch of a frown. "Kirsten, by all means, you can try. Just don't get your hopes up."

"Why do you say that? Do you know something?"

Grabbing Kirsten's hand, Rosemary escorted her back to the beanbag chair. The two sat together on the chair as Kirsten waited patiently for an explanation. With a quick glance over to Lukas, Rosemary finally spoke.

"Lukas is an enigma. You can only get so close. You're not the first to try or think you could."

"You mean his heart is spoken for?"

"If only the answer were so easy. The blackness of his eyes— someone's taken that light from him. That is what I think. There's someone out there who has the ability to light the way through that darkness to his heart. It may not make much sense, but that comes from three years of being his friend."

Kirsten leaned back and looked down the path that led through the kitchen at Lukas. He saw her and smiled at her before turning away. There was something to this boy next door that made everyone gravitate to him. At the same time, everyone feared the black hole at his core. She looked back at Rosemary and wondered aloud, "Maybe he just hasn't found the right girl yet?"

Rosemary smiled back at this naïve eighteen-year-old. She motioned with her head to another of her friends in the kitchen. "Kirsten, you seem like a good kid, and I'm not going to stop you. The girls of this faculty are very fond of Lukas and we hope nothing but the best for him and that he finds the girl who'll chase his darkness away. If it is you, I will forever be indebted to you, but . . ."

"But, what?

"The rumor is the answer is sitting in his back pocket. But I've said enough; there has to be some mystery for you to solve." Rosemary squeezed Kirsten's hand and got up to rejoin her friends in the kitchen.

"Back pocket . . .?" Kirsten muttered quietly as Rosemary

wandered away into the light of the kitchen.

· · ·

Meanwhile, what seemed like miles away, Lukas stood alone now at the center of the room. The celebrations continued all around him. Paper plates, cups, half-eaten pizza, broken glass were littered all around him. He seemed to be the epicenter of some hurricane that had just taken place. He was the calm in the eye of the storm, alone in thought. His head was slightly raised and tilted at an angle as if looking at the sky. As if on cue, his left hand reached into his back pocket and gently stroked it, as if rubbing a rabbit's foot. Oblivious to Kirsten observing him, he now was looking above the door frame leading to the kitchen. He closed his eyes for an instant, then turned to Ram with a triumphant smile that lit the room.

Kirsten slowly made her way to the kitchen and stood at the spot Lukas just vacated. She looked up at the door frame and saw a crucifix perched above. Looking over to where Lukas now stood, she couldn't quite see any bulge in his back pocket. Her head leaned to one side, confused and in awe.

· · ·

The last partygoers left just after 3 a.m. Kirsten had long since left. She had secured a kiss, albeit on the cheek, from Lukas upon her departure. A small victory in her world. Lukas stayed behind as he usually did to assist in the cleaning while sipping on his vodka cranberry concoction. He surveyed the mess around him. Within the stately and elegant Victorian house, the anarchy of a university party had left the interior in shambles.

Little did anyone know, though some could suspect it, such was the condition of Lukas Wunand's soul. Not even Lukas was aware that night how soon the walls around his soul would begin to crack, no longer sheltering him from an invading past that, at the best of times, was hauntingly beautiful.

chapter three

In the dingiest bowels of the Faculty of Business on the pristine campus of St. Peter's University were the offices of the Student Society. They were called "offices," however, the stark reality was it was a large room with the remains of mammoth wood desks and chairs long since discarded by the academic staff. The president of the Student Society was elected for a one-year term at the end of the previous year and ran the faculty's student government, organizing career fairs, student parties, club activities, and anything else to enhance student life. The election was much easier than most incoming students realized. Few students ran for office, unwilling to put in the extra time to organize activities as many could barely keep up with their own schedules. The ones who did run for office did so either to sincerely make their fellow students' lives on campus memorable or to seize an opportunity early in their lives to bathe themselves in power. At least, this was Lukas's vision of public office, the dichotomy of good versus evil, with little gray in between.

It was an early Monday morning in September, and the beginning of Welcome Week activities for new students was about to begin. Classes had started at the end of the previous week, culminating in the now infamous trivia/drinking competition at Rosemary's on Friday. The newly elected president, Tobin, arrived at 8 a.m. in a panic due to all tasks requiring completion. He had spent his Sunday on the phone organizing volunteers for the week's events, ensuring that no stone was left unturned while also being very careful to avoid any direct accountability for any activities, except one, which he completely forgot. As he descended the broad concrete staircase that led to his office, he noticed a tinge of light emanating from beneath the orange-colored door, a remnant of 1980s bright exuberance. He cautiously turned the key, cursing to himself that someone had been too absentminded to turn off the light. Opening the door, he found Lukas sitting with his legs up on his desk, smiling back at him with a grin that threatened to leap off his face and encircle his head.

"Wunand, you scared the crap out of me! How did you get in here? Who gave you the key?"

"Right. I'm not part of your club, oops, sorry, I mean elected student leadership." He chuckled as he twirled the pen in his hand triumphantly. "I do have a key, remember? The faculty magazine. The one I write for."

"Oh yeah, the one that contains nothing but filth and silly juvenile humor. You're not even the editor. I forgot I gave you clowns the key." Tobin smiled, and his tone appeared to mock Lukas. Tobin also had not forgotten the betrayal he had been subjected to by Lukas on Friday.

"Tobin, are you still pissed at me for Friday? Want to kiss and make up?" Lukas puckered his lips and closed his eyes before tilting his head back in laughter.

"Mark my words, buddy, I will get even with you one day. I promise I will." Leaning over, Tobin slapped Lukas's feet off the desk. "Why are you here so early? You told me you didn't have class Monday until after lunch."

Lukas rubbed his eyes and sipped on the white Styrofoam cup before him. "This coffee totally sucks." Getting up, he walked to the front of the desk and sat on it, facing Tobin. "Believe it or not, I came in early to help." Lukas's voice and facial expression took on a serious tone. Over his first three years on campus, Lukas's reputation as a dependable friend was almost legendary. While he never explicitly volunteered for anything, he seemed omnipresent around the faculty, always willing to help. In fact, there were only two places where you were unlikely to find Lukas on any given day, the library or a classroom.

Tobin smiled at his friend. He had been the benefactor of Lukas's good intentions far too often not to take Lukas's words at face value. "If you do me a big favor, maybe I'll forgive you. A big one."

"Sure. Name it. Slay a dragon, save a damsel, answer a question, anything."

"I forgot to order hot dog buns and wieners for the welcome back barbecue. I need them by noon."

"Wow. A welcome back barbecue with no dogs. Seriously, Tobin, you are slipping lately. No doubt you did get lots of beer."

"Our campus brewery rep would kill me if I forgot that!" The university campus was the breeding ground for beer companies to tap into new consumers just as they hit legal drinking age. The student body widely believed that administration officials and even student leaders received inducements somewhere along the way.

Reaching into his pocket, Tobin pulled out a paper and handed it to Lukas. "I called the engineering faculty last night, and they have leftovers that they'll sell us. If you can go over there after nine and pick them up, I would appreciate it."

"No problem. Though, of all the faculties, engineering! There are no girls there."

"No shit. Why do you think they have so many wieners and buns!" Tobin started laughing even before the punch line landed.

Lukas put his head down, ignoring Tobin's failed attempt at humor. With this mission, he would need some more coffee before heading out. He tucked the list Tobin gave him into the right front pocket of his jeans and headed down the basement corridor. The cafeteria was just opening and the smell of hot, cheap campus coffee appealed to Lukas. He sauntered through the cafeteria, humming to himself. The walls were painted a mix of baby blue mixed with the crimson red that were the school colors. The chairs, an orange-colored hard plastic, were arranged neatly around long rectangular plastic tables, assembled military style.

After all these years, he could make this march to the counter blindfolded.

University life began three years ago for Lukas, and this was the first place he went upon arrival that day. There were few people Lukas knew that first day. He was like some alien dropped on a faraway planet with an unquenchable thirst for black coffee and blueberry muffins.

"Hey, Lukas, what can I do for you this early morning?" bellowed the always jovial Willie, caretaker of the cafeteria. Willie's first day as cafeteria manager coincided with Lukas's first day at the school. A small, portly man in his fifties, Willie had been struggling to set up that day, and Lukas offered to help him move heavy boxes. Willie had owned a restaurant downtown for years when his wife suddenly took ill. The struggle to pay bills and be there for her eventually cost him his business. Upon his wife's passing, with his children long since grown and far away, Willie took this opportunity on campus to go back to work and, as he once told Lukas, "Pass the time." Even before Lukas could respond, Willie had produced a muffin and coffee. As Lukas paid him, Willie smiled, then just as quickly his face turned pale. "This is your last year, right?"

Eyes turned to the muffin, as if ensuring the proper quantity of blueberries were in it, Lukas avoided Willie's question with an awkward silence. Summoning all his energy, he extracted a smile for Willie. "Yep. Last year of driving you crazy, big guy." He reached over and punched Willie in the shoulder. The realization gripped him when he was unprepared to accept it: he was going to graduate and be on his way. As emotion trembled through his body, he moved away quickly to end the conversation. Willie had been his second father. On more occasions than Lukas dared to admit, Willie had been the one who had supplied him with rivers of coffee and advice when Lukas had overindulged in university life.

Lukas made his way to his accustomed spot in the dimmest corner of the cafeteria. No one could ever recall when it became Lukas's place. It did, nevertheless. The seconds would swim into minutes, which catapulted into hours in that spot. From his vantage point, Lukas could see everyone who entered the cafeteria and deliver his oratories before those who dared journey into his public kingdom. It was also where Lukas wrote his often witty and many times controversial articles for the faculty's underground monthly magazine. As he sat, Lukas gingerly fingered his beloved muffin before slowly peeling off the muffin top, piece by piece, and punctuating each nibble with a slurp of black coffee. He once told Rosemary he drank it black so he would hate the taste so much he could never get addicted to it.

He studied the students entering the cafeteria. Most who had early classes on the first day were the newcomers. He recognized the wild-eyed wonder and fear as they made their way through the gaping opening of the cafeteria. Soon enough, Willie had an extended line of patrons waiting impatiently. From across the room, Lukas mockingly waved at Willie and lifted his coffee in salute. Willie shook his head amid the usual morning panic that was his life and slowly turned his back, tending to a coffee pot needing refilling. In reality, it was a diversion to stifle a tear that had snuck up on him.

With the increasing numbers that flocked in through the cafeteria, Lukas suddenly realized it was time to move on his mission. It would take a good twenty minutes to get across campus. If he stuck around any longer, he would soon immerse himself in a conversation and before he knew it, Lukas would spend the day in the cafeteria. The truth was that by Lukas's final year, he rarely went to class. The back of the cafeteria was his true classroom now, where he was both teacher and student on any given day and during any given conversation. There was a subtle power that he wielded, special because it was not demanded. Unlike Tobin, who sought power and wielded it from a locked office in the basement, Lukas's world was open with no boundaries nor allegiances. It was chaos to those who sought structure and rules; it was a utopia for those who dared to think without judgment.

Picking up his blue backpack, he quickly discarded his muffin wrapper and cup and left the cafeteria. He could now hear multiple voices erupting from the Student Society office down the hall. One voice ranted loudly in a familiar tone over all of them.

"Jesus Christ. Look what that bastard did. Look!" Tobin yelled incredulously at those in the room with him. Lukas slowly made his way to the office door, leaning against the wall to go unnoticed.

Tobin stood at the desk, pointing at his computer screen. His two fellow executives moved for a closer look at what was now visibly blinking across his screen. One of them looked closely at it before smiling; the word "NEVERMORE" flashed on and off Tobin's computer monitor screen. Suddenly, a familiar heavy hand grabbed Lukas's shoulder. It was Ram, who instantly caught on to Lukas's prank.

"Oh shit, Lukas. You messed with his screensaver! Wow, he is going to come at you hard."

"No, he won't. When I come back with his wieners and buns, he'll be all right." Lukas paused, a devious look in his eyes. "Tobin's first class is Organization Policy in Room 222. Why don't you go take a look at what some poor misguided soul wrote on that chalkboard before you head to your class."

"You didn't? Did you?" Ram said as Lukas walked back toward the staircase.

As he reached the top stair, he yelled down to his friend, "NEVERMORE!"

Ram was still laughing as he entered the Student Society office and saw a visibly frustrated Tobin punching keystroke after keystroke in a vain attempt to erase the message left behind by his more than worthy adversary. In a calm voice, and with evident sincerity, Ram declared, "Man, I cannot wait to have me some hot dogs for lunch. Hope you ordered a lot of buns and wieners, Mr. President!"

chapter four

The overcast skies had now surrendered to the towering presence of a September sun. It was perfect weather for initiating new students during Welcome Week. St. Peter's University was one of the oldest of the "new world" university campuses. Its campus was sprawled out at the core of the city, at the base of a lush, majestic mountain. Long before humans, the mountain was widely accepted to have been an active volcano whose top was violently ripped off, leaving behind what at a distance appeared to be two peaks uniting into one grand mountain. The natives named it Mount Atahensic after the goddess, who, according to legend, fell from the sky. The Sky Woman, according to the myth, was the mother of the twin souls that represented the peaks that joined at her center. Lukas was aware of all of this, as his heritage traced back to the ancestors who for centuries thrived in this region.

Lukas opened the heavy wood door to the faculty's back alley. Staring straight ahead, thinking of his mission, he crossed the scores of incoming students. He did not notice one particular student who immediately stepped into his path, knocking him partially off stride.

Kirsten's thick brown hair was tied in a ponytail, and she wore the slightest hint of makeup, adding color to her usually pale complexion. She stood in front of Lukas, ensuring he noted her presence. Although she met Lukas for the first time on the previous Friday party, she felt comfort and ease within his presence. Comfortable enough to doze off on his lap the first time they met. She smiled at him and poked him gently in the chest. "Are you going to wish me luck on my first day?"

"Of course, good luck, Kirsten. Stats is a killer the first year, so pay attention." His concentration on the task at hand was now completely broken, as was usually the case in the presence of a warm smile. Suddenly he remembered how he required getting in Tobin's good books again and looked at her seriously. "Sorry, I can't talk now. I'll try to catch up with you later. I'm usually in the caf."

"Oh, I heard about you. The kingpin of the cafeteria, or so I am told." She laughed at Rosemary's scouting report on Lukas before rolling her eyes. She then leaned forward and kissed him on the cheek. "Well, good luck on your errand."

Unsure what to make of this show of affection—innocent yet daunting, as if a sudden weight sat on his broad shoulders— Lukas stepped back slightly. As he noticed her eyes probing him for a reaction, he caught himself. The smile was unforced and came naturally to him and apparently served its purpose as she slowly turned and retreated through the doors into the faculty just as he said, "Good luck on your first day!"

He wasn't sure if she heard. She kissed him so quickly and moved on, almost stealing away from him the moment. It was some adult game of tag. He was it, again. At first, he didn't spend any time overthinking the exchange that just took place. The back alley was a perfect wind tunnel, with trees that lined the back fence and obscured the morning sun. Just as he thought it, a gust of wind caught him and gave him a cold chill. He marched hurriedly out of the alley and into the open area overlooking the campus, finally feeling the embracing heat of the sun.

The business faculty stood on the outskirts of the campus. Its doors opened to the busy downtown traffic. On the edge of both the university campus and the upper reaches of the city's bustling business core, it was one of the most modern buildings on campus. Many who first visited the campus often mistook the building for a regular office tower. Built with gray concrete and windows resembling a convention center hotel, it was in many ways separate from the rest of the university. The only connection was the name presiding over the doorway in blue and red. It was only by walking through the back entrance of the building and crossing the alleyways toward the core of the campus that a student realized the majesty of St. Peter's University.

Lukas crossed the street and made his way to the center of campus. From the busy city street, a pathway extended up through the lush green lawns that lay across the campus like an inviting blanket, dividing the campus in two. Someone entering the campus from the main street would marvel as the trail ascended slowly toward the two-hundred-year-old stone buildings. The buildings were at the heart of the university, nestled comfortably at the base of the welcoming and protective mountain.

Lukas walked across and up the stairs of the platformed terrace that ran parallel to the greenery of the lower campus fields below. His destination would be a hundred feet or so farther along. As the sunlight heated his brown hair, highlighting the tinges of autumn auburn that naturally streaked his straight mane, he stopped.

Looking back, he finally decided to let himself ponder his relationship with the younger Kirsten. He worried that she had developed a fondness for him that extended beyond just friendship. They had met briefly on Friday and spoke at considerable length, her drinking a beer and him chugging vodka with a hint of cranberry. They talked about her mainly, where she was from and why she came to this school. He carefully avoided any direct line of questions around himself and was more than eager to let her ramble at length about herself. The moment came when the beer and the excitement of her first university party left her seeking the quiet calm of his chest and heartbeat. He didn't mind spending time with Kirsten. She was a good three years younger than him, and next year he would be gone from this school while she was only beginning her studies. He wondered how naïve she was in believing it could work.

He quickly shook the thoughts of a relationship out of his mind as a child would shake a loud rattle. More than anything, he worried about hurting her by not being the person she thought, or maybe even hoped, he was. He searched his soul, and his head shook the thoughts even harder. Satisfied with his conclusion, he picked up his backpack and continued his journey, thinking how long this trek took and how at least Frodo had a trusted companion in Sam.

It was early September and the last days of summer would be coming to a climax. Lukas had just turned twenty-one the preceding week. Today's journey may seem never-ending, he pondered, and the long march of life was yet to pass through the winter of adulthood. The truth was that Lukas had years ago entered an eternal cold winter, which he chose to ignore.

As thoughts rumbled through his mind, the ground and his shoelaces seemed to conspire against him, sending him clumsily forward. He hit the ground palms first with his right knee scuffing along the cement floor. He could feel the burning sting of an open wound on his knee. He gathered himself quickly up and nodded reassuringly to those who took an interest in his plight. Surveying his now torn jeans and the trace of blood on his knee, he laughed at his new battle scar. Moving toward the platform ledge, he took a seat to tie his shoes. The error of his ways was immersing himself too deep in thought, and now a price paid. His classmates would marvel at his fashion statement, the ripped knee, and wonder behind his back at the tale surrounding its creation. He giggled at the craziness of university gossip.

With his legs dangling precariously over the ledge, Lukas pivoted around, noticing the sun's radiating light on the lower campus grass creating silhouette works of art using the tall maples as its brush. Rarely did he take the opportunity to embrace the natural beauty that caressed this vast campus, choosing instead to hold court in the bowels of his faculty. He traced the beam of light from the football/soccer/rugby pitch marked neatly in a rectangle. The perimeter was defined less by the human-made white chalk outlines and more by the trees standing stoically along its boundaries. For years, Lukas spent countless hours with his buddies on the fields below. He recalled enjoying these surroundings sporadically, the mere splashes of time when he tumbled injured or winded, and how he used the calmness of the setting to summon the resolve to continue playing.

Today was far different in many ways. Each shadow cast by the coy and teasing sun captured this young man's attention. Satisfied he had soaked it all in, his eyes then caught a glimpse of a student straying from the asphalt path below. The figure moved toward the terrace methodically and steadily. Beneath a red maple, distinctive only because it was one of the first whose leaves had begun to erupt in a symphony of autumn colors, two squirrels stopped in their tracks and studied the approaching stranger. Uncharacteristically, the squirrels waited in complete trust of this person. Kneeling before them, the young figure reached into the red backpack they were carrying. Long fragile fingers began distributing food at the feet of the small creatures.

Lukas's attention was initially captured by the figure's out-of-place behavior. Someone had broken ranks from the steady line of students walking in unison. But it was the subtle act of kindness that made Lukas grin.

However, he was aware of a more intense emotion stirring deep within him—a feeling long since lost, now seemingly returning in prodigal fashion. It was the familiarity of the student's gait. The ebony hair flowing just behind her back and slightly past her shoulders. The slender arms and long fingers. The gentleness of her interaction with the furry creatures. The olive tone of her skin was eerily reminiscent of someone long since gone from his life. His eyes focused on this girl as he felt something quite dramatic taking place. His heart finally caught up with what his eyes and brain were absorbing.

"*Kara?*" The words torpedoed through his disbelieving lips. He wondered if he screamed the name, whispered the name, or imagined the whole thing. His heart rate accelerated as he vacuumed back the air —his heart seeking freedom from his chest. His eyes zeroed in on the young girl as she pulled herself back up. She wore brown leather sandals and light blue jeans. A navy blue blouse was partially concealed at the waist by a white sweater wrapped around it, knotted at the front. Fighting to overcome both the sun and the distance between them, his eyes searched every nuance of her frame. At long last, he summoned his courage to look at her face. Her face was petite, small thin lips with a tiny button nose. The eyebrows thick and dark as were her eyes. She blinked, and the flash of white accentuated the deepness of the eyes, and the sun appeared to pause on her face. Her skin glistened and looked invitingly soft to the touch. It was exactly how Lukas remembered it. On cue, the squirrels scurried suddenly away but not before chirping deliriously at her feet, content with her offerings. Her lips stretched to test the boundaries and limits of cheeks. The bright white teeth and slight overbite were apparent to this trained observer. There was no doubt in his mind. "Kara!"

Lukas did not listen to the footsteps behind him. All he felt was the hands on his shoulders pulling him back from the ledge. In his trance, Lukas had risen to standing at the edge of the ledge. The drop to the thorny bushes below was over twenty feet, if not more.

"Be careful, young man," said the voice. "That is quite a drop." The man speaking was balding with white hair. He wore a gray suit and carried a soft leather briefcase. Lukas quickly determined it was a professor of some sort.

"Thanks, sir," Lukas politely replied as he turned to face the man. At the same time, he was anxious to return to the ghostly apparition. He took a step away from the ledge and thought of a lame reason for his reckless behavior. "Um, I dropped something below and wanted to see if I could get to it."

"Well," the man looked ready to deliver an impromptu lecture, "you will have to go all the way around to get it. There are stairs farther down that will get you there much more safely." He pointed to the long concrete steps about a hundred or so feet away.

"Yes. You're right. Thanks." Lukas quickly stepped down from the ledge as to alleviate the fears of the man and then ignored him completely as he pivoted his body back toward Kara. He leaned forward and cupped his hands to his mouth and yelled, "Kara." Whether she heard him or not was one thing. He was hoping for a reaction that would confirm his suspicions.

The young girl's movements seemed to stop in the moments her name floated into the sky. All that moved was her head as she appeared to search for the source. Lukas's heart exploded, and he called out as loud as he could, buoyed by this small victory. She continued to scan the vicinity. However, she did not look up to see the young suitor bellowing her name. Seeming to draw a breath, she picked up her backpack and made her way back to the main path. *Look up, Kara. Please, look up*, Lukas thought to himself. The triumph was short-lived, and the defeat marked by the young girl disappearing back into the throng of students making their way to class.

Paralyzed by the moment for what may have been an eternity to some, Lukas awoke with conviction. He grabbed his bag and ran at full pace toward the stairs. He did not have time to calibrate the futility of his plan to try and catch up with this girl. After all these years, hope fueled his heart with fresh blood and energy. However futile the attempt might be, it represented a hope that for years lay hidden beneath a cumbersome and smothering unsympathetic blanket.

His arms extended like a seasoned sprinter keeping pace with his powerful stride. In no time at all, he had reached the stairs and vaulted down them, skipping three or four steps in some leaps. He paid no regard for his safety. The fuel burning had fermented within him for years. His thoughts sped as quickly as his pace. While physically he was racing forward, his thoughts warped backward to a far more complicated time for him. Bypassing and vaulting over memories he knew waited for him like landmines, he focused on the emotion raging within him —unleashed anger.

For years, Lukas caked layers upon layers of solid crust to block out the anger and frustration erupting within him. Always hoping it would never explode, always realizing the slow simmer would cook everything within him nonetheless. Now, it careened through his insides trying to get out. When he reached the asphalt path, he looked up for the first time. A crowd of students drifted along the path in front, looking alike in every way. Where was she? He continued his run, now slaloming through student after student. Finally, upon reaching the large oak doors of the main arts building, he conceded in silence—she could have been anywhere by now. He lost her the minute she blended into the moving mass of humanity. After so many years and with so many questions unanswered, Lukas was left alone with only his thoughts, emotions, and, worse, his fears. He took a step back to face the two giant gnomes that stood devilishly above the door entrance. They taunted him with their wild eyes. The threat could not be more explicit: enter at your risk. Lukas lowered his head and followed the students through the entrance.

His first few steps into the arts building were a visit to a new world. Scores of sculptures littered the great hall. The floor was marbled. Artwork lined the walls of the building, surrounding the door frames of each classroom. Lukas's eyes followed the interior stairwell, which spiraled to the upper deck. There were three more floors of classrooms. A bell rang, punctuating an end to Lukas's distraction. The clarity of the current situation was blinding. The girl he called Kara had disappeared somewhere amongst the sprawling classrooms of the university campus. Right before his eyes, he had found her and lost her.

Lukas sought refuge on one of the rectangular benches that littered the main foyer. He threw himself back, his head banging against the concrete walls, almost shaking the painting above him off its frame. For years, the emotions he had smothered were anger and bitterness. He wondered now for the first time what he would say to her if he managed to catch up with her. How much rage would he cast upon her with a tongue sharpened by hurt for so many years? He put his hands on his face and leaned forward with his elbows resting on his knees to obscure the curious from the emotion sketching itself on his face. The coating of anger he carefully protected in his race to reach her had peeled off and disintegrated, and out flowed the soft and warm emotion now taking over his being. Lukas could no longer run. He could no longer hide. Love, long ago conceived within him, finally broke free and was reborn. He felt the warmest of shivers.

The arts building was built with a cathedral-like ceiling with a stained-glass window at its peak to welcome in the nourishing sun. With watery eyes, Lukas watched the ray of light filling up the foyer all the way up to the sky. A cloud passed, and darkness fell upon the room again, causing Lukas to clench his fist. Lukas wondered if the sun could be so cruel as to illuminate Kara to him only to give way to shadow once again. He moved toward the ray and bathed himself in it, closing his eyes as his left hand reached into his back pocket and caressed the contents gently. The works of art, like the building that housed them, remained constant and timeless through decades of sunrises and sunsets. In contrast, it took one brief morning for everything to change about Lukas, or so he thought. He was too young and innocent still to understand: the change within him was an illusion, the sun merely illuminating one of its works, only from a slightly different angle.

chapter five

The relief was palpable when Lukas returned carrying buns and hot dogs just as the barbecue was fired up and the lines of students began forming on the front lawn of the faculty building. It was just before noon and Lukas's prolonged absence was duly noted. On other occasions, his return would be grandiose, and he would quickly immerse himself in the festivities. Not today, however. His world changed from the time he left in the early morning until his return. He avoided any unnecessary small talk and greeted everyone with a smile. His gait defied gravity and had an airy tone. Lukas returned only to fulfill his obligation to Tobin. He easily could have spent the rest of day searching classroom after classroom, hallway after hallway, for Kara.

Tobin did not let Lukas off the hook easily. The last prank, an ode to Friday night, tore at Tobin like sandpaper. He, too, however, noticed something strange about his fellow student. But it was Ram who observed the torn jeans and stalked after Lukas as the two walked together toward the cafeteria.

"What's up?" Ram decided to break the tightening silence.

"Oh, not much. Why do you ask?" Immediately, Lukas grew suspicious of the question. At the same time, he used all his energy to hold himself back from divulging how he had spent his morning.

"Well, last I saw you, I don't think you were oozing blood down your leg for starters." Looking down at his leg, Lukas saw the coagulated blood from his fall and the large rip at the knees. No one else dared call him out on it. Ram was a trusted friend, and his comment and concern touched Lukas.

"I took a little tumble rushing to the engineering building. No biggie. Thanks for asking, though. I'm okay." He patted his friend on the shoulder and then tried to change the subject. "So, how are things going?"

"Good new crop coming in." Ram motioned to some of the younger students assembling in the cafeteria for extracurricular signups. His head nodded at the skirt lengths. Lukas smiled back at him, and before he could say anything, Ram quickly interjected. "I heard there's a young filly who already has her sights set on you."

Knowing he could only be speaking of Kirsten, Lukas said, "Let us not get carried away, Ram. She's a good kid. However, just a kid." Lukas could feel his insides ready to explode with a revelation and skillfully peeled back the thoughts that were trying to leak out. "She's too young."

Ram laughed. "Things never change for you, do they? Always an excuse." Ram moved toward the back of the cafeteria and waited for Lukas to follow him.

"No need to save my place. I'm just grabbing a cup of java and heading off."

"Where are you going? Our first class is at 1:30. We have time to sit and talk and maybe grab a bite at the barbecue outside."

"I have some things I need to do before class." He planned to return to the arts building, however long it took to wait, watch, and hope.

Ram could sense something was amiss. Lukas rarely avoided any opportunity to hold court at the back of the cafeteria, especially early in the school year. He chose not to pursue it. Ram genuinely trusted his friend, and there was a glow about Lukas he never saw or noticed before. He trusted his instincts and determined this was a good thing.

"Okay, buddy, if you need me, you know where to find me." He laughed as he pointed to the back wall. Lukas turned and proceeded to get in line. Willie was, as usual, scurrying with his head down, fulfilling the orders at a fast and furious pace. Like some savant, Willie poured Lukas a black cup of coffee, never looking up to acknowledge him. Suddenly, a soft whisper floated through the air. It was so quiet it spooked Willie.

"Two milk and one sugar, please."

Willie looked up, eyes wide. "Mr. Black now wants milk and sugar?" he said, laughing. "Did the earth tilt off its axis?"

Lukas grinned and winked at Willie. "My coffee was a little too black for a bit too long." He paid Willie and floated out of the cafeteria, leaving the cryptic message to percolate in Willie's mind.

As Lukas walked, a frantic girl tugged on his backpack. "Lukas, I need to talk to you quickly."

The girl had curly blonde hair and wore a summer dress, entirely floral, with a jean jacket draped over her shoulders. Ally Rosen, the Vice President of the Student Society. As much as Lukas was in a rush, he knew Ally was not one to get overly theatrical and would never grab him like she just did without a valid reason. He dutifully followed her to a secluded spot in the corridor.

Seeing the intense look on Ally's face, Lukas's tone became serious. "What's going on, Ally? You seem freaked out." She was responsible for student activities and events within the faculty. Only Tobin had more authority.

"A girl was attacked last night."

"Oh shit." Lukas immediately knew the severity of the issue and shook his head in frustration. "Anyone we know?"

"No, but it apparently happened near this building. Actually, in the back alley behind here."

"Is she okay?"

"Yes, but, dammit, it started again. They still have not caught the perv."

Shrugging his shoulders, Lukas looked down at the ground. The university had seen its share of violence, both on and off campus, over the years. It came with the territory of it being located in the heart of a metropolitan city. There were always fistfights erupting, but this was something far more wicked and horrific. Since the latter part of the preceding year, a wave of violent assaults against women commenced. The university increased campus security patrols and initiated programs across the campus to raise awareness. The fact was, with a sprawling campus, not every corner could be covered at all times. Lukas looked up at Ally with resolve. "We have to do what we talked about last year. Have a buddy program. No girl should have to walk through the campus and campus ghetto alone. I'll do it at least a night a week. I'm sure Ram will. Don't worry; we'll figure something out."

Ally smiled at Lukas, and her small, fragile hand reached for his elbow. "I was thinking the same thing, and I knew I could count on you."

Lukas smiled and then his face turned pensive as his leg began to fidget. "What is Tobin doing about this?"

"That's the problem. He told me it wasn't his problem and not something the Student Society needs to be involved in."

"That is just the damn wannabe lawyer in him talking. Always worried about appearances and liability." Lukas was well aware that Tobin enjoyed power more than anything and hated making decisions and working equally as much.

"He is the president, and he's probably right, this is a university issue." She batted her eyelashes at him and winked, knowing full well Lukas would do the right thing regardless of the rules and regulations.

"Ally, don't worry. Fuck Tobin. Do what you have to do. If you get in trouble for it, blame me."

"Thanks, you're my hero." She leaned over and kissed him on the cheek as he smiled meekly at her. He raced up the stairs and back outside across campus, hoping the karma he just earned would be enough.

· · ·

In the far reaches of the cafeteria, Ally joined Ram and Rosemary, who arrived just ahead of her. Ally quickly broke the news of the assault to the disbelief of both Ram and Rosemary.

"I hoped this all came to an end when the school year ended last year." Rosemary paused. "Is that what you were talking to Lukas about?"

"Yeah. I told him I was getting nowhere with Tobin."

"Let me guess. Lukas had an idea."

Ally chuckled. "What else is new? We'll do the buddy thing. You know, what Lukas suggested last year. Anyone needing to walk home alone after a certain hour could sign up and have someone escort them."

Ram quickly spoke just as Ally finished. "I volunteer."

Rosemary applauded. "Good for you, Ram, thanks."

Ram shook his head. "Well, in truth, I'm sure Lukas volunteered me anyways." He looked at a laughing Ally, who nodded in the affirmative.

After thanking them both for their support, Ally leaned across the table. "You guys both know Lukas pretty well."

"Yeah, I guess so," Ram said.

"Does something seem odd about him today? He seemed so preoccupied."

Ram nodded. "For sure, something is up with him."

Rosemary leaned back in her chair. For years now, many had come to her inquiring about Lukas. Every smile, grin, or frown seemed magnified by those around him. Rosemary took the mother hen role seriously and wished that her friend would find peace away from the scrutiny. She also knew he brought on the scrutiny by giving up so much of himself and not allowing anyone close enough to give something back to him. Rosemary was a marketing major and aced social psychology. She could feel guilt buried within Lukas's psyche, which he desperately tried to exorcise with generosity.

"Maybe we should just let him be and not speculate about him."

Ally's neck reclined back, taking her head with her. Rosemary's tone was ominous, and Ally's reaction caused Rosemary to retreat into an explanation. "Lukas and I are friends, and there is one thing I do know about him: I trust him. I also know that he values my trust immensely. Let's appreciate the friend we have instead of over analyzing him."

"Well said," Ram added. He slid his hand down Ally's arm in a reassuring way. "Lukas and I will gladly help you."

Ally nodded. She would start a buddy system, under the orders of Lukas, and avoid the consternation of her fellow executive, Tobin. Rosemary shifted in her chair, uncomfortable with her recent words. Until now, she never thought for a second that maybe Lukas needed support. For so long, they had leaned on him. His absence now made her keenly aware how enigmatic his existence truly was to her.

chapter six

The leaves changed colors and fell by the thousands on and around the campus. For the students, with each fallen leaf, deadlines most surely approached, whether projects due or mid-term exams. The partying of September gave way to the silent remorse of October. Students worried as parents mulled the strange charges on the credit cards they had given their children. Campus life was always about the here and now. The future would take hold in May and June as graduation beckoned. There was never any past for a St. Peter's student. Well, except for perhaps one student.

Children see the month of October punctuated with a grand pagan ritual that marks its end, Halloween. Ghosts represent the joys of childhood. Within the walls of the business school, there was one ghost now, who, rumor had it, once walked amongst the living. Lukas, was now the ghost of the faculty, even to his friends. His familiar spot in the corner of the cafeteria was largely empty. No one dared sit in his chair. Supposedly, he came and went to his classes. He talked to anyone who would venture into his space. He gave back to the conversation the bare minimum. No more and certainly no less. Every word measured for efficiency. The hope flowed through his veins, slowly leaking from his being as September progressed. Small holes of doubt opened.

From the time he believed the apparition of Kara appeared to him until the calendar turned to the next month, Lukas became the best ghost hunter the world could have ever known. He spent every available second and minute retracing the path he took that day and staked out every permutation and combination of classrooms she may have entered. Upon the ledge overlooking the fields below, he sat cross-legged sipping a drink and nibbling on a grilled cheese or cream cheese sandwich. Often the occasional rains would force him to seek refuge in the elongated arms of the oak trees. He vowed he would not miss her again. While he remained dutiful to his heart, he remained equally so to his commitment to Ally. It was early October now, and Lukas perused the faculty bulletin board to see if anyone had requested a walk home on the night he was on duty. His hand scrolled down the dates until he finally found today's and looked at the name with surprise: Rosemary Cooper. She never requested an escort home before and, in fact, lived just a couple of blocks from Ram on the far side of campus. There was a method to everything Rosemary did. Facing her meant confronting an uncomfortable truth, and he knew what was coming. She was too damn smart and perceptive.

Punctual as always, he arrived in the main floor lobby at exactly 9 p.m. The day students had long since left the building, and adult students, with some enrolled in MBA programs and some in continuing education, now invaded the halls. Rosemary often stayed late in the library to do her work before heading home. Usually, if it were late, she would ask Ram to wait for her and walk back together, but tonight, she specifically set out to walk home with Lukas—not that he minded doing so. He volunteered, after all, and returned home late with regularity. His mom and dad were notified well in advance and by now were quite accustomed to it. His sister, on the other hand, often stayed up late waiting patiently for the safe return of her younger brother. Many of the students lived on campus, even if they were from the city or its vast suburbs. Independence was a rite of passage for those. Lukas's reality, like his persona, seemed to be a study of contrasts. His parents coaxed Lukas to live his life and not feel an obligation toward them or his sibling. But duty and responsibility remained driving forces, as was his devotion to his sister.

Her bright orange backpack slung over one shoulder, Rosemary waited for him in her customary oversized work shoes and ragged T-shirt, topped with a white windbreaker. She was pure grunge, and Lukas always felt comfortable around her.

As she walked toward him, she said, "Well, if it isn't my bodyguard, waiting like some gallant knight to take me home." Rosemary punched Lukas in the arm and walked right by him, leading the way.

When she tried to walk ahead of him, Lukas grabbed her arm. "C'mon, Rose, why did you need me to walk with you?"

"The ever-thinking Lukas! I barely see you anymore. Please, walk me home." It was as Lukas suspected. The inquisition was yet to come. If he didn't deal with it now, he would have to sometime. After a month of chasing a ghost and dealing with emotions even he couldn't explain, the safety and comfort of Rosemary were welcome.

"You're right, Rose. I know I haven't been myself. I know." His pace quickened to keep up with her as she crossed the campus. As they reached the lower fields, Lukas stopped beneath one of the lampposts and pointed to the spot he thought he had seen Kara.

"I saw her there."

Rosemary stopped and turned, shock at Lukas's revelation evident on her face. In total confusion, she looked at him and shrugged. "There's no one there now. It's just you and me."

With eyes blacker than night, Lukas looked at her. "I know there's no one there . . . now." Before he could finish, she walked back to him, grabbed his hand firmly, and led him to the outer edge of the campus.

Without saying another word, she darted down side street after side street before coming to the Victorian stone home she lived in with her roommates. The night was cool but refreshing. They sat on the cast iron bench on the porch, and she finally let go of his hand.

"I'm going to get you a drink. Don't disappear on me." Within seconds, she vanished into her home.

"*Disappear*. Nice turn of a phrase," he said as he rested his eyes, though not loudly enough for her to hear. The irony of the words provided brief enjoyment. Rosemary long suspected that a lost love lurked hidden within Lukas's psyche. He perennially refused to talk about it. In the last month, though, the wear and tear of Lukas's internal erosion became visible.

She returned with a heavily diluted mix of gin and ginger ale. Her father, a surgeon, extolled the virtues of gin as a surgeon's drink. Gentle surgery is what she prepared to perform. As she handed him the glass, she shifted her hips close to him. "Despite what you think, I still want to thank you for walking me. On behalf of all the girls, thank you."

"You know you don't have to. No one should be scared to walk home, let alone while in university." Lukas's face diverted from Rosemary, drifting off toward the night sky. "We are all still kids. Yes, kids do need to feel secure."

She reached out to him and grabbed his hand, forcing him to make eye contact. "You know not everyone feels like you do. Tobin could not give a shit. He doesn't want to be bothered by anything."

"Oh, Tobin is just Tobin."

"I don't know why you're friends with him. He only cares about himself and the title of president because it'll look good on his application to law school."

Lukas nodded his head sympathetically. He and Tobin were opposites yet friends. Tobin had found work for Lukas in the summer at his dad's law firm. It was money Lukas sorely needed for his studies. "I don't think you brought me here to bitch about Tobin. And I'm pretty sure you're not expecting me to hit on you."

Rosemary chuckled. One of the first things she'd said to him back in their first year was, "Don't even think about hitting on me. I'm not into guys." The memory of it still made Lukas smile. "Good God, you will never let me live that down. No, I wanted to talk to you. Actually, on behalf of people who care about you, we miss you. We never see you around anymore."

"I know, and I apologize."

"You don't need to feel sorry. I'm just worried about you. Not only me. The caf is not the same without you. We see you as a . . . well, a . . ."

"Character? A clown?" He looked at her as he dipped his index finger in the cup and then licked it. "Be honest. I entertain you guys."

Rosemary shook her head. "More than that. You are a leader. That's the word. Sure, you're funny and entertaining. It's much more than that. You have a presence. We feel comfortable when you're there."

"I'm like a La-Z-Boy chair, then."

"Oh stop it. You know what I mean." She tried to look into his eyes, but his head drifted off to the side. He slowly got up and faced her.

"I should probably go home now."

At the sudden display of surrender from him, Rosemary quickly threw her head from side to side. The witty retorts ended abruptly, as did the playfulness. This behavior was not like him at all. He seemed to be drifting, wanting to leave the porch and go out into the night. She rose to her feet and grabbed his arms, capturing his eyes with hers.

"You do not scare me. I can look into your eyes and see the darkness. It does not freak me out. I kind of like it. I want to know what has you rattled. What did you mean when you said you saw her there?" Whether it was her words or her gesture, he maneuvered himself back onto the bench, with her following.

"I saw her. I mean I think I saw her. The day I went to the engineering faculty."

"Who did you see? An ex-girlfriend?"

"It was a girl I haven't seen or spoken to since I was sixteen. Kara."

"You thought you saw her. You're not sure?"

Biting his lip, his head shook in disbelief. He didn't trust his response and couldn't tell the story without appearing insane. Rosemary's maternal nature allowed the words to flow. "I'm sure it was her. Even though she was older now. I know Kara. It was her."

"I gather you saw her from a distance."

"Yes. I was at the top of the terrace, and Kara was down below. I ran, and I mean I ran, to catch up with her." He emphasized the point by clasping his hands. "She vanished into the crowd. I tried to find her. That was it. Day after day I went back to the spot, waited, and looked. I couldn't find her."

Like a seasoned detective, Rosemary listened intently. She nodded thoughtfully, more for appearance's sake. Conclusions were formulated ages ago. "I have always been honest with you." She waited for him to nod back in response. "I think you saw what you wanted to see. Your mind played tricks on you."

"Rosemary, I called her name, and she reacted."

"I am not trying to belittle what you said. I took some psychology."

"Maybe one or two courses more than I did. I forgot you were in marketing." He emphasized the point almost sarcastically.

"Just maybe you actually believe you saw her because you someone with a resemblance and your mind so badly wanted it to be her, it fooled you, a bit. I take it you loved her a lot."

"If I didn't, you think I would be here right now?"

"Right. She obviously had a tremendous effect on you. It explains a lot."

"Glad all the pieces are sliding into place for you."

"Did she break up with you?" Rosemary dragged every word across her lips and let it hang in the air like fresh laundry. She took as long as humanly possible to position herself to study Lukas's response.

Buying time, he coughed ever so gingerly. His eye fixed upon nothing other than the large pine tree directly in front before smiling and getting up to pace the floor. It was obvious even he could not answer the question. At last, he spoke.

"I guess she did. I don't want to go into it. All I know is I haven't seen her in years. Seeing her again made me realize how much I loved her."

"You thought you saw her. If the love was so strong, it explains how this illusion could have been created." Heavy in thought, Lukas returned to his seat.

"As a friend and someone who cares for you so much, you have to move on with your life, Lukas. You are letting this image of a girl hold you back from being happy."

"You think I don't know that? You think I wanted to see her again? All those feelings. September was like a crazy rollercoaster ride for me. I keep wondering where she is and when I'll see her again. I just never sunk in how much time has passed."

"Is this why . . ." She hesitated, although the elephant clearly started dancing at the center of the room.

"Why I haven't slept with anyone?" He looked at her with the expression of someone many steps ahead of her.

"Geez, Lukas, it would explain so much. The girls talk. You seem to keep it in your pants as if you gave it up for Lent." The million-dollar question leaped off her tongue like a triple somersault into the air before him. "You are a virgin then or not? I mean you and this Kara."

Lukas smiled at Rosemary with a look both gentle and filled with foreboding at the same time. "You know me by now, Rosemary. I would never tell you one way or another."

Rosemary realized how much this girl once meant to Lukas for him not to even wish to divulge personal information all these years later. A deeper need began driving her thoughts, something quite selfish. "I think it's time for you to move on. You cannot waste your life waiting. I mean, look how miserable you have been."

The words simmered, each one weighed and measured by him. Rosemary could be a skilled surgeon or chef if she chose. Everything was cut in front of him like bite-size pieces, easy for him to digest. "I need to move on. I know. I get it. It isn't that easy."

"Lukas, you just turned twenty-one. Have fun. Enjoy yourself. There's nothing wrong with that. Some girls dig you. Give them a chance."

"Kirsten? Yeah, I figured."

"Yes, Kirsten, for sure, except it doesn't have to be her. Open yourself to someone. You cannot wait all your life for something that might never happen. It has been, like, over four years.

Time to let go."

He reclined back with his shoulders heaving forward from some invisible weight. A month ago when he returned to the cafeteria, everything seemed so different all of a sudden. The world he had known for three years, even his friends, seemed changed. A stranger is what he had become. There were months to go to graduation and if he was to survive and stay, he needed to find the actor's voice within him, learn his lines, and smile for the camera's eyes. The role he would play now is the part of the Lukas his friends recognized and not the Lukas who longed for Kara. Rosemary reached out and stroked his arm. "Your friends need you."

Leaning over, he kissed her on the cheek. "You may be right. I do miss you crazy kids." He punched her in the arm and gave her an exaggerated thumbs-up sign. "I need to get going. My parents are pretty patient with my nighttime antics. My sister will probably be waiting." Within seconds, he handed an empty glass to Rosemary and was down the street and in the distance.

• • •

The sigh of relief from Rosemary was audible in the still of the night. It was bittersweet, and an uneasiness stalked Rosemary with each thought dancing in her mind. She thought of her motives for bringing Lukas out this far tonight. She convinced herself fairly quickly of her pure ambition. She wished her friend to be content. The ugly gray veil must be lifted from him so he could find his bliss. Yes, she wanted him to find happiness.

She could see him at the bus stop. The lamppost close to where Lukas stood flickered intermittently, playing games with Rosemary's sight and calling attention to the lad standing beneath it. Rosemary grabbed a tissue from her pocket and dabbed her eyes. The light no longer flickered. Her eyes, too, were playing games with her. Just then another flicker occurred and Lukas, unperturbed, reached into his back pocket. From so far away, she could not ascertain what he held, but he studied it carefully before returning it to the sanctity of his pocket. The mass of her betrayal grew heavy with the gravity of her guilt. Nervous, she dropped her glass to the floor, and it shattered into sharp shards. She watched Lukas, his innocence and vulnerability, glowing under the street lamp. She wanted him to play a part in the entertainment of her and her friends. She so longed to be entertained for the rest of the school year that she forgot about what happens to the actor once the show is over. Rosemary had felt the slightest pain and a momentary tingling before she drew her hand back. Her vision became cloudy, and for a second, she could barely see Lukas. Broken glass can blind when caressing one's eyes with reflected light.

chapter seven

The journey home at such a late hour was not unusual for Lukas. He knew when the last buses and subway ran. He could close his eyes, he was certain, and still find his way. This night felt different.

Lukas still lived with his parents in the suburbs. Not a wealthy neighborhood in anyone's imagination. His current home appeared slightly more affluent than the neighborhood of his childhood. His parents, sister, and he moved farther west when he graduated high school, much farther from the hustle and bustle of the city.

He didn't look back at Rosemary, so he was oblivious to the vision of her on all fours, sweeping up broken glass with her finger wrapped in a makeshift tourniquet. The black hole swirling in the distance preoccupied his wandering mind.

He sat on the bus, eyes closed, with a Walkman partially exposed in his backpack. At such a late hour, the bus was empty and likely would remain empty except for the driver. Sleepily, he rocked himself to the music. If anyone could hear the sound that resonated with him, they would probably understand him better. It was a tiny clue to the mystery. He listened to songs written by those who exorcise inner demons with music. It was a wonder that such beautiful lyrics could come from such cavernous places of a lonely human soul.

He always found the irony in tragedy. The thin razor lines

between laughter and sadness. Immersed in his music, he forgot where he was, letting his voice escape, singing the Bill Hicks's inspired verse from "Ricochet" by Faith No More.

"Hey, dude, Faith No More, right?" The driver's head tilted back as he maintained his eyes on the road. Not much older than him, the driver's tattooed arms bulged from a short sleeve light blue bus company shirt.

Eyes now open, Lukas said, "Yes. Great band. Sorry, it is a bit loud."

"Man, don't worry about that. I like them, too."

Pulling off his headphones, Lukas moved forward to sit behind the driver. "Not many people are aware of them. They're not very commercial. Kind of out there."

"I hitchhiked to see them at a festival last year. Great show. Got pretty messed up, too, that weekend."

Although the driver couldn't see his face, Lukas gave a knowing smile. It was all a great lie. Drugs were not a vice of Lukas, though he couldn't let on and lose this connection.

"So, college kid, what are you studying?"

"Aw, I'm in the business school. Not sure why, though, it's not my thing."

"Not your thing. Oh boy. Like driving a bus is my thing!"

"I'm just treading water. Not sure where it's all heading."

"Well, enjoy the ride. Some of us don't have much choice, and I mean no offense by it." His head swiveled back quickly to make eye contact. The stubble on his face sat thick and uneven in spots. A touch of acne dotted his cheeks. His eyes were brown, resting comfortably atop his broad nose. He was certainly not much older than Lukas.

"If you don't mind me asking, how did you end up as a bus driver?" Looking up at the dashboard of the bus, Lukas saw a small Virgin Mary statue. A picture of a young male in full military uniform stared back at him from where it hung. It was a younger, wide-eyed version of the driver. Lukas studied the eyes and could see the sparkle captured on photographic film. He, too, once had that sparkle in pictures.

The driver followed Lukas's eyes through the rearview mirror and noticed that Lukas had zeroed in on his photo. He took one of his hands off the wheel and pointed at the picture before returning his fingers to the rigid plastic of the steering wheel. "After high school, I thought I could see the world. I wanted to serve my country. I bought into all the evil out there and how we had to fight it before it got to our homes. I read about it as a kid, so I volunteered for the military. Fuck it. I could not fire a pistol for squat. They gave me a truck to drive. Drove a military ambulance. I had no idea what real war was like."

Lukas leaned forward, intrigued. Grasping the heaviness of this man's story, he held his breath. "You saw combat?"

"Enough. Only one thing I learned." His head turned back to make the point clearly to his passenger. "All humans suffer the same regardless of race or religion. You wanna know what else? Evil wore the same face I did and the same uniform."

Lukas could not respond without weighing down the moment in hypocrisy. He, too, knew full well evil wore many faces. As the driver continued, Lukas nodded his head.

"Finding out the evil out there comes from within, man that messed me up." His eyes focused on the windshield in front. He stopped the bus for a potential passenger who turned out was waiting for another one on a different route. There was a long pause before the bus moved again, an even longer pause before he spoke again. "Death is not the worst thing I saw. People living without hope is more horrific to witness. I guess I realized how naïve and weak I was."

The words weighed on Lukas's mind. The loss of hope. Those words stretched out around his brain where they made themselves at home with Lukas's thoughts. Lukas believed once that he had seen the face of his true enemy. Hearing it looked like him was neither terrifying nor shocking. He knew he had scars, physical and emotional. The emotional ones could only have come from within. He was aware that the driver's ears were reaching out, waiting for comfort. He responded to the driver but digested the words hoping to find nourishment in them.

"There was meaning for you to survive and live through what you did. I am grateful you're alive. Hell, you and I would never have met, and I would never get home." The two new friends broke the tension with awkward laughs.

"The long and short of it, this was the only job I could get when I came back. Just driving people around. But it keeps my mind off things, and it pays bills." He drove slowly, enjoying the rare conversation. He glanced over backward. "Not many kids come to the front to talk to me, let alone college types."

Lukas knew what he meant and was ashamed of it. "Well, you have an important job, driving people to where they need to go. It's honest work."

"Ah. It is a job, no more no less." Silence drifted between them and settled. Uncomfortable with it, Lukas blew it aside.

"I thought you could use some company. But I probably needed the companionship more than you." He started to chuckle. "Not many kids in my school care about my music. Too out there, so you have one up on them." He reached over and extended his hand. "My name is Lukas."

Looking up in his mirror at Lukas, the driver thrust one hand behind him, reaching for Lukas's. "Nice to meet you, the name is Sean."

"Ever think of going back to school, Sean?"

"Naw, I'm too old."

"Never too old to change your path, Sean, never too old. I'm sure you have some stories and some wisdom to share."

"Really? You think someone would listen to me?"

"Sharing is part of healing. You went through some tough crap, I presume. Maybe the way to turn it into a positive is to impart some wisdom from it to others. I'm listening to you."

Sean's head bobbed forward and back. "You know the same applies to you?"

"Me?"

"Yeah, you were just itching to change the world, weren't you? Aren't you still?"

Lukas's eyes widened, the wisdom ricocheted back into his face. He looked out the bus window at the night stars. If Sean only knew how close to the bullseye he hit. Perhaps he did. Lukas pressed his eyes shut and thought back to the Lukas who once longed to change the world and wondered if he could find him. He wondered if the pin could be put back in the grenade, years after the explosion.

"You okay?" Sean could see Lukas's eyes closed from the mirror.

"There was a time when I thought I could change the world and make it a better place. It was all I longed for."

"What stopped you? Not that there's anything wrong with business school, but it doesn't sound like changing the world."

"I guess we all have our crosses to bear." The face of evil once looked back at him. The image in the mirror one night, years ago, was definitively his face.

Sean turned with a serious expression. "There are different types of war. The worse for me is not what I saw. What you don't see is something far sinister. The loss of innocence and youth. You can never get that back. I know." His words echoed around the emptiness of the bus and pulled Lukas's ears open wide before hiding inside. "I am sure your war was different in only the amount of blood spilled."

There were a good fifteen minutes to go to get near his parent's home. The bus was traveling through a familiar part of the city now, about to leave the outskirts for the new suburbs. He thought about Rosemary's words regarding moving beyond the past. It was now waiting for him just outside the window. There was something out there calling to him. "Can I ask you a big favor?"

Sean slowed the bus down. "Depends on what."

"Since there's no one on this bus and it's late, would you mind taking a quick detour and dropping me off someplace?"

"Yeah, sure. As long as it's not too far."

"Thanks. It's not more than a few minutes out of your way." Lukas gave directions quickly. Sean dutifully and with army precision arrived in a more decrepit section of the city. The houses were bungalows, many with shingles missing on roofs.

"Is this okay?" Sean asked. "I need to get back and finish off my route. This is where you live?" The question lingered in the air.

"It's where I grew up. My parents moved us away from here a few years ago."

"So you don't live here now? Why do you want to go here tonight?

"I need to follow my advice."

Sean turned all the way around. "For a business school kid, you are pretty complicated."

"I kind of realized tonight, I need to move on. A friend of mine convinced me. I just need to come back one more time. I have this strange feeling I need to do it tonight or else I never will."

"I see. Are you okay getting back? The buses only come once

every forty-five minutes."

"I don't think I'll stay here too long. I'll catch the last one."

"Just be careful. This neighborhood has gotten a little scary in the last few years."

Lukas leaned over and patted Sean on the shoulder. "It had its moments back then." He grabbed his backpack, stood up, and waved at Sean. "Have a safe ride the rest of the way tonight. Remember, you can still change directions. *You* are the driver." He winked at Sean as he descended the stairs.

Suddenly, the door opened and closed just in front of him, trapping him in the stairwell of the bus. He looked back at Sean, who tipped his cap to him with a toothy smile.

chapter eight

Propelled by unseen forces, gray clouds hurried past the moon. Far below on the residential streets of Morris Town, a solitary figure weaved his way through the streets and parked cars. It was now midnight, give or take five minutes, and the neighborhood silence was unsettling. Wandering cats along the side of the road offered only hints of life. A rustle of tree branches seemed to be the only sign of a three-dimensional world this night. Lights flickered from homes haphazardly. On a school night, the eerie quiet did not surprise Lukas. After all, this neighborhood always was working class and the home of many young families.

Lukas's family moved from this neighborhood because his parents wanted something more spacious and farther away from the buzz of big city traffic. Unlike most teenagers who were horrified to move and leave friends behind, Lukas put up no resistance in leaving his childhood neighborhood. Here he was on an October night, surprisingly drawn back to where his formative years were stitched together.

The streets were still damp from an early evening shower. The smell of wet grass and leaves nauseated him. The houses of his childhood remained as they always had. Some repainted, roofs redone, and trees wider and denser. His childhood home stood patiently waiting for him. The new owners repainted the window and door frames from a white to a contrasting black. The maroon tone of the brick façade appeared blotchy from the rain. The two inviting bay windows extending out to the street caught his attention. He could almost envision his sister's face pressed up against it in awe of the outside world. Their parents remodeled the sitting room at the front into a bedroom just for her. Hours upon hours, Lukas sat in the room with his back to the light, feeling the sun's warm embrace upon his neck and broad shoulders, reading to her. He was content to find the home well maintained, the lawn trimmed immaculately, and the perimeter fence freshly painted.

A gentle breeze sent a leaf down like a conductor's wand, brushing his cheek on its way to the ground. He lingered at his old home briefly, though it was not the reason he deviated from his journey tonight. Instead, he turned back to look up the long narrow street, the street lamps flickering as their bulbs gasped their final breaths. A dog barked in the distance, its sound echoing loudly, greeted by sporadic retaliatory barks. House by house, Lukas searched, until he settled on one, five houses up and one across. As his head tilted from side to side, an unintended smile crossed his lips. He stepped back, surprised by the emotion spilling out. Looking to the ground at his feet, he forced a frown on his face until he could reset his expression. Satisfied, he looked up again and instinctively studied the house from different angles. Warmth radiated within his core. He slowly crossed the street toward this one home, vacuuming in its details with each step like a chef savoring an aromatic broth.

Focus permeated every pore of his skin. Like a lizard camouflaged and invisible, he arrived on the steps of the one-story bungalow. Its green-painted wood porch and stairs remained unchanged by time. There were minor variances from his memories. The emotions coated them. He wondered if anyone noticed his presence this night. Admittedly, many of the current residents would recall Lukas, particularly in this location. He adjusted his backpack, taking in his surroundings. Who lived here now? There was a parked car, a Jetta, with rusted bumpers, and a child seat at the back. Instincts took over, and Lukas scaled two steps up, using the splintering handrail for balance. The last thing he wanted was a frightened family fearing this stranger on their stairs. He smothered whatever sound possible, including his breath. He sat on the top step next to the railing, leaving ample space next to him.

Silence and loneliness soon buried the nostalgia of his return. His hand extended to his right, farther and farther out, fingers hoping to touch a miracle. The coolness of the late night only accentuated the warmth missing. No one was next to him. He reached inside and raised the courage to glance to the emptiness beside him; the chipped railing was all he could see. His return to this place, once heaven on Earth to him, now bore a striking resemblance to everything else. The one spot where her presence warded off evil like an Egyptian Sphinx, and where he hoped to find her, now was vacant. Profound frustration overcame him. After Rosemary's sermon about moving on and forward, his hope, his last grip on the past, slipped away. Kara was not here where she had once always been. She had not been in years. His mind shivered as logic rained an icy cold over it. He now needed to convince himself that he had not imagined seeing her that September day.

His hands reached around and met below his navel, preparing for a silent prayer that never came. He persuaded himself of Rosemary's wisdom. The ghosts of the past jeopardized the good in his present He nodded and spoke just below a whisper to himself, almost hearing Rosemary's words. *Friends depended on him at the school. He could no longer appear to be weak or desperate. He needed to be strong and commit himself to wear a mask and play his part just for them, at least for the remainder of the school year.* It was his penance; he knew they deserved more than he had given, more of *that* Lukas. He descended the stairs and walked out into the street, turned and took one last look at what was, upon a time, Kara's home. Memories can deceive time, and the powerful ones toy with it.

Looking up and down the street, he hovered, no longer sure where the night would take him. Shadows forming on the blinds from the houses surrounding him seemed to be watching him. The carefully sheltered eyes followed him now. Rather than walk toward his childhood home again, he ventured into the less lighted section of the street. Moving closer to the park, the distance between the street lamps seemed to be measured in miles and not feet. The houses appeared more sinister with each step until he finally found the one house that taunted him.

With its rusted rails and cracked wood façade, the house appeared to be forgotten by humans, if not by time itself. Windows boarded up; there were no indications of life. The fence leading to the backyard was propped up by timber strategically placed. The gate swung open and closed to the beat of wind. Lukas moved toward the gate and stood at the entrance, surveying the lack of any color beyond that point. Gripping the gate, he dug his fingers into the tired wood, hoping to lock himself into place. The slivers of wood spiked his skin. He was oblivious to it. From behind him, he did not hear the encroaching footsteps of an older couple on the sidewalk until they called to him.

"Young man. You should not be there. That is private property."

Lukas turned to face the couple. He bowed his head in prayer, hoping they would not recognize him. Cautiously, he raised his head to look at them. In the night, he could barely make out their faces and could not tell if they lived here when he was a young teen. He could see the man gripping his wife's hand tightly.

"I was looking for something. I mean, I thought I saw an animal take off into the backyard. I was just curious."

"Well, you should not be hanging around outside at this late hour and especially on private property."

"You're right. I'll be on my way."

"Yes, I think that would be a good idea." The couple continued, and Lukas could hear the woman mention something about calling public security when they got back home. Slowly and sporadically, more prying eyes emerged behind the curtains and blinds of this neighborhood to the study this intruder.

Lukas's obsession with what lay beyond the gate mesmerized him, and he stood for minutes gazing into the abyss lurking ahead of him. Suddenly, Lukas dropped down to his knees between the gate posts. Fatigue had overcome him as did the weight of a million emotions. Off in the distance, he did not hear the vehicle approach nor the brakes bringing it to a stop on a nearby side street. The steps coming toward him grew louder with a sound caked in urgency. Expecting to see public security or even the police, Lukas's eyes exploded wide in panic and fear. Before he could even rise, let alone run, he felt two strong arms reach under his shoulders lifting him to his feet.

"Lukas, it's me, Sean. Are you trying to get yourself arrested?"

"Sean? What are you doing?"

"I came back to get you once my shift finished. I had a feeling you may need a lift home."

Lukas staggered free from Sean's grip and over Sean's shoulder could see the city bus parked on a side street with all its lights off. "Why? I know how to get back."

Sean looked at him and smiled. "Don't argue with me. I have good instincts for these things." He quickly looked over his shoulder. "Hurry up, though, and come with me. I think some-one called public security. I saw them lost on one of the streets nearby."

Following Sean's quick pace, Lukas jogged to the bus. Sean opened the door and slid into the driver's seat. The bus started abruptly as Lukas stumbled up the stairs and, with a worried look, toppled onto the seat across from Sean. Once the bus had rounded the corner and made its way a mile or two from Lukas's old neighborhood, he finally spoke again.

"Sean, what made you want to come back for me? I mean, I appreciate it, I just was wondering why?"

"It's just an instinct I have, I guess. Like I told you, they saw I couldn't fire a gun, so they gave me a bus to drive. I got pretty damn good at bringing back people from the battlefield."

"Well, thanks."

"Look, buddy, whatever it is that happened to you, I assume it is in the past."

"Sort of. Sometimes the past has a way of popping up around a corner when you least expect it."

"Whatever, it is, Lukas, next time, just hop on the nearest bus and take a different route."

Lukas laughed and leaned over to put his hand on Sean's shoulder, patting it gently. "Maybe the secret has all along been to find the right bus."

"Or the right driver. Now tell me where you need to go."

chapter nine

Summer and the end of the school year represented infinite joy to children of all ages. Lukas arrived home with a report card in one hand and a mask of determination across his face. In his mind, work remained. He was older, wiser, and more mature now, or so he was told on the final day of school. As an elementary school graduate, great things awaited him as well as new challenges in the coming months. Lukas slung his school bag across the room, knocking over a small table lamp and, more disturbingly, catching the attention of his grandmother, Ruth. She tore through the hallway and across the hard oak floors, entering his room without even a courtesy knock.

Ruth spent her days watching Lukas and his sister while his parents worked. Her husband and Lukas's grandfather would pick her up and take her home when he finished his shift as a head cook in a restaurant downtown. When he passed away, Ruth would stay over more often and longer. Ruth was not a towering or domineering woman. Nevertheless, her presence was noticeable whether or not she ever spoke a word. Her hair was gray and usually tied in a bun at the back. A flowery apron snaked around her waist as an appendage of sorts. Lukas knew that once the apron hung over the handle on the kitchen stove, she was done for the day. Ruth spent the day performing the regular household chores awaiting the return of Lukas and his sister, Maggie, from school. Amongst the noisier neighbors, presumptions linked Ruth's daily presence with the task of looking after Maggie. Within the walls and roof of this family enclave, the real caretaker of Maggie was her younger brother, Lukas. Ruth was merely a figurehead maternal figure for Maggie while her mom was away. In Maggie's world, the wonders of the universe were embodied in this young little boy she called Lukey.

Maggie was born a couple of years before Lukas. She did not cry much as a baby, a sign of her unique developmental path. Brought home from the hospital in the midst of an unseasonal April snowstorm, her parents harbored infinite hopes for the future of their daughter. Over the course of her first two years, their daughter did not develop at a normal pace. By the time Lukas was born, the heaviness of their daughter's condition had subdued their jubilation over having a son. When Maggie was five and in kindergarten, the reality of a child who saw the world differently from those around her became self-evident. Despite her difficulties communicating and making eye contact, she exuded a charm. Her brown hair, dipped in ginger, cascaded around her small round face and outlined a smile that could generate more warmth than a million suns. Her parents marveled at the glow of their daughter, whose brightness seemed always to shine a spotlight on her brother. From the time she set eyes on the rambunctious and energetic baby, it seemed she drew purpose from his being.

The devotion of sister to brother was far from one-sided. Lukas found a quiet confidence in this older little girl whose smile reassured him that even if his tummy ached or diaper needed changing, everything in the world hummed with a calming sound. His parents warned Lukas early on about his sister not under-standing the world as he did and how she was struggling to speak, let alone read. It was with a tremendous determination that Lukas asked or rather demanded Ruth teach him to read as soon as he could. Armed with the power to open a book and enter new worlds, Lukas immediately set about to bring his sister along with him on journeys of great adventure. On weekends, Lukas would tug on his mother's skirt or dad's trousers and beg them to take him to a library or bookstore. He would arrive with newfound treasures, a generous pirate was he, racing to Maggie's room and spilling these riches across her bed cover while she chortled with delight. From *Dr. Seuss* to *Curious George* to his favorite, *Winnie the Pooh*, Lukas took it upon himself to decorate Maggie's world with the most colorful of characters on the wildest of adventures. Lukas never complained. How could he? Such was his choice. The only source of frustration came upon the realization he would not be permitted to go to Maggie's school. His frustration lingered throughout his first years of elementary school. He could not imagine any school, even one with programs designed for children like Maggie, which would give his sister the unequivocal attention she deserved. In time Lukas learned the lesson of patience as he dutifully passed the time at his school, rushing home at a sprinter's pace to be with his sister in the late afternoon.

Lukas's preoccupation with his loyalties at home did not go unnoticed by his elementary school teachers. A model student with decent grades, each teacher sensed something profound within Lukas, as though he was preoccupied with a different world. A week before Lukas's elementary school graduation, the school guidance counselor requested a meeting with Lukas's parents.

In the car on the way to the meeting, Mr. and Mrs. Wunand wondered in silence as to what they were about to hear. A fear seeped through them, and as they walked up the steps of the school, they extended their hands together, holding them tight, each feeling the tremble of the other's. Lukas's dad looked at his wife and with a reassuring smile told her, "I am sure Lukas is doing well. He's just too quiet sometimes maybe."

"I hope you're right. Maggie is doing so much better now thanks to him. I don't want to think anything is wrong."

The meeting with the guidance counselor, a recent Ph.D. graduate of St. Peter's University, began with the handsome yet scrawny looking man extending his hand to put the Wunands at ease. He was in his late twenties at best. His hair was crew-cut short, his scalp visible on the side. His ebony glasses, thick and almost crushing his ears with their girth, slid slightly down his nose as he looked at them with an awkward smile. He towered over both of them, his long arms dangling from his short-sleeve dress shirt. His boyish demeanor was soothing to this anxious husband and wife team. No one so young could deliver bad news, or so they thought to themselves. Bad news usually came from someone white-haired or bald.

"Mr. and Mrs. Wunand, I wanted to meet with you to discuss Lukas and his development." He smiled as he receded into his chair, gesturing for them to sit as he reclined backward.

Grace Wunand sighed in a manner only her husband, Roman, could hear. He glanced over at her, offering muted support. Forever appeared to come and go before a voice spoke. "Is Lukas all right? Developmentally? You do know about his sister?" Grace asked.

The young man leaned forward and smiled. "Of course, I know about his sister. Everyone knows about Maggie. Lukas would never allow us not to know." He laughed. Each word dripped out of his mouth and onto them in a torturous fashion. He immediately continued. "Lukas is doing quite well. He has an abundance of potential and a thirst for knowledge most remark-able for someone his age."

Roman's smile was brief. He knew more was to come. "But? Something is troubling you about Lukas, or we wouldn't be here."

"Lukas is articulate, well-read, and tremendously caring, almost to a fault. I know from speaking to him and his teachers, he has invested so much of his time in his sister."

"Yes, we're so proud of our son. Without Lukas, I have no idea where Maggie would be. I honestly do not." Grace put her two arms up on the old worn wood desk, almost knocking over the pitcher of water sitting on it.

"You should be proud. But the heart of the matter is Lukas has sacrificed a lot of himself for her."

Almost gasping, Grace shook her head immediately. Roman reached over and grabbed her hands to calm her and prevent an outburst. "You stated that developmentally he's all right. What has he sacrificed?"

"Lukas is very much a loner in school. He does not spend much time with the other kids. He gets along with them but really has no interest in them."

"I guess he's not very good in sports," Roman said. "If he was, it might have been easier for him.

"According to our gym teacher, he is quite athletic. He's just so focused on going home to read and teach his sister that he's at risk of not having his own identity."

"Oh, he is just so good with her, and she enjoys his company so much. I'm not sure what would happen . . . if." Grace stopped and stared out the large rectangular window that ran along most of the side wall of the office. She was too timid even to say the words.

"Lukas needs to spend his time with kids his age and not have the responsibilities of his sister."

Redness filled Grace's cheeks, and defiance emboldened her. Her choice to work to help support the family was being prosecuted. Mr. Youttan rose from his chair and leaned against the side of the desk where Grace was seated.

"Mrs. Wunand, what I am telling you has nothing to do with you or Lukas's grandma watching Maggie. It is about Maggie having the opportunity to grow and blossom. She is after all a teenager. She can be more independent."

Roman raised an eyebrow, processing how much this young upstart knew about his kids. "How do you know about Maggie? You seem to know a lot."

"I've spoken to the teachers at her school on a few occasions. They tell me she's progressing beyond anyone's expectations. They believe she may be ready to join a regular class within a couple of years."

Grace's eyes widened. "Really? Are you sure?"

"Mrs. Wunand, Lukas has done so much for his sister and taught her so much of the world or, dare I say, the world as he perceives it. The challenge now is for Lukas to become part of a new world."

"Mr. Youttan, I truly appreciate how much thought you have put into this and obviously how much you care about our children."

"Mr. Wunand, it's not hard to care. It's hard to tell someone their child needs to be let loose into a world that may not be as forgiving or as embracing as the one they envisage."

"Yes, we're worried it will be a difficult transition for Maggie." Grace looked at her husband and spoke on his behalf. "However, to think our Maggie could even have the possibility of being in a regular class is certainly worth the risk."

Mr. Youttan tightly pressed his lips together and walked back around his desk to lean against his chair for support. "I'm referring to your son, Lukas."

"I'm having trouble understanding why this is such a concern. Lukas is only eleven. I agree less time with his sister would be good for him, but he will adjust." As he spoke, Roman clenched his hands.

"Lukas is tremendously idealistic. His compositions, school artwork, and everything about him speaks to this."

"All good qualities." Grace was quick to interject.

"Of course, admirable and noble. You both know the world doesn't work that way. Lukas needs to experience the world for how it is. If he doesn't do it soon, it will be tough to deal with things when he's older. He is starting high school in the fall."

Grace nodded her head forward as she brought her hands to her face. She looked over at Roman, and a truth buried layers upon layers beneath the earth was dredged up like a treasure with each holding one side. The realization stirred up emotions within her and her eyes watered. "Mr. Youttan, I am so sorry for being difficult. My husband and I both know you are right. What can we do for Lukas? I mean, how will we tell him he should spend less time with his sister?"

"One thing you can do is consider sending him and his sister to separate camps, whether a day camp or sleepover camp. The rest has been taken care of." His smile raced across each side of his face, almost extending around his head.

"Mr. Youttan, what have you done?" Roman looked at him as if the guidance counselor were his child.

"I'm good friends with the counselor at Maggie's school. I was over there today to speak to Maggie. A remarkable young lady."

"And?"

"Well, she wants to talk to Lukas and thank him for all he has done for her. She also wants to let him now it's fine to follow his path going forward."

Grace looked at Mr. Youttan. "Maggie agreed to this?"

"Trust me when I say this. She actually cannot wait to speak to Lukas."

Roman got up and paced across the room. "How did you ever get Maggie's buy-in?"

"Maggie sees giving Lukas his freedom as this great gift she is giving him."

Approaching the back of his wife's chair, Roman put his hands on her shoulders. The two took their cue from Mr. Youttan, who got up to usher them out. With enthusiasm, they both shook his hands.

Crossing the door frame, they proceeded down the hall with Mr. Youttan close behind when both parents stopped suddenly and turned. It was Grace who spoke.

"Thank you, Mr. Youttan. The school is quite fortunate to have young people like yourself working with our children."

"Grace, if I may, good fortune lies in those whose footsteps fall upon the same path as your kids." With those words, he retreated silently to his office and the next set of parents awaiting him to discuss their child.

Roman and Grace drove home with nary a word piercing the tranquility of the air between them. They wondered what awaited them when they arrived home. Pulling into to the driveway they could see through Maggie's window, the drapes slightly open. The slit created gave them a line of sight to their son, Lukas, as he entered Maggie's bedroom, book in hand, not knowing the Maggie he had known was about to play the role of big sister for the first time in her life.

chapter ten

The sun was exceptionally bright as Grace and Roman Wunand exited their automobile and slowly made their way up the stairs to their home. They had rehearsed their speeches along the way. Grace would speak to her daughter and Roman to his son. They glimpsed Lukas perched at the edge of the desk chair while Maggie paced in front of him in perpetual motion. They could see a book clenched between Lukas's fingers. His head tilted to one side, a confused looked on his face. Indeed, a rare occurrence to see Lukas seated, a student before his sister. It was often the other way around.

By the time they reached the top of the stairs, Ruth already had opened the door to intercept them. "Something major is going on. Maggie demanded to speak to Lukas even before she had her usual snack after school."

"Ruth, we know. Are they okay?" Roman's eyes shifted to the window, and Ruth looked in from this new perspective, through the clear glass.

"Yes. I have never seen Maggie so sure of herself. I'm worried about Lukas. He came home with a book and was all intent on reading it to her."

"Crap." Roman looked at his wife and gestured with his hand. Lukas had disappeared from view, and the bedroom door was open.

"Time to pick up the pieces." Grace raced past Ruth, who stood stoically, yet apparently confused and now worried.

Roman put his hand on Ruth's shoulder to reassure her before shuffling by her. "I'll explain later." He winked and followed his wife. As his wife entered and closed the door, Roman glimpsed Maggie and heard his daughter's voice before the sound muffled. "Mom, I told Lukas, as they said. Like they told me."

He looked down the hallway to the corner bedroom. The light emanating from the room was bright. Lukas's room looked out onto the backyard and, with summer starting, the bright early evening sun shone directly into his room. Roman rapped politely on the door while entering, uncertain as to the state of the young occupant's mind. He found Lukas sitting on his bed, staring down at the book in his hands. Rather than proceeding, he stood for an instant to observe his son. There was no indication of Lukas reading the book, rather he appeared to be feeling it, as if the words were jumping off the page and massaging his fingertips. Realizing the attention, Lukas looked up. The dark eyes met his father's, absorbing whatever light sprang forth from them. Roman realized how young and yet truly ancient his son was. The trepidation had lasted for a nanosecond before a grin on Lukas's face disarmed any threat of negativity.

"Dad, Maggie may be going to a regular school one day!"

"She told you that? What else did she say?"

The words slithered across the floor, and Roman could feel Lukas struggling with the response even before the words could crawl up to his ears. Roman realized, in his son's typical fashion, that no one would steal away the victory from his sister, even Lukas's disappointment.

"She told me that I didn't have to spend as much time teaching and reading to her. She said that to get to the regular class, she needed to do things on her own." Lukas's eyes circled the room as he spoke. His teeth protruded from his upper jaw and, with each syllable, bit hard down on his lower lip.

"Are you good with that?" Roman said while slowly positioning himself next to his son at the edge of the bed. He crouched down to make sure he met his son's gaze at his level.

"Of course, why wouldn't I be?" The thought of anything selfish instinctively upset Lukas.

"I wondered if you might be disappointed spending less time with your sister."

"For sure." His lips began to tremble slightly. "She told me it would be good for me to make new friends and have more time for myself."

"She is a wise young woman, your sister."

"I guess I never realized it until today."

"Well, she takes after her younger brother, I suppose." Roman patted his son on the back as Lukas sucked back a sniffle before laughing. "What book were you going to read with her to start summer vacation? It looks quite familiar."

"*The Catcher in the Rye*. I guess she would have to read it one day before she graduated so maybe a head start would help."

"Good thinking. At least you can still read it yourself."

"I plan to. Just maybe not today. I don't feel like reading right now."

"The edition you have seems quite old. I don't recall taking you to the library for it."

"Dad, it's your copy. I found it in a box of your old stuff."

"Wow. I forgot what a scholar I was," Roman said, grinning.

"Everyone had to read this, even back in your day."

"Let me check to see if it is mine." Roman reached for the book and flipped through the pages. "I used to underline sentences with a blue fountain pen." Roman opened a page and laughed.

Lukas immediately tore the book out of his hand and found the one line on the page underlined in blue.

"Oh, it's the line about marrying someone who laughs at your jokes."

Lukas looked at his dad and chuckled. "You thought this was an important line?"

Roman smiled as his wife entered the room almost on cue. "Still do." He rose from the bed and addressed his wife.

"Lukas had a magnificent talk with his sister."

"So Maggie tells me. Who needs parents anymore?" Grace giggled at her joke while staring into Lukas's eyes. Suddenly, Maggie appeared behind her mom, peering into the room. She maneuvered quickly around Grace to hug her father.

"Dad, I told Lukas it was time."

"Maggie, time for what?"

"He has read many stories about other people's adventures."

"Yes, I'm sure he has."

"You don't understand."

"Maybe not. Please explain."

Lukas fidgeted at the edge of the bed before locking his left hand tightly to his right. He could see his sister grow-ing frustrated with finding the words. Her eyes shut in peace, the words being collated together behind her eyelids, being assembled in an orderly fashion to depart through her lips. Her eyes opened slowly.

"I will be the one reading to Lukas one day. I promise I will, one day."

"What about the stories of people's adventures?" Grace leaned toward Maggie and placed her hand on her elbow, reminding her of her train of thought.

"Yes, the best part. I told Lukas it was time to start his journey."

Lukas looked up at the three faces staring at him, the book

now closed in his hands. A new façade now overtook the ancient appearance his father saw earlier. Lukas suddenly seemed like the child he was, and the adventure awaiting would come not from the pen of a stranger in a two-dimensional world.

chapter eleven

Heat and humidity marked the first days of July. The neighborhood kids assembled outdoors upon devouring their breakfast. Impromptu games, improvised and improved with rules added daily pushed their creativity. The children returned home at sundown, parched and exhausted, oblivious to the oppressive heat.

Lukas Wunand stood in the middle of the hallway having just finished a bowl of Special K cereal drenched in milk. The physical changes occurring within him were accelerating. Aside from the humming of Ruth washing the breakfast dishes, an eerie quiet permeated the household. Lukas meandered into his sister's bedroom and forensically studied it with his eyes. Everything was in place and orderly, in stark contrast to the utter chaos of his sister's everyday existence. Maggie left early that morning with her parents to a summer camp about two hours north of the city. It was a camp for children with developmental challenges recommended by Mr. Youttan, or Dr. Youttan, as Grace now referred to him. Maggie would be spending the next two weeks there, separated from her family for the first time. After considerable reflection, Lukas realized the feeling of loneliness was slowly buried by pride. The happiness for his sister coupled with her words for him invigorated him. It was 10 a.m. and he could hear the piercing voices of the neighborhood kids intertwined with high-pitched chirps of the sparrows in their nests. He ran into his room, dug out his baseball mitt, donned a cap, and raced outside. Ruth chased him down before he could descend completely down the front stairs.

"Lukas, I think you need shoes, don't you?"

Looking down at his socks, both mismatched in his haste, he shook his head in disbelief. "Oh shit!"

"What, young man? Did I hear you say what I think you said?" Ruth pretended to be angry. She took delight in witnessing Lukas's eagerness to venture outdoors. She long found him to be too pale and in desperate need of some Vitamin D.

"Oops, I guess I did use a foul word." Lukas smirked as he reached for the sneakers Ruth held out for him.

"Have fun, young man. I will make you lunch in a couple of hours. Remember your parents' rules."

"Yes, I cannot leave the street without your permission."

Ruth smiled and stared as Lukas raced down the street to join a group of children, some younger, some older, five houses down. She marveled at how quickly Lukas blended into the group. Although Lukas's appearances on the street were few and far between during his early childhood, his undeniable charm and non-threatening manner made him most welcome. The kids also recognized his natural athleticism and were sincerely happy he joined them. Satisfied, Ruth withdrew inside to complete her daily chores. For the first time in years, she would be alone in the home during the summer. The thought of sipping a cup of Earl Grey tea and maybe finally watching one of the afternoon soap operas in peace delighted her.

For the next couple of weeks, Lukas basked in the glow of being the new kid on the block. The irony being he had lived on the street longer than most. Many introduced themselves to him as though they never met him. In no time, Lukas became a valuable player on the baseball team his street had assembled. In the world of street baseball, the outfield position required a pure athlete. Any ball hit past the infield could roll forever, and the batter could easily circle the bases and score a run. Ryan Oldham, a seventeen-year old, stressed to Lukas the importance of playing center field one day on the eve of a big game against a rival street.

"Lukas, we need you in center field, okay? We cannot lose to Pine Street today."

"No problem, Ryan, nothing will get by me. You know that."

"I know that, Lukas. If anything does, run like hell to get the ball."

Lukas pounded his fist in determination. He had not yet turned twelve, and the senior kid on Dakota Street was counting on him. The boys took their positions on the field. The handful of girls who lived in the neighborhood avoided the boys in general and did their own thing during the summer. The exception was the girls who swooned over some of the older boys. Lukas's focus was on the task at hand, and he was naïve to the social game played under his nose.

The burden of living in a sprawling city in the mid-80s was the lack of green space. Kids made due with open spots on city streets where parked cars were mercifully few during regular work hours. Today's game took place close enough to Lukas's house, and as Lukas took his spot in the outfield a hundred or so feet away from his home, he could see Ruth standing in Maggie's bedroom, a cup of tea clearly in hand, watching. Looking away, he pretended not to see her. Making sure he digested his surroundings, particularly any obstacles he may face in tracking down an errant ball, his head circled the street.

The sun reflected on one of the only cars parked on the street that day, with a moving van parked just behind it. He watched as the movers maneuvered a large sofa into one of the most run-down homes on the street. The creaking of the dilapidated wood stairs burdened by the weight made him wince. As the movers made their way back down, a solitary figure seated amidst the hustle and bustle became visible. Obscured by the furniture and men moving up and down the stairs, he hadn't noticed her before. To satisfy his curiosity, he turned completely around. Her long hair and the light blue summer dress she wore with brown sandals reminded Lukas of characters from novels set in the south. Intrigued, he tried to make out her face, but she leaned forward, her head buried in, of all things, a book. A book! She was reading, oblivious to every distraction around her. Fascination danced within Lukas's mind, utterly diverting him from the supreme task entrusted him, chasing a white ball down an asphalt street.

"Hey, Who Nad!" They never pronounced his last name correctly. "Pay attention out there."

Lukas quickly turned around. The last time he felt so exposed was when his mom caught him eating ice cream at 2 a.m. It served her right, Lukas deduced at the time, for bringing home double mountain fudge. The sharp piercing of the scream annoyed him, especially since for a second, he reveled in the moment.

As he zeroed in on the game in front of him, a tiny flake of intrigue floated back and forth through the cavern of his mind. *A girl reading a book.* Perhaps he never knew how tight he could seal his thoughts and, for the next hour, not once did he even attempt to glance over at the girl. For all he knew, she long ago retreated inside.

The game meandered under the summer heat. The enthusiasm that roared wildly like a flame across the wild bush had peaked much earlier. The boys agreed it would be the last at-bat as Lukas made his way to his position. The beauty of summer baseball amongst children is each child kept their score, with every child

convincing themselves of an undeniable victory. With one out
to go, Lukas pounded his glove, leaning forward with his heels,
pushing his weight onto his toes.

Suddenly, almost on cue, a collision of bat and ball sent a
sonic boom in his direction. Without even looking up to catch
the flight of the ball, Lukas raced back instinctively, recognizing
the sound of a well-hit ball. Gasps popped in the humid air like
firecrackers. Lukas assumed the noises resulted from admiration
of such a well-connected hit. Upon looking, the horror of a worse
calamity than a run scored against him energized him. He could
see the bright blue rusted car parked in front of the house where
the girl sat reading. At best there would be a dent buried deep
into the car's hood when the ball landed, or worse, the windshield
would shatter into millions of pieces.

Lukas summoned the elasticity of every joint, tendon, and
ligament in his body as he dashed toward the intersect point of
baseball and parked car. Mere feet away from the car's side mirror,
Lukas timed his leap forward. With an outstretched left hand, he
slid partially across the windshield of the car. His eyes were closed,
braced for the pain he expected to feel around his hip as it thud-
ded against the car and dreading the sound of shattered glass. A
second or so passed, then another, and then another. Before long,
the chorus of congratulations and exaggerated guffaws reached
his ears. His left eye opened to find his brown, oil-stained glove,
partially ajar, with a familiar white objected nestled within. An
oyster could never hold a pearl as solemnly or protective as Lukas
did as he slid himself gently off the car.

"Lukas?" Ryan's loud baritone voice, while not the only one
thundering through the street, was certainly the most distinctive.

"Yeah. I'm fine." The repetitiveness of "great catch" and "way to
go" overcame even Lukas's thoughts. He smiled as he examined

the car before preparing to saunter back to the adoring masses waiting to greet him in the makeshift infield.

Just as he was about to take his first stride, a voice floated through the air, chasing his ear before finding it and devouring it with its vibration. "That was a nice catch. Thank you." The voice itself sounded surreal. The accent hinted at British with a trace of Hindi. So different from anything Lukas ever heard in the neighborhood before. Lukas signaled for his friends not to wait. He would catch up with them later. It was lunchtime anyway so despite Lukas's heroics, most were more than happy to be gestured away into their homes where cold beverages and sandwiches likely awaited.

Replaying the voice over and over in his head, his hand caressed the ball with every stitch brushed by the top of a finger. With a sheepish smile, he lowered his head as he turned to respond to the compliment. "Thank you. It was a lucky catch. My eyes were closed." His eyes remained closed and stayed that way as he stepped timidly toward her. The scene resembled a valiant knight returning from great battle at the feet of a victorious queen—she sitting at the top of the stairs, he, with head down, at the base.

Her voice trembled ever so minimally. Lukas could hear the nervousness as she spoke. "It's my father's car. You saved it from some severe damage. He would be so upset, so, thank you."

Temptation stoked the fire of courage, and Lukas raised his chin. He wondered what her lips looked like—imagining them formed by the caress of her soft words flowing over them. The smile came instinctively although his eyelids remained shuttered. She noticed his awkwardness.

"Are your eyes okay? The sun is not quite so bright today."

The grin extended, threatening to abandon his face, and as his eyes opened, he quivered despite the daunting heat. Her eyes were darker and deeper than his, pulling him in with ease. Her hair was jet black and straight, pulled back behind her ears. Her skin was olive, making his seem pale and unhealthy with an egg-shell tinge in contrast. Lukas felt sloppy in his sweats and T-shirt in front of this picture-perfect girl sitting so properly in her dress. Nodding to him again while waiting for some sign of life, she woke him from his reverie.

"Oh, my eyes are fine. I would have felt awful if something happened to your dad's car." Each word came out of his mouth slowly, so slowly that he could almost see the letters crawl through the sky. Her eyes never left him, and typically being scrutinized would be unnerving. Not today. Everything about this girl comforted him and relaxed him. Without a further word, he maneuvered to sit beside her on the front steps. Once seated, he sensed a change in her. Nervousness overtook her and resonated with him.

"Is everything all right? You seem edgy." He leaned closer to reassure her like he had done so often with his sister, and she recoiled in embarrassment. Lukas's head drifted down, unsure of what brought on this change. "Did I say something wrong?"

Lifting her head, she sniffed quickly and put her hands close to her chest. "My father will be back soon with the movers."

"Don't worry; his car survived. I'm pretty sure there's no scratch, maybe a scuff on it at worse." His hands motioned toward the car.

"No, it's not that. My father has old fashioned values. About girls and boys our ages."

Lukas's mouth opened wide as his head began bobbing. He thought he understood and desperately wanted to interrupt but intuitively allowed her to proceed.

"Let's just say he would not be fond of a boy sitting next to me on the steps of my house. I'm only eleven."

Her honesty made him comfortable, almost too much so. "Hmm. Well, if we got married, it would be allowed then." Horror flooded every crevice with him. If only he could drown fast enough. A vain attempt at humor. *So dumb*, he thought. Much to his surprise, the awkward silence he anticipated never came.

"Oh, I'm sure my father would love that." Her face lit up with a glow, soaking up every ray of the sun, devouring it from the sky in front of his eyes. "That is quite funny."

"Wow. I don't know if I should be happy you share my terrible humor or sympathetic or both." He looked into her eyes and the blackness of each melted together and intertwined. The reflection of his smile within her eyes baked into memory.

"Seriously, though, my dad would not be pleased for you to be here. I sincerely do not want to sound rude. I truly don't."

Lukas stood up and faced her with one foot leaning forward on the stair. "You don't need to explain. I understand. I don't want you to feel uncomfortable. I'll stand, and if he comes back, I'll just pretend I'm picking up my ball."

"Sounds like a plan. A good idea. I approve."

"What's your name? Are you allowed to divulge that info or do I need to cross the street and have you yell it across?" Lukas winked almost involuntarily at her, recoiling ever so slightly.

"You can call me Kara."

"Kara. I like it. I think I'll keep calling you that, so please don't change it." Lukas laughed again, enjoying the smile forming on her lips, highlighting her cheeks.

"And what is yours, if I may ask?"

"Lukas."

"A good old-fashioned English name."

"You just moved here today. Right? You're moving in?" Lukas

asked, the anxiety in his voice making each syllable tremble.

"Yes. We arrived late last night, and the moving vans were here early today."

"Where are you moving from? Overseas?

"Ah, I guess my accent gave it away. We lived in England since I was born. My parents are from India, and much of my extended family is still there."

"That must be exciting. England has so much history."

"I'm more than happy to move here. We didn't live in a great area. It was where my dad found work."

"Is he here because of work?"

"Yes, he's a university professor. He teaches physics or will be at St. Peter's starting in the fall."

"He must be brilliant."

"Yes, he does think so. I mean it's just that he still lives in the old world."

The excitement was evident in each of Lukas's questions. Patiently, he interviewed her and equally patiently, she answered his questions with her shoulders straight back and her hands across her lap, resting on her thighs. "You're going to Riel High School? That's where I'm going."

"No, sadly that is a co-educational school, if I'm not mistaken."

"Yes. It is." He paused and noticed a frown on her face. "Oh, you can't be with boys, not even in school?"

"No. I'm attending St. Mary's, an all girls' school." She started shifting in her seat, suggesting discomfort.

"Is something bothering you?"

At the concern in his voice, she looked up at him. "You're not bothering me. I cannot talk to boys. I mean I shouldn't be."

"Your dad is very strict?"

"Just old fashioned. My mom is probably more so. I hope you

take no offense. They would not think it proper, what with you standing here for so long."

Lukas put his head down sadly. Understanding her parents' way was not something he readily grasped. He grimaced before forcing a smile on his face. "I guess I should leave you be then." He backed away slowly and turned, watching her eyes as she followed his movements.

He took two steps forward when he heard the creak of stairs behind him and quick footsteps growing louder behind him. She reached out and touched his shoulders delicately and so rapidly that by the time he turned, she was completely still standing in front of him. She smiled at him as she spoke. "Thank you again. I did enjoy talking to you."

Before Lukas could reply, she turned just as the screen door behind her opened and a woman appeared in a colorful red and purple sari. Her black hair was tied at the back. She had subtle wrinkles under her eyes, which were charcoal. Hints of gray appeared randomly in patches in her hair. Her face was stern and severe. Lukas could smell the smoke generated by the fire that burned in her eyes. Anger tensed this woman's shoulders and appearance as she scolded her daughter in a language Lukas had never heard. She flailed her arms at Lukas like one would chase away a stray dog. The rant did not last long, but its power approximated a hurricane in the damage it inflicted. Lukas could see Kara's eyes watering and witnessed her shoulders slump.

"You're in trouble because I spoke to you. Darn it. Can I speak to her?"

"Lord no, Lukas. You must go home. I'm in enough trouble. Please. She means well and is truly a good person. Believe me. Don't think badly of her. She cannot help it."

Lukas's eyes drifted skyward to witness the clouds passing each other in the sky. He desperately tried to conjure a spell to make everything okay. He sighed and looked at Kara. "I'm sure your mother is a wonderful person. Just as I'm certain that your father is."

Kara tilted her head, confusion obvious on her face.

"They must be pretty special to have you as a daughter." Without waiting for a response, he turned and walked home.

The street was quiet with the children indoors enjoying their lunches and likely planning their return in the afternoon. Lukas anticipated Ruth wondering where he was while waiting for him with a grilled cheese sandwich and maybe lemonade. When he got to his front porch, he did not enter immediately. He sat and looked back up the street to Kara's house. He could see her sitting where he first saw her, with a book visible in her hand. All he could do was obsess over making things right for her. While he returned to his home in apparent retreat, a thought that brought happiness from the depths of his soul occurred to him. When he left his house that morning, his notion of beauty was defined by words on the pages of books that he read. In all the stories of princes and princesses, heroes and heroines, his imagination would flash images of what it was. However hard he tried, he knew he could never touch the beauty from those stories. He grinned as his gaze settled on the figure sitting on the porch. Now he had seen beauty in this world. His hand reached up gently toward Kara, pretending to caress her hair from afar, his eyes bright and full as the sun cast its light and engulfed his eyes.

• • •

Kara sat on her porch, staring at the same page of her book for the next few minutes. She would get another lecture from her mom later and would again listen to a repetition of the message when her father arrived. Stealing a peek up from her book and down the street, she could see the strange boy, one hand in the air, rhythmically moving it up and down, looking like a magician with an imaginary wand. She smiled and returned to her book, her hand reaching into the top of her blouse, pulling out a necklace hidden underneath. She closed her eyes as she kissed the sigil at the end of the chain before tucking it away. The fear of coming to a strange country was replaced with excitement and the comfort of being on the same street with her new friend. The sun reached its midday peak and bathed the street in its light. Looking up at it, Kara opened her mouth as if to swallow its light, laughing in delight at her childish gesture.

chapter twelve

It was late August when the reminder letters arrived for high school. The list of school supplies, clothing rules, and bus information were indicators that the carefree days of summer were soon to end. Lukas's sister returned home to a victory parade, sort of, in late July. Lukas, too, enjoyed his camp experience for much of early August. By now, Lukas mastered the art of subtle communication with Kara. Standing in center field on the days of street baseball, he would adjust himself so any balls hit in his direction invariably resulted in him finding his way near Kara's house. The conversations were short snippets on an individual day. Taken together, they told a story.

Lukas was ever so careful to avoid the scrutiny of Kara's mom or dad. There was no way he would put herself in an awkward position again. While Lukas longed for much more time with Kara, he grew satisfied with just being in her presence. He did wonder how long this would go on. On an unusually blustery August day, events transpired that changed their interaction forever.

It was early morning when Kara's dad left in his car to begin preparations for the upcoming semester. The winds howled in the morning, signifying the coming of the cooler months. Lukas stood in his driveway adjusting Maggie's bicycle seat.

"Maggie, see if it's good. I put it a little higher."

Maggie dutifully climbed on the bike and smiled, satisfied. "That is much better. Thanks." As Maggie disembarked to allow Lukas to tighten the screws, she began pointing frantically.

"Kara is crying. I see her crying. Something is wrong." Upon return from camp, Maggie learned quite quickly of her brother's relationship with Kara. Her enthusiasm was reassuring to Lukas, who wondered how Maggie would react to Kara's existence. In fact, Maggie became an impromptu messenger as her appearance on Kara's lawn was far from intimidating. Kara took an instant liking to Maggie. Through understanding Maggie and her struggles as a child, she gained a tremendous respect for Lukas.

Lukas immediately stood up and looked toward Kara's porch. She was not in her customary spot. His eyes searched and looked back to Maggie to calibrate with her line of vision. Sure enough, off to the side of a large red maple, Kara stood crouched down with her arms outstretched, appearing to sob. Lukas told his sister to wait for him as he raced to check on Kara. Maggie tried to remind Lukas of the potential fool-heartiness of his actions and potential for a confrontation with her ever-present mom. For Lukas, Kara's safety superseded any such concerns. Within seconds, he was by her side.

"Kara, what's wrong?" He looked down on the grass around the tree, and almost instantly the situation revealed itself.

"The birds. The babies. The wind pushed them out of the nest. They're all over. The poor things."

Lukas looked up and examined the tree, branch by branch, searching. In one of the upper reaches of the tree, a nest must have sat, as Lukas could see brown and yellow remnants of straw on one of the branches. The remainder of the nest no longer was visible.

"Where is the nest? Do you see it?"

Kara pointed a few feet away. Sure enough, a tightly packed and wound nest sat upside down on the grass. Walking to it, Lukas carefully picked it up. Lukas heard Kara's breathing grow more and more rapid, almost hyperventilating, as she pointed frantically at the baby birds scattered within a few feet of the nest. Without further thought, he reached out to her and held both her hands. It was the first time he had ever touched her. He felt the warmth flowing through her long narrow fingers as they trembled.

Eyes wide at the assertiveness of his actions, Kara looked at him.

With a slight smile, he said, "Everything will be just fine. We can save them. I need your help. Please go get me a small container and fill it with water. Small enough to fit in a nest."

Kara raced into her house and returned with a small plastic container filled with water. When she came back outside, Lukas glanced at her house and, in the windows, could see a slit appear through the silk curtains. There was no doubt in his mind whose eyes patiently observed from the opening in those curtains. For now, Lukas would not fear the consequences. Staying focused for Kara was the prime directive.

Lukas reached over and took the water and set it aside. He bent over to the nest and picked it up.

"Hold this. Keep it steady and stay near me." She followed him with the nest in hand as he bent down to study the ground. He carefully cupped each small bird he found, all almost featherless, with veins protruding from their thin skin. Most of them had their eyes closed while all five he found had chests that thumped visibly with rapid heartbeats. He placed each into the nest, using his fingers to push them gently close to one another to keep them warm.

"Shouldn't you be wearing gloves?

"I probably should but I'll just give them a good scrub after. I don't have time now to find a pair."

Once the babies were snuggled together in the nest, Lukas took the nest from Kara and fitted the small water container into the nest. With nest in hand, he walked around the tree, carefully plotting his next course of action.

"You're not going to try to climb to the top!"

"No, just high enough to keep them out of sight from any cats or whatever." After finding a branch that extended securely and shielded from the sun and rain, he began climbing. As he moved along the branch, Kara followed him underneath. Had he fallen, she would break his fall. Methodically, he reached the end of the branch and secured the nest. Once satisfied they were secure, he shifted his weight and slid off the branch, landing ten or so feet below on his side, mere feet away from Kara.

She raced over to him with both hands, reaching down to help him up. Lukas placed his hands on hers, and one swoop later was up on his feet, his body close against hers. Silence could be priced in gold as their eyes met. Each saw the other in the tunnel of their vision. A sharp chirp from near the top of the tree pierced the air, causing Lukas and Kara to simultaneously step back.

With a smile, Kara broke the silence. "Thank you. I think you need to go now." Lukas knew exactly what she was trying to tell him and took no offense. Her eyes betrayed her as she looked at something in the background. Before he could cross the street back to his side, she added, "Do you think they'll be okay?"

"The birds?"

"Of course, the birds."

"Yes, I do. I think the mother already came back looking for them." He pointed to the top of the tree where a plump robin sat. Kara smiled as her eyes grew wide.

Looking beyond Kara, Lukas could see Kara's mother peering

from the window, her stern look locked almost in concrete. He walked home concerned less with Kara's mom's reaction to his indiscretion. Something more disturbing troubled him. He knew the robin would likely abandon the nest, baby birdies and all, since humans had desecrated it with their touch. The baby robins would likely not survive. Lukas vowed Kara would never find out.

Having observed the whole scene, Maggie sat patiently on the curb. When it came to Lukas, nothing surprised her anymore. She winked at him with a wide grin. "That was fun seeing you together."

Days later, Kara stood patiently at the edge of her lawn awaiting Lukas's appearance outdoors. Lukas promised he would check on the birds in three days. If he didn't know better, she stood guarding the tree daily. He saw her from the window of sister's room. Maggie could sense his pensiveness.

"Why aren't you outside? Kara is waiting for you. I think."

"Maggie, you are too right. I just don't know how or what I'm going to do."

"The birds. She wants to check up on the birds."

"Yeah. I'm sure of that."

"She needs you, Lukas. The poor girl is waiting. Why are you scared to go out?"

Lukas inhaled and as he did, he coughed with all the air he sucked in. Maggie was right, as usual. Despite her sometimes simplistic view of things, she usually was right. The night before was a sleepless night for him. Knowing what he needed to do was not an issue. Dishonesty upset him more.

"Please go see her and make her happy," Maggie demanded in an impatient manner. Her teenage voice shrieking with excitability.

"Calm down, sis. I'm going."

He left his house with his laces untied and socks that did not match. The trek toward her house could have passed for a turtle marathon; only a turtle run would have been more exciting. Lukas stared at the tree and outstretched branches. He prayed he would see a head or two protrude from the nest or any sign of life. Drawing nearer did not settle his nerves down. Kara fidgeted upon his approach.

"Where were you today? I wanted you to check on the birds."

Although the answer was self-evident with Kara wearing a Sunday dress, he asked anyway. "You mean, you haven't checked yet?"

"Good joke, Lukas. See how I'm dressed? You think my mom would let me climb a tree in this?"

"Kara, I don't believe she ever would let you climb a tree. Speaking of which, did she say anything about the other day?"

"No, of course not. She was having her tea and listening to her TV show while I was out."

Lukas looked at the window behind Kara. The blinds were shut tight in contrast to the opening and the eyes peering at him during his previous mission. He shrugged and moved toward the tree. His eyes lined up the nest in his sights but, to his dismay, there was no movement, no sign anywhere of a mother robin. Lukas easily climbed the tree. With no nest to carry, the climb and crawl along the extended branch took a mere instant. The pause before looking inside the nest lasted an eternity. Kara positioned herself directly below, in his field of vision. He knew his facial expression needed to be carefully considered and managed. A bead of sweat began to trickle down from his temple and settled on his cheek briefly before dripping to the lawn below.

He straddled the branch, shifting his body weight forward as his outstretched fingers wrapped around the branch. The nest lay silent just ahead of his sight and appeared to draw closer to him.

Carefully, he moved his head forward until he finally could see over the straw enclosure. Horror mixed with fascination caused his heart to skip a beat. In the corner of the nest were the baby robins just where he left them, snuggled together. Only now they were lifeless. He reached in with a finger and placed some loose straw over them. In and of itself, the gesture was pure nonsense and the reality pulled him down. He suddenly lost his balance, fortunately catching the branch with his hands to steady himself. The action drew his face closer to the birds.

Death had never looked at Lukas before, nor he at death. When Ruth's husband died, Lukas did not visit the funeral home as he was considered too young. The feeling within him humbled him. He had seen life three days earlier. Today it was gone. In trying to save the birds, Lukas learned how much of a persistent adversary death could be. The quietness of mortality deafened Lukas with its heavy steps on his heart. Before he could face Kara, he looked up between the branches and leaves of the tree and a sliver of sunlight shimmered through the thickness, almost blinding him. In between the leaves and the sun, way high in the sky, he could make out birds flying overhead. He wondered what death was. Looking closer at the baby robins, he sensed something powerful, a presence not in the bodies of the robins. A presence in everything around him. A comfort from an unknown source soaked him. A gentle breeze guided a leaf against his cheek.

Kara reached up and tugged at his sneakers. "Well, is everything okay?" Her voice was hesitant, fearing the answer or worse, silence.

Lukas opened up his mouth wide and nodded to her. "Yes. They're all gone. The nest is empty. They must have flown away and off to a better nest, probably higher up." The words were crisp, confident, and clear. Reassurance pouring from his mouth slid into her hungry ears. She gleefully clasped her hands together.

"Lukas, you did it! You saved them."

"You and me. Not just me." By the time he finished, he had shimmied backward down the branch and tree. He stumbled slightly as he hit the ground. "I'll leave the nest there for a day or so, just in case they come back." A plan soon was conceived. Pointing at the clouds, he continued, "Looks like it's going to rain soon. I probably should leave in case your mom has finished her tea."

"I feel so much better now. I knew I shouldn't have to worry. I knew you wouldn't let me down." Her eyes shifted from side to side as her head angled toward the ground.

Lukas's hands clenched together, trying to hold back every urge to hug her. To resist temptation, he turned and ran home, racing up the stairs to witness Maggie staring at him with an approving grin from her window. He put his head down and spent the rest of the day in his room, where thunder could be heard in the distance. He wondered if the thunder signified approval for his deeds or a warning of punishment for his dishonesty.

The night came early for Lukas for he had plans. At 4 a.m., he arose from his bed. A little drizzle tickled the window in his room. An alarm clock was set and proved unnecessary as Lukas lay awake most of the night. His blue-striped cotton pajama bottoms and white Jockey T-shirt were all he had on as he tiptoed through his house and unbolted the front door before sliding out into the thick of the night. Sunrise tauntingly awaited time to signal its entrance for the next day's show. Lukas needed to complete his mission before the sun rose and the first neighbors awoke. No one could see him and especially anyone who potentially could mention what he was doing to Kara.

Once outside, Lukas raced into his backyard and, guided by the light coming from the street lamps, found a garbage bag. He zig-zagged his way across the street and in seconds stood before Kara's lawn staring up at the red maple. He looked at the windows and could tell the blinds were fully drawn. He could not hesitate or risk exposing himself. In his haste to climb the tree and retrieve the birds, his palms skidded along the branch, ripping his skin. Crying out in pain was not an option nor was the luxury of self-pity. In agony, he shifted the nest to its side and emptied the contents into the bag.

Stumbling on the wet grass, his pajama pant legs soaked in the moisture. He looked around for a garbage bin to discard the bag amongst the driveways along the street. Not finding one, he proceeded to return home, deciding to use the trash container in his driveway. The last clouds from the rain floated off into oblivion, revealing to Lukas the stars in the sky. He looked down at the bag and its pure plastic coldness and stopped in his tracks. Thoroughly distracted by the throbbing pain in his hand, he nodded to himself. Returning to Kara's front lawn, he crawled under the tree and up to the small garden beneath the window at the front of her house. With his bare hands, he dug into the earth. Satisfied with the depth, he carefully removed the robins from the bag and tucked them into the earth close together before blanketing them in the soil. After pressing down firmly to level off the top, he closed his eyes and prayed for the souls of the birds. This was Kara's house, and where they belonged.

As he rose, his eyes blinked as a glow of orange burst on the horizon. His hand ached in pain. In the sparse growing light, he could now see the slivers of wood buried embedded in his hand and caked in dirt. A feeling of utter dread ripped through him; he could feel someone watching him. Cautiously, he rose and turned in a full circle, wondering if a stray dog, raccoon, or worse, a skunk was nearby. Noticing nothing, he breathed again, his eyes drifting up. To his chagrin, he could see a noticeable slit in the window blinds, and worse, two eyes, piercing and ominous, were quite visible. Without hesitation, he turned and scurried like a squirrel back to his home.

The next day Lukas's parents were surprised to find a trail of soil mixed with blood leading to Lukas's room. They opened his door to find him lying in bed in a bottomless sleep, his pajamas wet and reeking with the smell of stale earth. Grace called Roman to Lukas's room while exchanging worried glances. Maggie's door opened, and she marched confidently to her parents just outside of Lukas's room. Maggie put her fingers to her mouth and, in an exaggerated fashion, signaled her parents to come to her room. When they entered, puzzled and worried, she closed the door behind them, excited to tell the tale. "I saw what happened, Mom and Dad. Please do not be mad at Lukas. He did well."

When the tale was told, Grace and Roman Wunand shook their heads in disbelief and pride. Grace bit her lip and marched through the house and entered Lukas's room. She sat at the edge of the bed and observed her son as he slept before leaning over and placing her hands on his forehead. She brushed back his hair and kissed him on the cheek. That day, Lukas went to see a doctor and arrived home with a bandage and a prescription for antibiotics. When his parents did not demand an explanation for his condition, Lukas's curiosity grew restless.

"Aren't you wondering what happened to me?"

Roman reached over and grabbed his wife's hand squeezing it slightly, a signal he would answer. "You know, Lukas, you're not as good a spy as you think. Your sister told us what you did."

"She saw me? Geez. I thought I was super quiet. What exactly did she say?"

"It was all about a girl."

"You're not mad?"

"We're grateful you're okay. Mad, not at all. You truly like Kara, don't you?"

Lukas was silent but couldn't conceal his smile.

"You don't have to answer."

"Thanks, Dad. I figured you knew the answer."

The following week school officially started. Lukas left earlier and arrived from school before Kara's bus from her girls' school. Lukas arrived home and drank a glass and a half of milk before heading outside to await the return of Kara. He paced up and down the street across from her house. Her door opened, and her mom swooped out onto the porch. Lukas halted on his side of the street and turned to face the opposite direction, hoping to avoid scrutiny. Suddenly, a voice with a distinct accent, almost like Kara's, only older and slightly lower in tone, snuck up from Kara's home and trapped him.

"Mr. Lukas, why don't you come wait for Kara on our steps?"

Convinced the antibiotics were causing a delirium so far-fetched it was unbelievable, Lukas froze. Whether he knew it or not, a squirrel with a peanut within its clutches looked less paranoid. The voice continued. "Mr. Lukas, please come sit on my steps and wait for Kara."

In shock and fearing the most monstrous of consequences if he did not follow the orders, he crossed the street with his brows pressing tight on his forehead, unsure of himself. He arrived at the base of the steps and looked up to this woman, who in the month since he had known Kara filled his heart with pure terror.

"Did you not know I speak English? Is that what surprises you?"

"No, I mean, are you sure I can stay and wait for Kara?"

"Is that what you want to do?"

He wondered if he was falling into some complex web or a

game of cat and mouse. Recalling the eyes following him that night and the day they found the birds, he decided to move forward in trust. "Yes, I really would like to wait for Kara. Only if that is fine with you?"

"Of course, it is, young man. I will bring you a glass of lemonade. Kara tells me you like lemonade."

"Thank you. I would like that."

She motioned for him to take a seat before making her way into the home, only to return with a glass of lemonade. In one motion she maneuvered herself next to him. He thought he would be uncomfortable in her presence yet found her to be quite gentle. The stern face he had been accustomed to had given way to a kind, gentle woman who, without question, loved her only child. Lukas finally smiled at her as he sipped on his lemonade. She smiled back, and he could see the source of Kara's beauty.

"Do you like our garden? The one beneath the window?"

Lukas gulped on his drink and followed where she was looking. It was no doubt it was the spot. When he said nothing, she continued, "It is a special garden. There are many things I hope that grow beautiful out of that which is planted in that garden. Do you understand?"

"I think so."

"Mr. Lukas, I know Kara thinks of you very highly."

"That is nice. I appreciate that. I think highly of Kara. She's my friend."

"I know you think highly of her. I do not doubt that. You know, her father and I came from a destitute place. We made many sacrifices to go to England and now move here. Our one child is what we do everything for and let's say maybe we are overprotective of her."

"I understand, and I . . ."

Before he could continue, she put her finger to her lips. "I want you to know you are welcome here anytime, young man. You will always be welcome."

Lukas bit his lip and struggled to direct his feelings in an orderly manner. The only words that passed his lips were more than enough to elicit a broad smile from Kara's mom. "I care about her."

She reached over and patted him on the cheek. "I know you do."

Just then an orange school bus pulled up at the corner, and Kara came toward them, marching with her head down and pink backpack swinging in her hands as she hummed to herself. A few feet away from her home, she finally looked up, and her pace noticeably slowed as she witnessed the sight of her mom and Lukas on the front steps. Her faced contorted in disbelief.

Lukas waved at her and yelled out. "Hi, Kara! Your mom and I have been talking and waiting for you."

Kara glanced over at her mom and then at Lukas. Both shared the same silly grin. Placing her bag down, she angled her head to the side to examine her mother from a different perspective.

"Yes, Kara, Lukas and I had a very pleasant chat."

"You did, are you sure?" She saw her mother's expression look exasperated and rephrased her question. "What did you talk about?"

"I told Lukas he could come to our house anytime he wants. He will always be welcome here."

Kara could not contain her emotions. The worry on her face was chased away by pure joy. "Really, Mommy. You are serious. He can even sit with me on the steps?"

"Most certainly he can. I trust this young man."

"What about Dad?"

"I will speak to him. I am not without my charms."

Kara looked at Lukas with both excitement and bewilderment.

Her heart thumped beneath her dress as his eyes and hers met. Kara's mother got up slowly and made room for Kara to sit.

"Kara, I will get you a glass of lemonade. I'm sure the two of you have lots to talk about after your first day of high school."

Alone on the front seats with Lukas, Kara moved closer and leaned her shoulder against him. The two sat silently that evening, cherishing the moment together. Words were not needed to convey the shared feelings.

chapter thirteen

The buzz in the air and the frenzied activity in the bowels of the St. Peter's Faculty of Business cafeteria unnerved Rosemary as she entered. Without the benefit of a calendar, Rosemary sensed midterm exam anxiety taking over so many of the first years. Nerves were shot, patience thin, and the school chapels became busier than ever as students sought forgiveness for their sins, just in time for midterms.

Rosemary no longer looked across the cafeteria for Lukas in the far corner. His absence since September from the depths of the building tempered her enthusiasm for being here. If it were not for her coffee and chocolate croissant fix, she likely would stop venturing this far down aside from the Student Society meetings. While her intentions for having a one on one with her friend came from her heart, the selfish nature of it played on her mind. The bandage around her cut finger reminded her of that.

Upon entering the cafeteria, she noticed that a line was forming far from where the food counter stood. Instead, the line was at one of the desks pushed against the wall nearby. It was where the school announcements, handouts, and student newsletters were placed. It dawned on her that today was the day the monthly "magazine" came out. To say it was a journalistic endeavor severely strained the bounds of credibility. Plain and simple, it was a satirical eight-page collection of pure juvenile delinquency. It created the cult following of pied piper proportions; only Lukas never did play the flute. In an industrious month, the paper ran for sixteen pages. Lukas's contribution ranged from the serious to the utterly bizarre. One month, he included a fake classified ad section complete with someone trying to sell a "dead parrot." Another month, there were fake classified ads for items such as a peep show booth maintenance man, a casting call for a fictitious school play, and people looking to adopt lost students.

Rosemary entered the line, her curiosity getting the better of her. She tugged on the shirt of the young male in front of her. "Why the fuss?"

"The magazine. It is out. Everyone is trying to get a copy."

"Yes, they usually print enough for everyone."

"Um, I need to look at it as soon as possible."

"Why?"

"They put the stats exam answers in it. Our big midterm is this afternoon."

"Hmm, I see." Rosemary suddenly felt a surge of joy, hoping that her intuition was right. A first-year student walked by her with a light blue booklet in his hands. His eyes focused on the page in front of him, and she could see his lips moving and head bopping in unison to the words. He was memorizing the damn page! She abruptly shoved him in the shoulder, almost toppling him.

"Sorry. Can I take a quick look, please?"

"Geez. You need to chill. Besides you're graduating, why would you care about the stats answers?"

"I need to take a quick look."

Reluctantly, he held out the paper for her to read, ensuring it would never enter her hands. As she perused the page, there was no longer a doubt whose fingerprints were all over this one. "Thanks and good luck." The student jammed the paper under his eyes, returning to his memorization ritual. The page had a heading entitled "Secret Stat Answers" and then fifty numbers with letters ranging from A to E next to each. The first-year stats exams were traditionally multiple choice since both prof and school were too lazy to create an exam requiring any subjective grading. The page was signed, "Your friendly neighborhood Statman."

Ram entered the caf with a chuckle and a laugh. From his expression, Rosemary figured he either was in on the plot or quickly caught on. She surmised that Ram was not so quick on the best of days. Therefore, he surely knew about this well before. She cut him off and pulled him aside to speak in private.

"Lukas put the stats answers in the magazine? What the fuck is he thinking?" Her voice exuded anger. The initial emotions of joy were now muted realizing Lukas may have stolen exam answers.

"Shh . . . Rose, calm down. Lukas did it, of course. He was in the computer lab all weekend."

"I knew it. But, you know Lukas could get expelled for doing this! How did he get the exam?"

"My friend, Rosemary, you are not thinking clearly. Would Lukas do something so dishonest?"

"Oh shit. You mean the answers are incorrect."

"Yep. He used a random generator program and, voila, fifty multiple choice answers. The joke is on all of those trying to cheat."

"That is so Lukas." She reflected on the return of the prodigal enigma and convinced herself that all was well with the world again.

"That's not the best part. Each one is different."

"You mean everyone has different answers. No two has the

same?" A rhetorical question if she ever heard one.

"Yep. Can you imagine when they start comparing answers? They will be totally flipping out."

Rosemary put her hand on her face to control her laughter. Lukas must have spent hours putting his plan together. His "A" game returned to the delight of his friends. "So, where is he?"

Surprised by the question, Ram's eyebrows twitched. "He is where he always is. Correction, he reclaimed his throne." Ram turned and nodded to the far corner of the room and the last seat on the last rectangular table. Sitting with his feet up on the table, wearing sunglasses, and holding court with a bunch of students was the prankster himself. Sunglasses were an added touch worn by him on occasions like this, allowing him to sit back and observe unseen.

Excited to see his old self back again and wreaking havoc on the faculty, Rosemary walked toward him. He acknowledged her approach with a raised Styrofoam cup. "Cheers, Lady Rosemary. Welcome to exam day at the Faculty Lounge." He swiveled to the side and extended his feet to kick out an empty chair for her to sit. "The throne awaits, my Lady Rose."

Rosemary shook her head. The stark reminder of how over the top Lukas could be caught her off guard for a second. The students at the table moved back to allow Rosemary passage to the seat Lukas ordained for her. Positioning herself in the chair so she could stare directly at him, she cast a look that spooked him.

"Rosemary, did I do something wrong? You seem freaked out a bit."

She leaned forward to him to whisper, not wanting everyone else at the table to hear. "I wanted to know how you were doing. I was worried after our talk the other night." She paused, realizing by his reaction that her scrutiny could indeed be considered unsettling. After all, Lukas's behavior could not have been any more than she could have wished for after their talk. But there was something about it that seemed distinctly wrong.

"Gosh, Rosemary. I'm the last person you need to worry about." He lowered his glasses to the edge of his nose to give her an earnest wink before tucking them back up, covering his eyes. "I wonder what all the fuss is about today. Seems to be quite a commotion."

"You know perfectly well what is going on. It appears some anonymous person published the stats exam answers. The wrong answers, of course."

Lukas leaned forward almost dropping his cup. "Do not be so melodramatic! I'm sure they're the right answers." He paused and after a slightly dramatic silence, said in a quieter voice while sipping on his cup, "For some exam somewhere in the universe."

"All I know, Lukas, is some poor souls are going to fail and fail their stats midterms badly because of this."

Lukas's face exploded in expression. He could not hold back the delight from his face. "Poor capitalist bastard business students." He rose slightly from his chair to announce with a mock toast. "To the REVOLUTION!!!"

Rosemary shook her head, the monster having been repaired, unleashed, and out into the wild again. She got up and patted him on the knee. "Glad you're back!" She saluted him in a manner only he could appreciate. "Permission to leave for class, sir!"

Lukas played right along. "Permission granted, private!"

Rosemary walked away and passed Kirsten heading into the cafeteria. "Hey, Kirsten, you might find Lukas in back of the caf if you choose to look."

Kirsten smiled. "I heard he returned to his spot. I'll catch up to him later. First, I need to get my hands on those stats answers.

That's why I'm here."

Without saying another word, Rosemary continued moving on, rolling her eyes out of sight of Kirsten. *Oh boy, dumb capitalist is right*, she thought. Remembering she had three hours of classes ahead of her, she decided to make a pit stop at the snack counter, which now had a sparse line.

"Hey, Willie, a medium coffee, please." She reached over for the cup and poured in a dose of milk. The flowing white of the milk mixing with blackness fascinated her and gave her pause. "Willie, how did Lukas take his coffee today?"

"Oh, he's back to his usual. Black as black can be. Don't know how that kid does it. Pure straight up coffee must be burning a hole in his gut."

She stirred the milk, not saying another word. Looking back at Lukas as she left the cafeteria, the doubt escaped the cage she thought was secured. Sure, Lukas was back to his old escapades and in his routine again. Could she truly expect her speech impacted Lukas so dramatically as to call off his obsession with this girl so swiftly? The vibrant expression on Lukas's face, when she previously asked him if he loved this girl, danced before her. Rosemary knew she would never forget the depth of sadness in his face. In her spare time she read up on psychology and human behavior, and the metamorphosis she witnessed defied logic. Of course, the aberration was Lukas's behavior in September. The detour completed, Lukas had found the path again thanks to her. Yet, her motherly impulses implored her to accept that Lukas never deviated, even for a second, and to question anything led into unchartered territories. Resolve cemented itself and Rosemary continued her journey to class.

• • •

Meanwhile, Lukas sat with the magazine in hand, reading it aloud. A good portion of it had been authored by him, whether it was credited or not. Laughter filled the cafeteria. The bell rang as the next round of classes commenced. A changeover took place at Lukas's table, with students coming and going. The constant was, of course, Lukas. Pretending he didn't understand the chaos bouncing through the room, and watching with scientific delight as his grand experiment unfolded before him, he sat patiently as new disciples settled themselves. Yes, this in many ways, like much of what Lukas did, represented an experiment, a sociological one.

The sunglasses masked the truth swimming in between the white and black of his eyes. For years, walls were built to conceal and protect emotions. Built out of false anger, the crumbling of those walls was inevitable. Whether Kara appeared to him physically or merely in the spirit that morning was irrelevant. His soul awoke to find itself torn, the other half missing, and the revelation that she was a part of him profoundly moved him. Now that he had this wisdom, he knew he needed to protect its spirit. So, he found a place hidden within him where he would keep those feelings close to his heart and warm. The physical world on this campus now was foreign to him. He did not belong here—he never did.

He observed the students milling about that day. Many excited they were going to get a shortcut to a good grade on a midterm about probabilities, means, and arithmetic sums, pure logic. Many were studying how to market products to consumers. Many were learning how to run a business, efficient organization structures, and most cynically, how to strive for affluence. Yes, he chose to enter this world to hide because it was the last place anyone would ever find him. Well, anyone looking for him who knew him as a child. Sean's words rose to the surface, identifying his thirst for a perfect world. He promised it to Kara—her entrance into his life confirmed its existence once again. Time, space, and matter conspired to have him here today, surrounded by the familiarity of strangers.

He looked at these kids, older than children, more naïve. There were mere months left in the production, and he would take on the role with passion and bravado. Impersonating what the mirror portrayed only required he bury his true being and lose himself for a while longer. These kids needed him, and this would be his way of earning the forgiveness he sought. He hoped forgiveness would come and maybe playing this role would suffice as his penance.

On that bus ride home, Lukas pondered the role of an actor. A great actor not only entertained but also inspired and taught. Once the students finally settled in with their snacks and lunches, they looked to Lukas to precipitate a discussion. Without glancing down, he reached into his backpack and pulled out a paper. Tucking the paper into his magazine copy, he opened up the magazine.

"Well, let's see what crap they put in here."

"Stats exam is on the last page," shouted one of the students at the table.

"No, no, something else. Absorbing. Here, I'll read it to you."

The students now, whether initially wanting to pay attention or not, were taken in. None had been at the table an hour earlier when Lukas introduced the same act. A good performer sometimes has multiple performances in a day.

Papers could be heard shuffling and ruffling as everyone around the table tried to decipher the source of Lukas's oration.

"What the fuck are you reading? I don't see it anywhere."

"It's not in there. It's a poem I just chose to read."

"A poem. Are you serious? What does it have to do with any-thing? We are not artsy. You're kidding, right?"

"No, not kidding at all. No one is forcing you to listen."

A girl at the end of the table leaned forward and placed her bag on the table to get everyone's attention. Lukas recognized her from the party, a friend of Kirsten.

"I know this; it's T.S. Eliot. 'The Hollow Men'?"

"Yes," said Lukas excitedly. "I know it's an old one. Nevertheless, very appropriate in any age, especially amongst all us business students." He winked at the girl, her face reddening with the sudden attention.

"Okay, Lukas, the joke is over. Take off the sunglasses. Amusing, I suppose, to be reading poetry here today."

Expressionless, Lukas put his feet up on the desk. Noticing his yellow untied laces on one shoe, he leaned forward to fasten them. "No joke. I thought it would be nice as a change of pace to throw in some literature now and then." Finally succeeding in tying the lace, he reclined back in his chair, almost tumbling completely back. "Every day, whoever wants to can come and join me here at this table so we can read together. Bring whatever you want. Yes, even if it is an old *Mad Magazine*. Love that 'Spy vs. Spy' shit."

Faces looked more glazed than a donut. For every snicker, there was enthusiasm. Some students missed reading stories and poems and found the reprieve from business cases welcome. Lukas returned to the poem and continued reading it. Those who departed did so quickly with dismissive glances at him. Others drew their chairs closer, some asking Lukas to repeat stan-zas. As Lukas read, a corner of his mouth expanded higher up his chin, a smirk gracing his façade. The story of Johnny Appleseed was one of the first Lukas had ever read as a child and remained one of his inspirations.

chapter fourteen

Never before had the St. Peter's Faculty of Business been a breeding ground for literary genius. The weeks following the infamous stats exam episode marked a renaissance of sorts for business students. Any casual passerby to the basement cafeteria could be confused by the sounds of a student, using a myriad of accents and voices, reading from various literary works. What had begun as pure jolly and satire instantly became ritualistic in the hands of one Lukas Wunand.

The rumors spread around the faculty quickly. Soon enough, the curious would wander into the secluded corner of the cafeteria and sit at Lukas's table. Whether first years or graduating students, Lukas cared not who they were or why they were there. He acknowledged some were there to enjoy the spectacle or share a laugh, maybe even at his expense. The truth is an audience is an audience. To a skilled showman, the audience could be the show itself.

Within a couple of weeks, two tables needed to be pulled together to accommodate the participants. Yes, the audience had become active in the readings. Lukas encouraged those around him to read and assigned parts or pages to his fellow students. Rosemary marveled at the pure joy that emanated from the back of the otherwise dreary basement. Students looked forward to these moments. For some it was a return to a long-lost love, reading for the pure enjoyment of it. There would be no tests, no requirements to interpret the work, and no obligations. Even Kyle, who struggled to get through university, began a daily pilgrimage to the back of the cafeteria when his class ended.

Ram was first to highlight the distortion in the picture. Rosemary may have sensed it, but she chose not to pursue that line of thought. It was in the week leading up to Christmas with final exams approaching that Ram forayed into the world of unpleasant truths. One morning, before Lukas arrived, he found Rosemary alone, savoring her morning coffee.

"Rosemary, has Lukas been to class recently?"

"Not really. I can't say for sure. He comes and goes."

"I don't think he's gone at all. He's in a couple with me. Since early October he's been AWOL."

Rosemary paused and placed her cup down. She knew full well an inconvenient truth lay exposed. She pursed her lips and shook her head solemnly. "He does spend all his time here. I sort of noticed that, too."

"He comes to all the parties. He drinks more now, also."

"I guess he's living the life now. Maybe he's enjoying his last year a little too much."

"Well, it's not that I'm worried about him. No one has his head screwed on more than him."

"He has been all over the map since this year started."

"I thought he was over the girl stuff. Moved on and all that, thanks to you."

"Yes. I don't know anymore. Maybe I'm imagining things."

"And Kirsten? Any action?"

"Goodness, she wants him badly. He talks about her and everything. It just never goes further. He keeps her at a distance."

"That boy. Well, hopefully, persistence pays off."

Rosemary shook her head and changed subjects as the cafeteria gradually filled. Yes, Kirsten was a regular at the table with Lukas. Yes, Kirsten followed Lukas at parties, trying to find a quiet moment alone with him. If escape artists needed training, Lukas would be the perfect mentor. Sheer intelligence would get Lukas through his courses; this was of no concern to Rosemary. Nor was she concerned about Lukas finding a job once he graduated. He had worked the summer at the firm where Tobin's dad was a partner. So, as long as Tobin was not completely put off, Lukas had a full-time job. More disconcerting was his utter contempt for his established norms in the faculty. Perhaps it was just her imagination.

Christmas exams came and went with the New Year beginning with a foreboding. Campus security was heavy as students returned to the faculty in January. Ally broke the news to her fellow executives that assaults against women on campus increased in the months leading up to the holidays. The crimes were occurring more and more frequently around their faculty.

"Campus security will be more active on our grounds as a result. We need to do something." Ally looked over to Tobin, who sat passively at his desk.

"Look, we have to let the school police take care of things. We cannot have people panicked here on campus." Tobin got up and walked around his desk. He pointed to a large wall calendar that extended across the elongated back wall of the Student Society office. All the scheduled activities for the winter semester were painstakingly posted on it. "We have career days, guest speakers, and so many activities planned in the next couple of months. We cannot make more of this than needs to be."

Kyle, who was the sports rep, looked up cynically. "You mean you're worried about the school's reputation, aren't you?"

Tobin's eyes squinted as he brushed back his blonde hair and grabbed it at the back, squeezing it before speaking. "I do not want anyone thinking we have a problem here."

Upon realizing the insinuation, Ally looked stunned. "You think it could be a student. That's even more of a reason to do something. We have to protect each other. That is our responsibility."

"Ally, stop being melodramatic. We cannot hurt the reputation of the school by being alarmist. Guys, I know what I am doing. Fear mongering is not an answer." He stepped back and looked around the room before pounding his fist on the calendar. "All these activities are high profile for us, especially those graduating and anyone seeking summer employment. I do not want any potential recruiter or sponsor backing out." He grabbed his black leather briefcase and walked to the center of the room. "This discussion is over. Let security do its job. Oh yes . . . nothing gets out about our discussion!" He then stormed out of the room, leaving his fellow executives casting glances at one another.

Ally shook her head defiantly and muttered under her breath. "Fucking asshole."

chapter fifteen

A flowing white blanket caressed the trees and lawns of St. Peter's campus, hiding autumn's imperfections. Much like the mood within the school of business, the snow could hide the secrets of past seasons, framing them in the form of the footprints that violated it. Despite the vain efforts to misdirect discussion of the violence now closing in on the faculty, fear itself fell out of the lips of the students.

The waves of insecurity found the intense shore of Lukas's thoughts soon enough. Ally chose to let Lukas hear the punchline of the executive meeting from a different source. A punchline, indeed, to a sick joke. Violence, let alone sexual violence, was abhorrent to Ally, who grew up in a home where she witnessed its very horrors. Sincere trepidation tore through her when she heard Lukas from across the cafeteria requesting her presence. She could never resist his charm even during the heaviest of moments.

"What's going on, Lukas? I guess you wanted to talk to me about the exec meeting."

"Yeah. I heard Tobin was a real douche. I do not understand him sometimes."

"Look, I've bothered you enough over this issue. Others need to step up."

"I have something in mind to send Tobin a message."

"He's still our president, Lukas, and your friend. I don't want to start anything." She settled back in her chair, her fingers subconsciously twisting in small circles the edges of her hair just above the ear. The anger in each twirl and each tightly wound thread of hair was palpable. Lukas dipped his index finger into his coffee and slid his lips across the finger before sucking all the coffee off it.

"Tobin needs to be put in his place. Well, at least taken off his high horse."

Reminding herself that it was he who had summoned her today, that she hadn't been the one to incite him, she inhaled deeply. Buried within her, voices sang in delight. The allure of witnessing Tobin usurped appealed to her immensely. Her left hand reached out to Lukas before giving the back of his right an enthusiastic rub. "Thanks again, Lukas. I appreciate your concern. Please do not jeopardize your friendship." A soft tap on one of Lukas's knees preceded her departure.

· · ·

Lukas watched Ally as she walked. He knew her childhood story and what she witnessed. Although she claimed the past was long ago lowered into a final resting spot far away, the footprints sprawled across the pure blanket of her soul were visible to him. He shook his cup deliberately, watching the dark liquid shift from side to side, daring to leap its boundaries and potentially burn his hand. His grip on the cup tightened as he raised the beverage to his lips and in one sip devoured the contents. What he intended to do would wait until later that night. He pushed back his chair and extended his feet up on the table. A nap waited for him. Sleep and he were acquaintances, though not necessarily friends. His mind was forever jealous and alert, guarding against subconscious thought. It's how he managed to stay focused on his purpose and devotion to his buddies. The subconscious, however, lurked in the background, tireless and seductive.

The last of the stragglers left the bottom floor shortly after 10 p.m. Lukas arrived in the cafeteria and sat patiently. Ram agreed to join him and partake in his plot. Curiosity sat heavily on Ram's massive shoulders. Lukas pulled out a silver key, set it in front of him on the table, and began twirling it in a circle. He imagined a game of spin the bottle and practiced to see if he could get the key to spin and stop at the same spot. Tapping his foot impatiently, Lukas looked at the clock. Soon enough, he could hear Ram's heavy steps coming down the stairs and his feet stomping the snow off his boots.

"Hey, buddy! Sorry, I'm late. I had a class all the way on the other side of campus and lost track of time."

"Ram, you were about to miss the fun." Lukas gave the key a final spin, grimacing when he witnessed where it pointed. "Christ, it never points to the girl I want to kiss." He shook his head as he picked it up in his hand, gripping it like a hawk would a worm.

Ram looked around the room. The act was so convincing, Ram could be seen staring where the key pointed almost expecting a girl to appear there. "Man, you are one strange dude. I doubt you wanted just to spin a key around all night."

"You know me too well. Okay, follow me to the offices." Ram dutifully followed his friend out the cafeteria and down the hallway to the Student Society office. Lukas turned the key and flipped the light switch. The fluorescent bulbs protested at first before hiccupping to life. Lukas stepped aside to allow Ram to enter in front of him. Ram stood and looked around the room, trying to gauge Lukas's intentions.

Seeing his friend struggling to get his bearings, Lukas said,

"Look over *there,* Ram." Whatever clarity of action Lukas possessed, Ram did not. Lukas pointed directly across the room at the oversized wall calendar hanging. "My canvas awaits." He paused to squeeze Ram's arm tightly. "I mean, our canvas!"

"You are not planning to mess with Tobin's calendar, are you? I mean, are you planning to steal it?" Ram's thoughts jumped haphazardly to every possible conclusion.

"No, I would never steal it. How would we ever know when the Business Achievement Awards were! Think of the kids, Ram!" Lukas chortled, laughing crazily while trying to contain it at the same time. Putting his hand on Ram's shoulder, he patted it three times before sauntering over to a desk. He opened drawer after drawer before finding a blue marker he fancied. Raising it in the air, he motioned like a conductor with an army of musicians at his disposal. His hand eased the cap off the marker before turning to the wall-sized calendar in front of him.

Ram stared at Lukas with his mouth gaping, even though the madness of his friend should by now not surprise him. The option of interrupting his buddy never crossed his mind. He chose the option of leaning against one of the desks to enjoy the performance taking place. Unlike Rosemary, who overanalyzed cause and effect in perpetuity, the moment was paramount for Ram. Energy consumed Lukas as if attracted to the lightning rod of Ram's presence.

Lukas motioned in a circle at the calendar. The blue wand in his hand taunted the canvas in front of him. His eyes leaned forward to study entries on certain dates. Tobin meticulously documented every campus activity for the faculty on his calendar. If it was not entered here in big print for all to see, it was neither going to happen nor of importance. Finally, Lukas turned to Ram. He smiled at him before moving on to the board again, changing his facial expression to a frown in the process. "I thought Tobin was much more thorough than this."

"What do you mean? The bugger has everything on his damn calendar. Shit, I think his folks' birthdays are up there, too."

"No doubt, but there are some clear omissions." Lukas paused before moving closer to a date on the calendar before pulling back and looking at Ram. "I don't want you to get in trouble. I'll understand if you leave, and if you stay, I never saw you."

Ram smiled back. He walked over to a small fridge in the corner of the room and pulled out an aluminum can. It was beer the sports reps for the faculty stashed away for themselves. He peeled back the tab and the snap pop of the gas escaping exploded through the room. "I am not going anywhere. I'm not going to miss this."

Lukas's face erupted in delight. His eyes widened, and the corners of his mouth pushed his lips to his cheeks. "All righty then, let's see where to begin." The blue marker danced on the paper as he scribbled in the boxes one after another, his pace quickening as he went. Ram would lean over at times to get a better view, especially when the print was too small. Suddenly, Ram slipped off the desk and landed on the floor. The pain as his butt crashed to the ground was muted by the delirious laughter spewing from his lips. Lukas raced over to make sure he was uninjured, picking up the beer can that scattered its contents along the floor. "You all right?"

"Oh man. You are crazy. Seriously." Ram got up, grimacing, although his pain reflected the sorrow of partly spilled beer. Laughter, soon enough, overcame the pain. "What is this you have for March 2? Guest Economics Lecturer, Fidel Castro!"

"Yes, I was surprised myself that Mr. Castro would take time from his busy schedule. Hell, if it's on the paper, he must be coming."

Ram moved on to March 9, "Ponzi Day, Clothing Optional."
He stared at Lukas, shaking his head.

"Well, how can anyone have a real Ponzi day and not be naked?"

Within an hour, and before Ram could consume a second beer,
the calendar glowed in bright blue ink. Each previously open date
filled with an event existing solely in Lukas's imagination. For
some real events, Lukas added small clarifications. For example,
the Accounting Club Wine and Cheese had the added caption in
small, bold print, "Bring your own weed."

"He is going to be so freaking pissed at you when he finds out."
Ram's voice got low and almost in a whisper.

"I'll just have to throw him off." Lukas's head darted back and
forth across the paper in front of him before settling on a spot.
"This would indeed be a memorable day and most appropriate."
The pen jiggled across the paper to his personal rhythm. Satisfied with his creation, he took three steps back. "That will throw
him off, I think." He laughed, not caring if Tobin ascertained his
identity or not.

"March 29 Final Beer Bash: Lukas Finally Gets Laid." Ram
nearly choked on the words and the aluminum can popped as he
squeezed it. "Lukas, that is too much." Again, the big young man
stumbled while leaning on the furniture. His laughter exploded
from every crevice of his being. A quietness crept across the room,
smothering the sheer pandemonium. Lukas's expression resembled pure stone: his eyes fixed and focused, his mouth shut with
lips parallel and his head bowed down slightly. A trembling and
unsteady hand reached out to Lukas as Ram attempted to console
him. "Oh, I'm sorry Lukas. I didn't mean to make fun of you. I
guess I overdid it. You know, laughing about you getting laid."

Lukas raised his head to face his friend and nodded to him

while putting his hands behind Ram's head and clasping his thick black hair. Like a light switched turned on, Lukas's face came alive with a glow. "Please laugh about it, Ram. It's a good one if I must say so myself. I know everyone wonders about me."

"About you getting laid? Man, it is going to be the lead story on the news." Ram's shoulders slumped as though a significant weight departed off his back. The tension of avoiding that one topic with his friend profoundly affected him. Ram put his arms around his friend suddenly and squeezed him tightly. The exposure of vulnerability touched Lukas.

Lukas was grateful that Ram pulled him tight enough as not to be looking at him in the eyes as he would not notice the lonely army of tears forming at the boundaries. He blinked his eyes to dry them against the lids before stepping back out of the clutches of his friend. "Well, I kind of realized it would be a pretty big event if I did get laid that night."

"Pretty big event for us. Imagine for you!"

Fidgeting with the marker, Lukas walked back to his creation and gave it a final inspection. Ram was about to voice his concern for Tobin's reaction the next day, but his friend vanished through the door and out into the hall, stealthy as a ghost. He noticed an empty flask of vodka by the desk. Ram had only left Lukas alone for a few minutes to go to the washroom. Sadness tugged at Ram as the fluorescent rays were smothered with a flick of a switch.

chapter sixteen

No one was certain exactly when Tobin entered his office or how long he sat staring at the bright blue markings that violated his sacred canvas. All anyone figured was Tobin was alone with his thoughts before Kyle opened the door to find him sitting at the edge of the desk, taking in all of the entries on the calendar. The anger trickled across the room and hid behind the door, waiting for him. Kyle could tell instantly something had unsettled his class president. He could see Tobin's backside and ironed white shirt pulsate. Tobin's hand clenched and unclenched before he reached back to the base of his neck and tugged at his cropped blonde hair.

"Everything okay, Tobin?" Kyle's voice slid out as if to tippy toe to Tobin's ears. He had witnessed Tobin's outbursts before, and the tell-tale signs of an approaching one were apparent.

"Look what the bastard did. *Look!*" He shoved aside papers on the desk in a fury so Kyle could sit next to him. Although Tobin's logic told him who the perpetrator was, he needed confirmation.

Kyle moved forward cautiously, well aware traps were set. Not knowing what to expect unnerved him. His curly black hair could feel the tension. The board came into full view as he grew closer, unsure whose heart was racing faster. He felt Tobin's eyes fixated on him as his own finally settled on a spot and began reading. Halfway through the entry, a smile escaped his lips, which he clenched tight. Resistance proved futile, and the laughter became loud and bordered on delirium. "Holy shit. March 23, Lecture on How to Succeed in Porn." If only he could have chained the words, yanked them back in. The hot breath of Tobin tinged his neck.

"You think this is funny. They ruined the calendar. They desecrated me . . . I mean, our faculty's property." Tobin slammed his right fist on the desk to emphasize his point.

Kyle pushed off the desk, continuing his enjoyment while moving out of physical proximity from an irate Tobin. He looked at Tobin and smirked. "Oh c'mon. It's funny. You have to hand it to him."

Tobin's fist clenched in frustration as Kyle, in his mind, missed the point. "I am sure it's fucking brilliant. That is not the issue. It's an insult to me to have all this made fun of by some delinquent. Don't protect him."

Kyle, without thinking, responded, "Lukas. I guess you think it's him."

"Of course, it's him. First of all, he has a key to this room, and some of the stuff can only be from him. I recognize his style."

"Tobin, don't jump to conclusions. And frankly, even if it was him, who cares? Take the joke and move on."

"Oh brother. Just let him get away with it? We're in business school and supposed to be grooming professionals to be employable and have careers. It's not elementary school where one person can do what he wants."

The flaring nostrils and piercing eyes warned Kyle enough about pursuing the argument. There never was a doubt that Lukas would have the audacity to perform such a stunt. Trying to calm Tobin only meant he was taking sides and causing more infuriation. He chose to ignore Tobin and moved back to the wall to read more. "Tobin, did you see this one?" His finger shook in front of the day in March.

Tobin moved closer and looked, shaking his head. "Well, at least, one date will be memorable." Just as he spoke, the room slowly filled with the usual crowd and in seconds, Tobin's calendar became the center of attention. He sat impassively back, observing each person who dared venture forward to admire Lukas's work. He looked next to the waste basket and noticed the discarded mickey of vodka. Gasoline poured onto a fire could cause less of an explosion than the combustion within Tobin's gut. He waited patiently, watching the clock in the far corner, expecting the performer to arrive before his adoring public. The pen he gripped ruptured. The royal blue stream of ink splattered onto his desk, dotting his white shirt and drenching his hand. The crimson color invading his cheeks were a mere warning of the eruption to come.

· · ·

Beneath the classrooms, auditoriums, and teachers' offices of the faculty, chaos often reigned supreme in the cafeteria where the milling of students contrasted the seriousness of the Student Society office. Today was much different. The chaos and subversion began taking root in Tobin's empire.

The calm figure strolling to the beat of his headphones as he navigated the stairwell to the basement behaved unmindful of the commotion in the corner office. It would not be unusual for Lukas to wander by the office to announce his presence on any given day. Rather than basking in the aura of the pandemonium, he chose instead to head straight for his customary cafeteria spot. While Lukas reveled in creating satire and observing the vibrations of his pranks, this one was born out of protest. There was a message in his madness. However, he too wondered if he pushed far too many buttons this time.

Entering the caf, he paid no heed to the looks and sporadic fingers pointing in his direction. His target was the coffee station. Though, even a witty repartee with Willie felt forced this morning. Willie could see the pensiveness in Lukas's gaze and avoided anything except the most minuscule of words.

"Willie, you forgot my muffin, or are you out?" Lukas seemed puzzled by Willie forgetting his usual morning snack. Perhaps, of all days, there were none left. Lukas's stomach gurgled from hunger.

"No, I *could never* forget. Someone bought you a muffin and told me to let you know she left it at your spot." Willie pointed to the far corner of the caf and at the solitary muffin placed strategically in front of his usual seat.

"Who bought it? Kirsten?"

"No, it was Ally," Willie said. "I asked her why and she said she owed you one, big time."

"That was sweet. Thanks." Lukas backed away, humbled by the simple show of gratitude. Instinctively, Ally must have known it was he who subverted the Student Society calendar. She understood the protest. No longer feeling the gravity of uncertainty, he hurriedly made his way to his spot. While adjusting the chair to sit, he noticed a small note next to the muffin.

"Thanks, Lukas. I appreciate it. You are the 'tops.' Get it. Love, Ally"

He folded the note neatly and tucked it in his wallet. The recognized good deed revitalized him as he reached into the inside pouch of the jean jacket he wore that day and fumbled with a small glass container, emptying the contents into his coffee. He gently took his cup and shifted it to mix it. Sipping it slightly, he bit his lip and eased the cup down, bracing himself for the inevitable confrontation to come.

Kirsten appeared out of a crowd of students and sat clumsily across from him, shaking the table and his cup in the process. A drop or two of the coffee escaped the cup and splashed the table. Lukas immediately wiped the puddle it made with his hand before rubbing his hands dry across his thighs.

"Your coffee seems very watery." Kirsten was quick to observe the lighter color of the liquid that escaped.

"Something wrong with the filter, I suppose." Lukas avoided eye contact with her. "Um, nice to see you today. In between classes?"

"Yes, actually have one in a couple of minutes. Saw you here alone and thought I would say hello to my favorite senior." Holding back her real intent, she smirked at him.

"I take it you heard about the calendar." He raised his brow and smiled at her playfully.

"Of course, it's fricken hysterical."

"I haven't seen it yet today."

"Oh, don't play with your words, Lukas. We all know it was you." She reached over and poked him in the arm, rubbing the back of his hand in the process.

"You know it was just to make a point. I didn't do it to hurt anyone. I left all the original calendar entries intact."

"I certainly get it. No need to be defensive. It's hilarious. Some people here need to stop taking things so seriously. You remind us of that." She slid her hand down to his hand and squeezed it before looking at her watch. "Now I need to get going. Mrs. Hyatt takes attendance."

"Have fun while I sit here alone to face the consequences." He elongated each word in a sorrowful fashion. Part of him wished she could stay and deflect the furious winds that would for sure blow his way. The other part wanted her out of harm's way.

She took two steps forward before swiveling to face him. "I'm sure it will all be worth it anyways. You may have to wait until March 29. Something tells me it'll be worth it then." She winked at him and continued on her way, having delivered her message.

As she turned, Lukas smiled back. Realizing the corner he painted himself into literally and figuratively, he rubbed his eye. Yes, Lukas gets laid on March 29, and the calendar is the final word on what goes on in the faculty, he surmised to himself sarcastically. Well, he knew there were worse things to worry about, and that was quite a self-fulfilling prophecy. Lukas wondered if he was a madman, genius, or a fool. All sorts of characters wandered the halls of purgatory, and he would, one day, be classified into a category. All in due time, he supposed, as he was about to face an earthier judgment.

Rare, perhaps, was too strong an adjective to describe the frequency of Tobin's appearances in the cafeteria. When he did not bring his lunch, he usually ate outside of the confines of his faculty. Being a Student Society executive and with parents who were university alumni of some stature, he dined at one of the private restaurants on campus. His hard footsteps signaled the energy behind the quick driving anger. Without a word, he knocked aside the seat Kirsten had vacated and leaned forward to prepare his siege.

Lukas could feel the heat emanating from the mouth and the flaring nostrils. He could almost feel Tobin's knees reaching toward his own below the table. A physical confrontation worried Lukas only ever so slightly. Tobin's flash temper was self-contained by his aspirations to remain ever in control and power. Any physical confrontation would be politically damaging with someone popular like Lukas. If worse came to worst, Lukas knew he could conjure his inner demons to defeat Tobin. He feared them more than Tobin himself.

Each waited for the first words. Tobin stared intently at Lukas as if sizing up his adversary. Lukas looked at Tobin and noticed first the blue dots spread out across his white shirt and the dark blue stains on his hands. His lip quivered as every ounce of muscle worked together to suppress the grin ready to announce itself. Fortuitously, it was Tobin who cut through the silence.

"I don't know what you were thinking. I presume you did it because you were wasted."

"Wasted? You think that's the reason?"

"I saw the vodka mickey in the garbage. You wouldn't be the first to do something stupid while drunk."

"Alcohol had nothing to do with it." Lukas grew frustrated by the suggestion. He did not understand the potential for the excuse being a path to forgiveness.

"So a sober person would desecrate faculty property?"

"Seriously, desecrate! It's funny. Humor. Lighten up. I mean, I'm getting laid on March 29. Let's talk about that instead."

Tobin shook his head as the shades of red began appearing in patches on his face. He pushed back on the chair and tapped his foot, visibly perturbed by the lack of remorse. Without a word, Rosemary suddenly appeared beside him and pulled up a chair. Her intent could not be any more transparent other than to divert the danger from her friend.

"Look, Rosemary, this is a pretty serious discussion we're having."

Lukas could see both Rosemary's hands rubbing together in excitement and could feel the tenseness in her muscles by how rigidly she sat. "Tobin, let's go to your office to continue our discussion. We'll kick everyone out and close the door."

"I'm good with that." Tobin leaped from his chair, almost toppling Rosemary, and hurried back to the office to empty it for their private meeting.

Rosemary rolled her eyes and spoke to Lukas. "You sure you want to be alone with him? I can demand to be with you."

"I appreciate the offer and support, but I have to deal with consequences of what I've done. I understand that now. I have to face Tobin alone."

Before Rosemary could even formulate a rebuttal, Lukas hurried across the cafeteria with his head down to avoid eye contact, leaving the Styrofoam cup behind with crumbs surrounding it.

Before she could even get up, Ram came toward Rosemary in a hurry with a worried look.

"It's going down now, isn't it?"

"Is it ever. If looks could kill. Tobin is livid."

"Our boy can handle himself."

"I don't know anymore. I used to be a hundred percent sure of Lukas. But he seems different. I can't put my finger on it. This whole calendar thing. It's almost too much. I know he's mad about the whole sexual assault issue." She reflected for a moment and then reconsidered. "I guess maybe it is good that we have him. Why, though, does it have to be him always?"

Ram sat across from her, careful not to take Lukas's seat. He considered every word as his mind closed in on the events of the preceding night. "I have to tell you something. I was with Lukas last night. I probably should have stopped him. It's just that he was in such a zone and, let's be honest, it is quite a stunt. People are worked up only because Tobin made it an issue."

"Do not feel responsible if you could not stop Lukas. I know what that is like."

"No. That's not what I wanted to tell you."

Elbows on the table and arms crossed, Rosemary leaned forward, waiting for the rest. She knew it was serious because the sweat was forming on Ram's forehead.

"Last night, when we were about to leave, I saw a mickey of vodka near where Lukas was standing most of the evening. I don't know how much he drank. Could have been the whole thing. I honestly did not notice."

Rosemary pressed her lips inward and leaned her head back to look at the ceiling before leaning forward again. "Vodka. It is his drink of choice. Shit. I've never seen him sneaking drinks." Her eyes circled the room hoping to find an answer or an excuse somewhere. The cup on the table distracted her and tugged at her like a child demanding attention. Her hand reached out to it and brought it beneath her nose as she peered inside it. Her nose twitched from the unexpected smell while her vision noted a translucent quality to the blackness. "Shit, take a whiff of this."

Ram grabbed the cup, smelled its contents, and then dipped a finger inside before licking it. "There is alcohol in here for sure."

"Damnit! Lukas is drinking. I wonder how often now and when this started."

"Well, since we only noticed now, let's hope it just started. I just don't understand why."

Rosemary shrugged her shoulders and sighed. Thoughts raced at miles a minute around her head in tight circles, all around an ugly conclusion. Lukas had been told to forget. She told him to forget and move on. She desperately wanted to take the cup, walk over to the garbage pail, and slam it inside with such brute force as to stifle time. She pounded the table to emphasize her words. "We need to watch him. The two of us need to look out for him."

"For sure. Maybe it's just a phase. Last semester and all that can make a guy squirrelly."

"I do hope so, my friend." She held her breath for a second; a silent prayer followed her words. Both Ram and Rosemary wondered about Lukas's state of mind. They could only watch as he now set out to face his adversary far from the friendly confines of the cafeteria.

chapter seventeen

By the time Lukas made his way down the long shoe-scuffed hall-way, Tobin's evacuation of the office was complete. Those forced to leave could only glance as Lukas passed by them. The majority could lick the sweet taste of tension in the air. Even Lukas's all-knowing grin could not dilute it.

"Close the door, Lukas." Tobin sat at his desk with his feet up on it. His eyes switched back and forth to Lukas and his beloved, now tarnished calendar.

Lukas entered and closed the door behind him, leaning against it, silent.

Tobin reached into the wastebasket by his desk and pulled out the mickey. "I know this is yours. Be honest, you were drunk last night."

Lukas noticed the calm demeanor that Tobin seemed to have slathered himself in now. The sanctity of the office certainly brought out the diplomat in him. Lukas shook his head defiantly. "I didn't do this because I was drunk." He smiled slightly and elaborated. "I did this because you need to understand that some things are more important."

Tobin's brows slanted, trying to find a path to understanding Lukas and failing. "I'm trying to give you an out, an excuse."

"I don't need an excuse. I know what I was doing."

"Really. Destroying property is some big joke. This is the office of the elected Student Society, and you have embarrassed it because you thought it was funny."

"Tobin, I did this to make a point. All these rules and procedures you have. The whole purpose of the Student Society is to be here to enhance the experience of the students."

"And you think what you did does that?"

"Not doing more to prevent sexual assaults on those very students is the issue. What is the point of all these events if girls cannot feel safe? Why do all this if people live in fear?"

"Oh, get off your soapbox. We're a business school. I cannot control what goes on outside these walls. I will demand respect for the Student Society within them."

Lukas grew frustrated. "Wake up, Tobin. Get out of your office now and then. Not everything is ironed and pressed in the world like in yours."

Tobin put his head down in disbelief. "The worst part is I thought you were my friend. I got you a summer job at my dad's firm. He even asked me the other day if you were coming back full time."

Moving toward one of the chairs, Lukas threw himself into it. The ensuing discussion was one he hoped to avoid. "Tobin, I am grateful for the summer job. I just don't think it's for me. I did not do this to hurt you or embarrass you. I'm trying to make you see things differently."

Tobin's colors changed yet again. "What do you mean, not for you? You're not coming back?"

"No offense, but I have no interest in being a lawyer."

"Fuck. I pulled for you and had to convince my dad."

"I do appreciate it. It's just not for me."

"Not for you. Who do you think you are? Seriously. Stop all this holier-than-thou shit. These past few months all you have acted with is disdain for this faculty and its students."

"Disdain? How so?"

"I put up with the crap you write in the magazine. I get the humor part, and while childish, people look forward to it. Poetry and book readings in the cafeteria! You're telling me you're not making fun of us."

"I love to read, and others do, too. Why does every thought have to be about this faculty? There's more to life."

"These kids do not need to be distracted by garbage outside their studies. We are trying to build them a viable career path."

Lukas put his elbows on his knees and smiled briefly before looking intently at Tobin. "I think people aspire to more than the confines of this box you want to seal them in."

"Maybe it's just you."

"No, I have faith it's not just me. If now and then you would join us in the cafeteria, you would see that. People like to think and ponder greater things in the universe."

"Soapbox derby time for you, eh, Lukas? Stop trying to make everyone buy into your vision. Look, you could have run for office and chose not to."

"I'm not much of a politician, Tobin." Lukas's words rolled out of his mouth as subtle as a live grenade.

"I could get you expelled for all of this."

"Expelled! All I did was bring some humor into this office and show you how meaningless calendars were without the experience of life."

It was no longer apparent whether or not Tobin listened to Lukas's words as he stood up and moved impatiently toward him with his hand extended. "Give me your key."

"My key? Are you taking away my office key?"

"Yes. I cannot trust you anymore to have access to this place.

I won't go to the administration, though I can take away your privileges here.

Lukas stared at Tobin, who stood above him, almost giving him no room to move. Pushing back on his chair, he dug deep into his pocket for the key. The silver color key passed from finger to finger before landing in Tobin's outstretched palm. Tobin noticed the strange white mark on it. "Just a mark I put to remind me it was my key."

Tobin looked at it more closely—it appeared to be a "K" in a whitish ink—and placed it into his pocket before moving back to his chair. "I don't think we have anything more to say to each other."

The words hung over Lukas and dripped down slowly over him, syllable by syllable. The tone was cold and dull-edged. The anger and emotion of the previous words were all erased by the lack of emotion now in the room. Lukas turned toward the board and the bright blue ink that glistened under the fluorescent lights. It was the only warmth he presently felt. "I won't say sorry, Tobin. I did appreciate you getting me a summer job. I just don't belong. The highlight of my summer was watching one of the other interns covering up a stain on his white shirt with liquid paper. Maybe my almost setting the photocopier on fire topped it."

Tobin sat impassively. Neither smile nor frown betrayed him. Even the blue smudges on his shirt, the residual of his valiant attempt to rub out the ink, looked faded.

Lukas shrugged in quiet despair, realizing how great a distance would need to be traveled to connect the dots of where these two men were. The silence swung like a pendulum with a sword's edge and cut through the room, immersing Lukas into an imaginary bath of ice water. He shivered, arousing his determination not to be defeated. Rising from his chair, he walked across the room, circling one desk after another while surveying the calendar from afar. As one eye, and then another, began following Lukas, Tobin visibly grew unsettled.

Reaching into a desk drawer, Lukas found another blue marker. He stood and stared at the paper in front, searching for the current date on the calendar. The pen grew closer to the paper, and he could hear Tobin shift in his seat, mesmerized by Lukas's next move. There was none as Lukas took the cap and placed it back firmly on the pen and tossed it back into the desk drawer. He turned to Tobin, acutely aware that his movements were carefully scrutinized.

"That is what not doing anything looks like." Lukas's words were sucked lifeless as Tobin put his head down and went back to focusing on the papers on his desk, totally ignoring him.

Lukas moved to the later months on the calendar. "Man, some guy named Lukas is going to get lucky one night." He smirked and made his way to the door. His hands touched the aluminum handle when a voice spoke from behind him.

"Let me tell you what your problem is. It's like that song you like. The one by that grunge band you listen to, Alice in Wonderland, or something like that."

"Yeah, the group is Alice in Chains, just for the record."

"Whatever. It has that line in it about the sun and being down in the hole."

"Yeah. Great song. It's about longing to recover from addiction or depression."

"Exactly. I'm not sure why you like music that is melancholy and about losers who whine about stuff."

Turning from the door, Lukas could see Tobin's fist clenched on the table. "The song is 'Down in a Hole.' Because you have no empathy and don't get it, don't judge."

"Enlighten me, I'm curious."

"Sure, it is written through the worldview of an addict. The singer is acknowledging his self-destruction and the longing to return to the comfort of the womb."

"And you think that's special? Returning to a womb, or is this really about wallowing?"

"Beautiful that such words can climb the walls of such bleak desperation. I mean, to sing about eating the sun to the point of scorching your tongue and never tasting anything again. How can you not be sympathetic to a loss of idealism?"

"Exactly my point. Self-indulgence is reckless and leads to misery. If he's been eating the sun and got burnt, I pity you because you have been munching on the sun since I have known you."

Lukas looked through Tobin and wondered how deep he needed to search to find substance. Turning the doorknob, he opened the door. It was only when the hallway light flooded in that he realized how the fluorescent lighting had masked so much darkness.

The faculty became a different place from the moment Lukas entered the office to the time he reopened the door to make the trek back down the hall. His face, usually barely holding back a grin, looked stoic and almost embedded in steel. Striding down the hallway, his gait slowed, and his hand reached into the pocket. A profound sense of loss overcame him that went beyond giving Tobin back the key. The cafeteria loomed in front of him, and he could hear the voices bouncing off one another. He fingered his ear, poking within to open up an imagined blockage. Voices that once merged as if in harmony now sounded shrill and made him feel uneasy.

Ram and Rosemary were on the edge of their seats by the time he got to his spot. Forcing an exaggerated smile, he sat, noticing their feet tapping and twitching. Interrogation would not be allowed, so he wore his most trusted mask from his gallery as he spoke.

"Do I need to lower the cone of silence because you guys seem itching to talk? Let me guess. You want to know if Tobin's shirt comes in other colors of ink?"

Rosemary ignored the attempt to lighten the mood. She stared at the cup, which they placed back where it had been. "We know you probably got raked over the coals by Tobin."

Lukas reached for the cup and gulped as both his friends grimaced before them. "All is good with Tobin and me. He agreed not to court-martial me. It'll go straight to the firing squad."

Ram shook his head. "Stop kidding around. He isn't going to report you or anything, right?"

Lukas flipped the empty cup over. His eyes rotated around the room before narrowing to mere slits. Now and then, he found his friends in his sight and tilted his head, acknowledging them. "I appreciate your concern but my escapade last night indeed moved Tobin. What course of action he will take, I am clueless."

"I'm glad because we were worried. Tobin can be a real dickhead." Rosemary punctuated the words with a finger raised toward the ceiling. The upside-down cup mesmerized her, and her eyes darted from the cup to his eyes, looking for a clue. Ram and she exchanged glances. Lukas sat impassively, his composure maintained throughout the awkward silence that followed.

"Kids, I'm going to read now if you would like to join me. I picked up a good new book on my recent bookstore trip." He reached into his backpack and pulled out a black paperback. It slid across the table next to his cup. His fingers thumped to a rhythm for some song.

Rosemary grimaced and swung out her arm, catching Ram

across his chest with a glancing blow. "I think he wants us to leave, Ram."

"Shit. It seems that way. He would rather read than talk to us."

Lukas rolled his eyes. "I would love to talk to you. Probed and prodded by you guys is a different story."

Rosemary could not prevent a grin breaking out on her face. "It's all good, we have class besides."

Ram began getting up and motioned for Rosemary to follow. Curiosity got the best of him, and he circled back to Lukas's spot. "Hey, buddy, have you gone to any classes today? This week? Since Christmas?"

"Three questions. Did I just come out of some lamp?"

"Three wishes, not questions, Lukas. Seriously, are you good with your courses?"

Lukas placed his two feet up on the table, toppling the cup. Leaning forward, he reached for the book and placed it on his thigh, tapping it. "Ram, I am in the school of life, as you are. And let me tell you, I have learned a lot and whether I pass or fail is not really up to me. It is the most unjust of courses I have ever taken." His face had grown grim. The smile which followed seconds later was most welcome to Ram and Rosemary. "Don't worry, I'll be done and out of here in June just like you."

Ram moved toward him and punched him in the shoulders playfully. "Great, glad you're doing well. Honestly, I don't know how you do it, never going to class." He walked away with Rosemary, who seemed distracted as she walked. Just as she was about to leave the cafeteria, she looked back to Lukas, expecting to see him reading or reciting his book to a fellow student who wandered into his realm. Instead, his hand extended toward his back pocket. She was startled to see him pull out something again and look at with an intense glare before tucking it back into his jeans. He then opened the book. Shit, she thought he was joking. She nudged Ram. "Did you catch the book he was reading?"

"Yeah, something by Hermann Hesse. The title was *Demian*. Black creepy cover. You know it?"

The words gushed abruptly out of Rosemary. "Yep. Damn heavy."

• • •

No line was drawn in the sand to separate Lukas and Tobin in the days and weeks that followed. Neither spoke of their confrontation to others in any detail. Both kept a respectable distance from one another. The cold war between the two young men sucked much of the energy out of the faculty. Lukas continued publishing his satire as well as his alternative curriculum. Tobin's agenda of bringing the business world closer to students accelerated with more public speakers and job fairs. The failure of the two to interact created two solitudes within the walls of the faculty.

One day, just as the last snowflake was melting in late March, Lukas arrived in the cafeteria to find all the chairs lined up with geometrical precision facing a solitary figure, Tobin. For a moment, Lukas hesitated before crossing the barrier between the hallway and his domain. Tobin's back was to him. Upon noticing the heads turning toward Lukas, Tobin finally faced him. With an icy frown, he stared Lukas down before dismissing his presence and returning to his audience. Lukas's pace accelerated as he drifted by Tobin to complete his usual trek to the back of the cafeteria and Willie. He nodded absentmindedly to Willie's friendly monolog, straining his ears to hear Tobin's speech. The words rattled him, and the coffee held in his hand splattered onto his bare hands burning him. He grimaced as his anger snuffed out the pain.

"I am sorry to tell you. A girl was assaulted last night in this building. I am as appalled as you are. Privacy prevents me from telling you more. The faculty is safe. There will be an extra security guard assigned to this building for the rest of the year. If you need to speak to me about it, we can talk in private. I called this meeting so that you do not hear it from anyone else."

Lukas instinctively searched the room looking for Ally. As an executive, she should be here with Tobin. Willie's words penetrated the sound barrier. "Lukas, that is awful. Crap. Poor girl. These assaults have been going on since last year. I hope they catch the bastard."

"You and me both."

The crowd broke up, and Tobin retreated to his office. Some students were stunned, others visibly shaken, and some were angry. Kirsten spotted Lukas and rushed toward him. Lukas silently felt relief she was there.

"Kirsten, where's Ally? I need to speak to her."

"My goodness. No one told you?"

"Told me what? I just got here."

"Ally quit school when she found out about the girl. She told Rosemary she was disgusted and this place was unsafe for a woman. She feels responsible."

"It is not her damn fault. Where is she?"

"Apparently she found out what happened and called her mom. She went back home."

Lukas stumbled uncharacteristically and grabbed a nearby chair to stabilize himself. Eyes wide, Kirsten said, "Lukas, what's wrong?"

A veil fell upon Lukas and cast him back into his past. Whether the memory was real or imagined, it mattered not. He was not cognizant of where he stood in space nor time. The silence throttled Kirsten with worry. "Lukas, sweetie, are you all right? Please say something."

"She left just like that. Disappeared without telling me." Turning his back, he brought his hands to his eyes to stem the flow of tears waiting to erupt. He thought how his sins remained not fully paid and how many more people would pass in and out of his life as retribution.

Kirsten tugged on his belt, forcing him to face her. His brave dry face wore a chiseled smile. Looking at her, he recalled there were acts left to be performed. "It will be good for her to get away. Time heals all wounds. Maybe she'll return when the dust settles."

"That is what I love about you. You always find the pot of gold after rain." She leaned forward and kissed him on the cheek.

"Kirsten, just promise me you'll be careful around the faculty. Especially at night. I mean if anything would happen to you, I'm not sure what I would do." The words dripped out and fell to his feet forming together and flowing to reach her.

"So you do care, you bugger. Don't worry; I can take care of myself. If I can tame you, I can handle anything."

He laughed and thought to himself, *An experienced tiger handler knows the most dangerous cat is the one you think you have completely under control.* "Be careful, Kirsten."

chapter eighteen

The earth passed through four seasons for everyone except for Lukas in Morris Town. Without tracking them formally, there were two distinct periods in Lukas's world. The school year, when he and Kara were separated, represented his period of reflection and focus. The end of the school year up until the beginning of the next was marked by the sun at its zenith in the sky and his time with Kara. The only interruption during this period was his brief summer camp interlude. He enjoyed the comfort of returning to see Kara and her smile when his parents brought him home.

Neighbors were accustomed to observing, from the seclusion of their living room windows, two figures sitting side by side on a porch. Quite often each had a book in their hand, existing in their private worlds with an unseen connection between them. Kara radiated harmony in Lukas's presence. She, having spent the school months at a traditional girls' school, enjoyed the new perspective of this interesting boy. Kara knew that any boy who can break the resistance of her mother and earn her trust wore a unique aura. Around him, she felt a confidence that she did not feel around anyone else. When she first arrived home wearing glasses, it was he who told her how "cool" they were and wished out loud he could wear a pair, too.

Such it was that Lukas and Kara grew up together and went through the awkwardness of their physical changes feeling accepted. Lukas respected the unwritten rules of his relationship with Kara. The physical distance between them was a requirement. Often Lukas would sidle closer to Kara to feel her warmth and slide away slowly when he heard her father's car approaching. Lukas was the first to notice when his muffler began acting up.

The seasons passed quickly and, in their youth, went by unnoticed at first. With each new day, the quiet footsteps of the future grew louder. Both heard the sound. Each ignored it to remain mindful of the bliss of the present.

One day, just after he had returned from summer camp and a month before Lukas's sixteenth birthday, Kara looked thoughtfully at the sky. She positioned her glasses higher up on her nose, and Lukas could hear her breathing growing unsteady. The oppressive humidity took its toll even on the heartiest of souls, so Lukas did not make much of it. However, he sensed Kara drawn into deep contemplation.

"What are you thinking of? Is the answer in the clouds?"

"Why do you think I have something on my mind? It doesn't necessarily have to be anything, or maybe it is something." She giggled as her hand went to her lips, surprised. "I realize I sound more like you every day."

"I can see it in your eyes. They're swirling in circles." Lukas moved closer and studied her face. "Tell me what it is that has you daydreaming so. Please."

"I was wondering what the view must be like from way up there."

"My thoughts have gone there often. I would imagine if everyone could be up in the clouds or sky and look upon the earth from a different view, maybe they would understand better."

"Understand better?"

"Yes. Appreciate the beauty of all this creation."

"Would they not see all the wars, disease, and hunger?" She asked him while tilting her head, testing him to an extent.

"They would see what exists, survives, and thrives in spite of all that scares and worries us in our quiet times. The beauty exists in finding the human soul hidden by the shadows."

Kara shook her head with her teeth glistening as her eyes opened wide. "I knew you would have that type of answer. I knew it."

"Is it a wrong answer?"

"No, not at all. I can only imagine what my father would think of it."

"Your father?"

"Remember, he's a physics professor. Everything has to be solvable and explain by mathematics. There can be no feeling or intuition. No, not in this world. It's quite funny at times, especially now hearing you."

"And what do you prefer to talk about?"

"Lukas, if you haven't figured that out yet, maybe you need to sit back on your porch." Her voice was firm in mock anger.

Lukas's face turned sour with a frown that could soak up the sun and spit it back in the form of clouds. He rose and, with head lowered and shoulders slumped, took two steps down before Kara could even regain her composure.

In a state of panic, she jumped out of her spot, the book that rested on her lap tumbling down the stairs, and she ran toward Lukas. Impulsively, she reached out. Her soft hand gripped his elbow as her fingers gently caressed his palms. In Lukas's heart, time dissolved and melted into his blood. By the time he turned, her hand had long since pulled back and she had retreated to retrieve her toppled book. He could see the frenzy of activity over her indiscretion. He felt remorseful taking her out of her comfort zone with his playfulness and despised seeing her disturbed.

"Kara, I'm kidding. I'm not mad. I was only pretending to be upset with you. I didn't mean anything by it." He moved to his spot and stretched out his legs while shaking his head, angry with himself.

She sat next to him in total silence, staring straight ahead. Finally, she put her hands together on her lap and faced him.

"I should have known you were kidding. I panicked because I . . . I thought I hurt you. I was scared."

"You didn't hurt me. You could never hurt me."

"I touched you. If my mom or if my dad would have seen, they would forbid your presence here. I have to respect them."

Lukas did not fear much other than Kara hearing his heart singing. He knew he needed to muffle the music within him for a while longer. Provoking something within her fascinated him. It also filled him with a sense of great responsibility. He tried to say something as her voice sentenced him to silence.

"You are so much stronger than me."

"I don't understand."

"Not in a boy-girl tangible way. You are stronger inside. You have confidence I don't have."

"I don't think that is true."

"Oh, yes it is, and you fully know it. Look at me panicking like that because what did I do? I touched your arm."

"Kara, it's not like you did anything wrong. You were concerned about hurting my feelings."

Kara leaned back and turned to her house. Her eyes darted up to the window pane. After a moment, she shook her head at Lukas.

"I'm not expecting you to understand. You're so far ahead of me in many ways. All I can ask you is your understanding and patience."

"Well, you have no problems with that because I am totally in left field right now. You didn't do anything wrong." Lukas grinned and tried desperately to hide the delirium within. Whatever just happened, above all else, showed him that emotions were lurking within Kara that Lukas alone had drawn out. He whispered softly to himself as he returned to his book.

"Whoso pulleth out this sword from this stone, is right wise King born of all England."

"What did you say? Sounded like something from King Arthur?" Kara asked.

"Nothing much, just think about something I read in school last year." Lukas smiled back at her, the twinkle in his eye blinding her to his lie.

"You can be a strange boy sometimes."

Lukas laughed and looked up at the sky. "I wonder what they would see if someone was watching us from above." He looked over at her, raising an eyebrow, waiting to deliver his words.

Seeing the look in Lukas's eyes, Kara could only follow his lead. "I assume you are going to tell me."

"From way up there in the sky, whether it be bird or plane or whatever, I'm pretty sure all they would see are the two of us side by side on these porch steps."

"Not the trees, not the flowers, not the green grass? Are you sure about that?" Kara gleefully asked, playing along.

"No, all that matters is right here." He looked over at her and smiled.

The putter of her father's ailing motor tore through the air. She looked up at Lukas, who on cue, picked up his book to make his way down the street and home. The car pulled into the driveway and Kara's dad smile meekly at Lukas, barely acknowledging his presence.

Lukas was up about three steps on his porch when Maggie opened the screen door with her head bobbing and face about to explode in expression.

"Maggie, what are you so excited about?"

"I saw the two of you."

"Like, seriously. You watched us from your bedroom window."

"Naw, I had trouble seeing. I was on the curb watching. I just ran inside to get an apple." She held a bright red apple in front of him. "You want a bite before I start?"

"No, it's yours. Tell me why you're so excited."

"It looked like the two of you were about to kiss. Why didn't you?" Maggie began stammering as her immaturity rose to the surface.

"You know why! She can't help it, I mean . . . ."

"So, you do want to? Don't you? I hope I'm there to see it."

Lukas reached and grabbed the apple from Maggie, who pretended to be upset. After looking at it carefully, he returned it to her. His eyes gravitated back to Kara's porch up the street. He could see her talking to her father, who kissed her on the forehead before entering his home. Kara returned to her seat and continued to read.

"You did not answer my question, little brother."

Lukas looked at his sister. He had forgotten that despite her eighteen years, for many of them, she saw the world through his voice and, as a cardinal on a wire, sat patiently waiting for the next words to come out.

"Maggie, you have become an intelligent young lady. I think you know the answer."

"I see it in your eyes." She grabbed both his arms and pulled him close to her. He could see his reflection in hers. She flung his arms away and took two steps back, a wide grin parading across her face.

"What has you laughing now?"

"Lukas, all I could see in your eyes was her."

"Stop joking."

"You need to kiss her."

"Don't start that now." Tired of his sister's game, Lukas walked passed her.

She smiled as he stumbled on the last step, distracted in thought. Looking over to Kara, she saw the young girl gathering up her book to retreat to the confines of her home.

To herself, Maggie muttered, "My brother can be so naïve."

chapter nineteen

The summer wound down with an unholy precision. On the last Friday before the beginning of the school year, Lukas and Kara walked along the sidewalks of their neighborhood. Kara's mom had given Kara some letters to mail to family overseas. Lukas volunteered his company and asked her mom if it would be acceptable if he joined her. It was all a formality. Her mom did take great delight in granting her approval.

Along the way back, they passed the small children's park and noticed the sad quietness that day. The children had grown older in the neighborhood and no longer were the echoes of shrill laughter heard. Littering the sand were cigarette butts and beer bottles. Graffiti dressed in black desecrated the blue-painted garbage tins. Lukas grimaced with each four-letter word they encountered. Kara stumbled slightly, and her gait stalled. She scowled as she shook her white sneakers with bright yellow laces.

"Everything okay, Kara? Did you get sand in your shoe?"

"I'm not sure. It hurts a little. I'll survive."

Lukas could see the pain on her face as she tried to step forward. He motioned to her to grab a seat on the nearby bench. When he approached, he could see the bench covered in a brownish foul-smelling liquid with a toppled beer bottle nearby.

"Kara, let's have a seat over there. It's humid today, and we can take a break." The swings nearby gently swayed in the warm breeze. Kara looked over and nodded her approval.

The duo sat next to each other, both staring at the desolate playground in front of them. Kara knew the summers were dwindling in number before they completed high school. Although in separate schools, while enjoying each other's company less frequently over the winter months, the certainty of the summer was comforting. She looked across the barren landscape and felt an uneasiness she could not readily describe. Lukas could sense it, too, as she pushed herself forward and began gliding to and fro to the rhythm of the swing. Her thoughts hummed toward him in the form of smothered words meant for only him to understand. He watched as she swung her legs forward and extended to give her a greater lift.

When the pace slowed, he waited for the swing to guide back in place as his eyes carefully measured every inch of her. The same melancholy that twisted free inside her found an abode within him. The passing of time pressed against his chest. He tried mightily to fight the tension within him. He always missed not seeing Kara once school started, but today the sense of loss frightened him.

His sister's words just weeks earlier awoke in his ear as if replayed with the twitch of a play button. The late afternoon sun cast a long shadow out of Lukas's frame. Kara's focus was on the wildflowers shimmering in the distance.

"Lukas, look at those pretty flowers. They're dancing."

Lukas turned his head to the flowers but only for a second. The sun blinded his eyes. When he blinked, he found himself gazing at Kara. "Yes, beautiful is more the word." He watched her chest heave with breath and her hands holding on the chains of the swing for balance. Her eyes were illuminated by the sun, impervious to his hypnotic trance. Her lips pressed tightly together, and

Lukas knew then and there the answer his sister wanted to hear.

Kara listened to a movement next to her, and before she could react, Lukas was walking ahead toward the flowers. Reaching down, he gently caressed a pink one, and then a yellow one, before settling down and kneeling before a white one. His hand reached and snatched it from the ground. Fascination locked Kara into her seat, and she could feel her heart racing as he approached. He moved toward her and dropped to both knees.

"Kara, a beautiful flower for a beautiful girl." Her hand trembled with uncertainty, so he skillfully placed it within her grip.

Smiling, she brought the flower close to her heart. "Lukas, I don't know what to say. I mean, I'm a bit overwhelmed." Her upper teeth bit down on her lower teeth as the emotions splashed onto her rocky shores, loud and powerful.

Seeing that she was struggling with his gesture, Lukas lifted himself up. It took great restraint for him to return to his seat as he beat down every ounce of being, which wanted to hug and hold her. When she raised her head again, her face fell upon seeing him back in his swing chair. Her hands slid beneath her as if to restrain any chance of pure spontaneity asserting control.

"It's just a simple gesture. I know you liked the flower and wanted you to have a little memento before school starts."

"Yes, thank you so much. It's a nice little memento." Her fingers stroked the flower with each word. "I guess we should get back. It's almost supper time. My mom will worry."

"Sure." Lukas watched as she lifted herself off the swing and unaccustomedly marched ahead of him. When they turned the corner and were within a few feet of her house, Lukas picked up his pace, unnerved by her silence, and slid in front of her.

"Kara, I need to say something to you." His heart took possession of his actions—Lukas had not thought of what he was going to say.

Kara's lips trembled with Lukas's words and her eyes watered. "My goodness, is everything all right?

Her body shivered in front of him as she gripped the flower tighter. Suddenly, she quickened the pace and continued past him before reaching the stairs of her home. The surprise paralyzed Lukas enough to allow her to make it to her porch before he ran toward her.

"Please, Kara, wait. I . . . um . . . wanted to tell you something." For the first time, he was speechless. Not that Lukas did not have many quiet moments, but this time even his wandering mind stood in utter tranquility. No words ricocheted off the walls in his brain. No words settled on his lips. He was utterly frozen in front of her. The words he so very longed to say sought refuge from his blinded tongue. In defeat, he put his head down.

"Yes, Lukas. What is it that makes you so anxious?" Her voice trembled despite her attempt at courage. The flower clutched tightly to her chest.

"Well, just put the flower in water, okay?" He smiled as his shoes toppled over on another as he turned to go home.

"For sure I will. Thanks, Lukas." Her words had to catch up to Lukas as he was already halfway up the street. She sighed, almost knowing the words that lay trapped within Lukas.

Lukas entered his home and made a hasty entrance past Grandma Ruth and right into the path of Maggie. Maggie rolled her eyes at Ruth, signaling she needed to speak to Lukas alone. Ruth returned to her chores as Maggie followed Lukas into his room.

"Ah, sis, must you always follow me?"

Maggie closed the door and pretended to be insulted. A look of whimsy overtook her face. She enjoyed her role as Lukas's advisor although she lacked any experience when it came to such things.

"The flowers! I saw her with them."

"Geez, Maggie. Must you watch us every second? Besides, what makes you think I gave her a flower?"

"Lukas, I'm your older sister but a girl, too. She was holding it so tightly to her chest. I can tell from here. She practically suffocated it."

"Really? You could tell that. I mean, why am I even talking about this?" Lukas leaned back on the edge of his bed and threw himself back, staring at the ceiling. Within seconds, both hands were over his eyes. On the one hand, he hoped Maggie would go away. On the other, he hoped she was right. Damn, she had a certain instinct with these things.

"Little brother, you are almost sixteen. It is nice to like Kara as much as you do. It is. Yes, I think it is."

"You think it is? Not a good time to be unsure." Lukas smiled and rose up and tossed his pillow at her.

"Okay. I'm sure you like her. I'm just disappointed."

"What? Disappointed!" Lukas looked at her intently.

"Yes. Did you tell her how you feel? I bet you didn't."

"Shoot, Maggie. To be honest, I had no idea what to tell her. My mind is starting to go blank when I'm with her now. It used to be so easy but now every time I'm with her, it gets trickier."

"My God, Lukas! You are in love. You are!" Maggie leaped into the air, both feet landing haphazardly and causing her to stumble sideways. Lukas groaned and rolled to his side on the bed, realizing he said way too much. His eyelids squeezed tightly together in the hope of turning back time and undoing his words. It was then he could feel a tug on his arms as Maggie with brute force jerked him upwards to his feet. When he opened his eyes, she glared at him with neither smile nor frown, looking as thoughtful as she had ever looked. She then spoke.

"If you cannot say it to her, just kiss her. On the lips. Short and sweet with meaning."

Lukas stepped back and shook his head, hoping to erase the words just entering his ear. "You think I need to kiss her."

"Yes. If I am right, it would be stronger than any words."

Looking at his sister, Lukas saw someone before him he had never seen before. Someone suddenly older and much wiser than he ever imagined he could ever be. His heart swallowed her words whole, knowing the truth. He stepped forward and, to her utter shock and amazement, hugged her tightly. "Thanks, big sis."

"You're going to do it? Kiss her?"

"I don't know about that. Thanks for caring."

"It is not that hard. I know you want to." Maggie left her advice behind and was out of his room in the wink of an eye.

A car pulled up in the driveway, and the voices of Lukas's parents filled the air. The distraction of their arrival relieved him. He needed to run away from his thoughts and raced toward the door to greet them. He arrived at the door just as they walked up the stairs hand in hand, the late afternoon sun bathing them in a golden yellow aura. Following the distant rays, his sight settled far up the street at the solitaire figure sitting on her porch. There was no book in her hand. He could see a single flower, which she twirled between her fingers.

chapter twenty

The early evening shadows stretched across the street, reminding everyone that the sunlit hours were shortening. Lukas followed the shadows up the street. Halfway to Kara's house, he noticed she was not outside and slowed his pace until he stopped. Turning his back toward the sun, Lukas could see the darkening skies and encroaching night. He could turn back home and commence another school year just as he had the preceding years. Partially turning back home, he felt the warm ray of sunlight on his cheek. Whatever logic tried to navigate his body was no match for the vastness of emotions tearing through him. He shifted back around with devotion to his initial journey, arriving at the base of Kara's porch before another thought could even cross his mind.

The screen door to Kara's house stared at Lukas tauntingly. He dared not knock at this hour. Her mom or dad would interrogate him, finding fault with his sudden forwardness, and not allow Kara outside. Rather than sit on her steps in his usual spot, Lukas chose a seat on the curb of the street. He fidgeted and passed the time kicking pebbles away from the curb and into the storm drain nearby. Back at his house, he could see his sister sitting on their front steps. The laser-like glare emanating from Maggie forced Lukas to tuck his head down lower, almost touching his knees. What was he doing? The feelings caressed every cell within him. Unfortunately, the warm waves he felt merely drowned whatever words he could assemble for Kara. The sun plummeted to the horizon as Lukas sighed as if reprieved. He lifted himself off the curb to face his sister and the inevitable lecture. Suddenly, the squeak of the door in the background paralyzed him. The permutations and combinations of who had emerged raced through his mind. Then a voice, soft and airy, comforted him.

"You're out late."

"I just went for a little walk. That's all. I took a break here. I just wanted to see the sunset. It's so breathtaking from the front of your house."

"I don't think my house has any special powers over the sun. I am sure the view is lovely from your house." She smiled, disarming him in the process.

"Now that you're out, do you want to walk with me up the street?" Realizing the moments with her would be few and far between drove him to action.

"It is getting a little late."

"I promise it won't be too far and not too long. I can ask your mom. She likes to give permission."

"Lukas, I can give you a greater challenge, and you can try asking my dad." Her laughter turned to horror as Lukas took a few steps toward her, clear in his intent. "I was joking, Lukas." Her hands signaled him to stop.

"I should have known."

"I'll join you on your walk. No need to ask my parents as long as I'm back in a few minutes."

"Great."

They walked side by side with their hands swinging at their side, tantalizingly close to brushing one another, each imagining they did. Lukas stopped at the corner, motioning for Kara to join him on the curb. Before she could even crouch down, he had positioned his hoodie on the curb to cushion her.

"Always a gentleman."

"Just a force of habit."

"Do not take it badly. It is an excellent characteristic, it surely is."

More than half of the sun appeared drowned at the horizon, while the remainder resigned itself to its destiny.

"Kara, we are going to be sixteen and in a couple of years going to a college."

"Time does fly. Maybe a bit too fast sometimes. Are you concerned about the future? Is that why you're mentioning it?"

Lukas looked up at the sky and away from her, hoping to find a response. In his heart, the response waited for him to find it. Biting his lip, he turned to her. "I was just wondering if when the time comes, we'll still be sitting here." He paused briefly and, without looking, sensed Kara listening intently. "I mean, the two of us together."

If his ears were not overcome with the heavy beat of his own heart, he would have heard the sonic boom that was Kara's sigh. Her legs trembled slightly. The meaning behind Lukas's words resonated with her, only adding sugar to hers. Her toes curled as she waited for Lukas to speak on her behalf. Looking over at her, he hoped to find his next words written across her face. His eyes focused on her necklace and the figure at the end of it. It had gone unnoticed by him as usually the top button of her blouse was closed. Kara followed his eyes.

"Do you want to see my necklace?" She reached up and lifted the chain up over her head and handed it to him.

"It's interesting. It is a Hindi symbol, I presume. Who is it?"

"It's Ganesha, a very revered god in my religion."

"I never noticed it before. It is quite wonderful."

"You do not wear any symbols on you, I noticed. Not even a cross."

Lukas reflected before speaking. "My family is Catholic. At some point, my ancestors were converted or so the story goes." He paused and observed her patiently awaiting more information. "I'm not very religious and cannot see myself wearing the symbol of one in particular."

"Well, the symbol of Christ on the cross is a noble one. Maybe that's how you should think about it." Kara's eyes met Lukas's. "He's someone who preached love as being the answer and died sacrificing himself for others. That is a pretty good symbol to hold dear. You cannot go wrong honoring that."

The sun nearly had finalized its exit for the night, and its remaining light found Kara's welcoming eyes. Lukas gently held Kara's necklace and thoughtfully considered her words. Lost in her, feelings scaled the walls of his soul and overtook his heart. The dying sun, thoughts of time passing, and the uncertainty of the future overcame him. She reached to take back the necklace as he shook his head with a smile meant for no one else on Earth except her. Opening up the necklace, he lifted it over her head until it rested on her shoulders. Her heart beat heavily as she silently put the necklace back in its place. When she looked up, his face appeared before her, and she could feel the warmth of his breath. Instinctively, she closed her eyes. Her lips parted in anticipation.

The streetlight flickered slowly before bursting into light. On cue, Lukas's lips danced with Kara's. Both sets of eyes closed reverent to the emotions within their hearts. While he would forever remember the moment, he would not ever get straight the length of time their lips locked. All that counted was it was not forever, and it ended too soon. Lukas's body jerked back violently, and his eyes opened wide to the false light of the streets. Before he could piece back together the shattered glass that was once an epiphany,

Kara was up and running back to her home. The spasmodic sobs he could hear cut into him. Blood leaked from every pore of his being in the form of confusion.

Finally, his mind reconnected to his body. Racing to reach Kara before she reached her home, his voice escaped just as he was a few feet behind her.

"Kara, please, what's wrong? Talk to me."

His voice paralyzed her. With her back to him, she put her hands to her eyes to soak up the tears. Looking at her house and to the now darkened sky above, her chest heaved at the words forming like bitter acid. She turned to face him with reddened eyes and an angry look that frightened him.

"You have ruined everything. Everything has changed. You kissed me. Now I can't see you again. Never. Do you understand what you have done?"

"My God, Kara. Don't say that. I kissed you because . . . I love you." Lukas threw the words out like a life jacket to her.

"You don't understand."

"Kara, I am not going to apologize for how I feel. Never. I would kiss you again if I could."

"Then I cannot be with you anymore." With those words, she abruptly twisted and raced into her house, leaving Lukas stunned on the darkened porch, alone. He looked at her windows to see if her parents had seen the interaction and saw the drawn, uninviting blinds. Feeling dizzy from the life that drained from him, he staggered to the edge of the curb. Sitting with his head buried in his hands, the sense of loss overcame him. It was the depth of his love for Kara that gave him the strength to hold back the tears. In the night, he licked his lips while his lids came together tightly. His hands reached for an invisible cross he visualized around his neck. He formed his hands around its imagined shaped and conjured an image of Kara, which he clung to for what seemed like forever.

The gentle drizzle of a shower awoke Lukas from his hypnotic state. He maneuvered his way through the hallway of his home deftly and with silent purpose. The door to Maggie's room was closed, and his parents were in the basement watching television together. He made his way down the stairs and wished them a good night. Roman and Grace both sensed something amiss with Lukas's early retreat to his room.

"You're going to bed quite early."

"Yes, Mom. I'm tired, and school starts Monday. I'm just going to read a little."

Roman gripped his wife's hand, unsure of his son's emotional state. "If you need to talk, we're here."

Lukas appreciated the concern and sat at the edge of one of the stairs. In replaying the events of the evening, he rummaged through the rubble and found the moment. He licked his lips, thinking of Kara's pressed against his. Looking at his parents, a twinkle flashed from his eyes, lighting up the dimly lit room. "Tonight was pretty awesome. Yes, pretty awesome." He convinced himself and his parents. Their relieved reciprocal smiles were his cue to depart. Roman looked at his wife and shook his head.

"Roman, what do you know that I'm missing? Lukas is acting strange, right?"

Roman reached over and kissed his wife on the lips with a sheepish grin on his face. "I think it is safe to say our boy is somewhat smitten."

"Kara? They're just kids. Childhood friends."

Roman winked at his wife and put his arm around her. "He's growing up. Of all the things in life, this is a good part."

Grace pulled her husband's arm closer to her and smiled.

Lukas put on his pajamas and lay in bed staring at the ceiling light above him. Suddenly, a light knock on his door preceded clumsy footsteps entering. It was Maggie.

"I was expecting you."

"What happened? You did go see Kara?"

"Yeah, I did." Lukas enjoyed the buildup as his sister stood in the doorway, fidgeting. "I told her I loved her and kissed her." Maggie's face exploded with excitement, and she clasped her hands to her face to stifle a shriek.

"Tell me. How did Kara react? Give me every detail."

Lukas sat up in bed and stared at his sister. "She doesn't want to see me anymore."

"Good Lord. Oh my goodness!" She saw the seriousness on Lukas's face and started to tear up. "I was so sure."

"Sis, don't be sad. I wasn't so sure until I kissed her and now I am."

Maggie wiped her eye, smiled weakly, and returned to her room confused.

chapter twenty-one

The world did indeed change for Lukas in a way he could not possibly describe. Emotions rolled around together in the playground of his heart. He could not herd them any more than a farmer could herd hyper sheep. There was a noticeable change in the routine Lukas had grown accustomed to: the lack of Kara in his life. Although they took separate paths during the school year, there were moments here and there when their paths converged either on the street, on her porch, be it after school or on weekends. While he longed for the summer and days on end with her, he now truly appreciated how mere moments should be cherished.

Kara was like a heavenly ghost to Lukas. She avoided him with steadfastness, abstaining even from eye contact. Despite Maggie's pleas to approach her and "fight the good fight," Lukas decided to respect her wishes. Only he saw the pain in her that day when she ran from him. He chose to give her time and hoped for the day when she would let him into her world again. Holding on to their kiss kept his heart beating and stoked the fire within him. Like the cold winter ends eventually, he convinced himself the change in seasons would bring him back to a special time.

He badly underestimated Kara's resolve. Determination became Lukas's friend one Saturday morning in spring, and he went to his bookshelf, selecting a paperback. It was his father's well-worn, highlighted copy of *The Catcher in the Rye*. Snapping the book against his thigh, he proceeded out the door with his blue hoodie slung over his shoulder. He brushed by a gleaming Maggie, who instinctively knew where he was heading. So it began. From that day forward, on weekends and after school, Lukas would walk down the street and take up a position directly in front of Kara's home. Sitting on the edge of the concrete curb, book in hand, Lukas read. Within days, he moved on to a new book in a workman-like fashion. Often, he would see the window drapes open and a set of eyes watching him. Kara for her part proved resilient in her stubbornness. She stopped sitting on her front porch and stayed indoors while avoiding Lukas's side of the street.

One day, sometime in early May, Roman Wunand drove by and, instead of ignoring his son's existence on the curb, pulled his car into the driveway and observed his son from a distance. *Geez, he is barely reading*, Roman realized and then rushed into the house, summoning his wife.

"Grace, we need to talk about Lukas. Something is going on."

Grace looked up at him, smirking. "Now you notice! Roman, this has been going on for months now. It's about Kara. The two of them don't even wave to each other, let alone talk."

"Well, something must have happened."

A quiet voice mixed in with the parental ones as Maggie emerged from her room. "I know what happened. Promise me you won't tell Lukas I told you."

"Sure," said Roman as he brushed his daughter's hair, putting her at ease.

Maggie explained her role in Lukas's misadventure and what Lukas had told her. "You know, Mom and Dad. It is kind of my fault. I told him what to do."

"Maggie, your brother has a mind of his own. I think you gave him some good sisterly advice." Grace smiled at her daughter and looked over at her husband. "I think our boy needs some womanly advice."

Roman nodded and laughed. "Of course, I will speak to him when he comes in. Right after supper."

"I didn't mean about a woman. I mean from a woman."

"Well, I had the talk with him. You know. *The* talk. I think I can handle this."

Maggie shook her head at her father and put her finger to his lips. "Mommy's right. Lukas needs her advice."

Roman stepped back and looked at the two women. "Okay. I know when I'm out of my element."

Lukas finally entered his home just as supper made its appearance on the table. Trapped in his misery, he did not notice the three quiet but smiling faces at the table. It was after he loaded the dishwasher and made his way to his room that Grace followed him. Silent in her gait, Lukas was startled to find his mom behind him as he entered his private domain. It was rare that his mom spent any time in his room, ensuring he had his teenage refuge.

"Mom, you startled me. Is anything wrong?"

Motioning for him to sit on his bed, Grace grinned and took a seat on Lukas's desk. "I was going to ask you the same thing. You tell me, honey."

"Uh-oh. Have you been talking to Maggie?"

"Yes, and she truly is worried about you, like your dad and I are as well."

"I know, Mom." Lukas's mind drifted back in time, cobbling together what Maggie knew and what she possibly could have divulged. In the world of Maggie, it could have been anything. "What exactly did she say?"

"Well, she told me you kissed Kara and Kara refuses to talk to you now."

"That pretty much sums it up."

"She said you also told her how you felt about her."

Lukas's face dropped while he stared at the old faded wood planks that were his floor. Grace reached over and gently lifted his chin. "You should not feel sad or ashamed of what you did. You were honest with your feelings, were you not?"

Lukas nodded and bit his lips, not in sadness but in frustration. His hands tightened. Grace could sense the tension in him. "You know, Mom, I am so confused."

"No kidding, you are."

"It's just that when I kissed her, I know she was kissing me back. I know that for sure, I felt it."

Grace looked at her son sympathetically. "And you're confused because she told you after she doesn't want to speak to you."

"Yes. Kara freaked on me, Mom. She ran from me like I was dangerous or something. Like she was scared of me."

Grace looked around his room and laughed. "Lukas, did you ever consider that maybe she wasn't scared of you, but herself?"

"I don't understand."

"Think of all the emotions you have to deal with. Maybe Kara is going through something similar."

"Mom, I definitely put her on the spot then. Her parents are very strict and if they knew what I did . . . Well, maybe that is it. How do I fix it?"

"You obviously care about her."

"Yeah, of course. You think my butt enjoys sitting on the hard concrete?" Lukas smiled.

"Well, from a woman's perspective and not solely a mom's, do not give up. Only you know how you felt when you kissed her, and only she knows how she felt. If Kara is worried about her parents, maybe you should speak to them."

"Good lord, Mom. I don't think I've said two words to her dad through the years."

"A little secret between us. Moms have the real power." She poked him on the shoulder.

Lukas laughed. "I have no doubts about that."

After kissing her son on the forehead, Grace backed her way out of the room and pointed her finger at his chest. "What you are feeling inside is a good thing. Don't ever forget that, and let it lead you."

"Thanks, Mom. This talk was ultra-helpful."

"By the way, when your dad had the birds and bees talk with you, was that also helpful?"

"Mom, he gave me a book to read. See the one on the middle shelf? That was the talk."

She shook her head. "I knew it. I knew it. What I said about real power. Case closed!"

chapter twenty-two

Motivation is a wondrous thing. Execution of it is awe inspiring. Realizing the nuance between the two locked Lukas in turmoil. His mother's advice struck a chord with him, only he suspected the intended audience was tone deaf. The warm days went from off and on to steady. With them came the appearances of Kara outdoors more frequently. The sight of her, albeit from his exile, spurred him into action. After supper one evening, Lukas waited on his porch patiently. Then the solitary figure of Kara emerged, paper in hand, heading for the grocery store to run an errand for her mother. Lukas waited until she was a block up the street before making his way to her home. Stopping in front of her door, he had no inkling of words which he could use. His mother arming him with a sword was all well and good, but she forgot the part about the two-headed fire-breathing dragons on the other side of the moat. Not knowing if he would be facing her father or mother also troubled him. While her father rarely answered the door, often secluding himself in his study correcting exams or preparing for a lecture, with his luck, he would land the bigger beast.

Little did Lukas notice how long he stood before the white door. Just as he raised his hand to knock, the door swung open. An older version of Kara stood before him. The long dark hair highlighted in wisps of gray, looking much younger than he remembered her.

"Mr. Lukas, what a pleasant surprise to see you. It has been so long."

Lukas's eyes popped open in genuine surprise. Either this woman was the greatest of all actresses, or he had accidentally slipped into a fifth dimension. His lower lip quivered as the words shivered on his tongue. "Um, well, I don't know what to say." He thought and wondered how much he needed to divulge. In her eyes, he could see Kara, and the words danced across his tongue, leaping over his lips. "What I mean is, I thought you were angry with me."

"What gave you that indication?" A frown crossed her face. "Let me guess, my daughter?"

"No! Not at all. It's just that Kara is unhappy with me and won't speak to me."

"Interesting. It certainly explains a lot." She took a step outside and moved onto the porch before sitting on the top step. "Please, sit next to me. It seems we need to talk."

"Kara didn't tell you? What exactly did she say to you?"

"My daughter can be quite sullen and quiet at times. She has not said much about you recently, and I dare not ask. Perhaps you should tell me."

The dragon before him could incinerate him with a breath. That much he was painfully aware. He closed his eyes and imagined speaking to his mom. "Well, last summer just before school started, something happened."

Kara's mom leaned toward Lukas, studying him. "What happened?"

He took a deep breath, almost coughing. "I kissed your daughter."

"On the cheeks?"

"On the lips. It was not frivolous or anything like that. I told her how I felt and kissed her."

"Go on."

"She ran off and told me we could never speak again."

Her eyebrows widened. Lukas could almost feel a sense of shock. There was no fire visible from her nostrils. "Lukas, you sincerely do like my daughter?"

"Yes, I told her so. I told her . . ."

"You need not tell me. Save those words for her. They are too precious to waste upon my prying ears."

"You're not mad at me? I thought Kara was upset because I did something I wasn't supposed to do."

"Young man, we may be a little old-fashioned and traditional to you, however, I was a young girl once."

"I shouldn't have done it. I should have respected her."

"Lukas, when I stated you were always welcome, it was because I trust you implicitly. Your coming to see me this evening confirms it."

"Now I'm totally confused. Why is Kara angry with me?"

"Oh, I don't think the emotion is anger. I cannot answer for Kara, though. You need to find the answer directly from her."

"What if she won't talk to me?"

She slid her hands from her thighs to her knee and rose from her seat. "I will leave that up to you. I suspect you know her better than anyone, whether you realize it or not. She just left to go to the store. She is by herself, and it may be a good time to find out." The door closed behind her, and Lukas was left alone on the stairs.

His head spun in a million circles. Clouds formed all over. It was not Kara's mom or her father who spurred her reaction. It was all her. Lukas could see threatening clouds forming on the horizon. The rain was on its way. He leaped past the bottom step to make his journey to catch up with Kara. His walk turned into a trot and then into a run. From behind the curtain, Kara's mom pressed her lips together tightly, unsure of what she was hoping to happen.

Kara, too, could see the storm clouds approaching. Carrying a bag filled with two cartons of milk, she crossed the park and was heading into a wooded section when she saw an unaccompanied black dog. Instinctively, she placed her bag down and moved toward it from behind, trying to see if there was a collar with a tag on it. With no owner or anyone else around, Kara took it upon herself to help what she thought was a helpless animal.

Lukas raced up the path through the park. In the distance, he could see Kara. Satisfied with finding her, he stopped running, taking pause to consider his words. So caught up with Kara being within his sight, he failed to notice the danger in front of her. When he observed her reaching out, the menacing dog that was before her filled his eyes. Although the dog was not large, its muscles were taut and its powerful jaws, decorated with sharp white teeth, heralded the danger it posed.

The dog turned in one quick movement to face Kara, snapping at her in the process. She fell backward, barely avoiding its jaws. Lying flat on her back, she quickly maneuvered herself to a sitting position as the dog moved ominously toward her. With its tail straight out, the threatening growl grew louder to Lukas as he approached from an angle.

"Kara, stay totally still!"

"Lukas, please don't."

"Stay still."

"Sure."

"When I yell, roll to your side."

"Okay." Her voice almost shrieked in terror. In her heart, she feared more for Lukas than herself.

Lukas moved within a few feet of Kara and the dog. As its body crouched lower, its hind legs began to dig into the grass, always staring at its prey. "Roll! Roll!" Kara moved to the side, hearing the dog's growl exponentially grow louder before becoming muffled. She turned to see Lukas's forearms in front of his face, the dog's white teeth buried deep within one of them. Red blood flowed down Lukas's arm like a mountain stream.

"No, Lukas. No!" She cried out in horror. With her last scream, another figure approached from behind, moving quickly toward the dog. With all his might, the figure swung with his fist and landed a series of blows on the dog's snout before it finally let go of Lukas's arm, yelped in agony, and retreated into the woods. He turned to face Kara. It was her father.

"Your mother sent me. She said this young man was looking for you. A storm is coming, and you had been gone long. Thank goodness."

Kara sobbed as her dad hugged her. Out of the corner of her eyes, she could see Lukas kneeling down, clutching his blood-soaked arm. His body completely doubled over, and his head rested on his knees. His head shook abruptly, and she could see his teeth clenching. The image of him fighting the pain seared into her brain. Her heart crumpled inside. The helplessness grounded her to the spot.

Lukas squeezed his hands tight in an attempt to focus the pain at his fingertips. With each passing second, the pain overcame him. It was the faint sobs of Kara that broke the spell agony had cast upon him. Biting down on his lip, he contorted his face before looking up at Kara. The smile he presented to her took every ounce of energy he could muster. Kara's face lit up with joy just as the setting sun's rays settled on her ebony hair. The pain ceased to exist.

Kara raced past her father and knelt in front of Lukas. She pulled his arms away from his stomach to survey the damage. One arm was maroon with the blood of the other. A gaping oozing wound just below his wrist caused her to grimace. "Help!" She turned to her father and begged. "Daddy, please come help."

Kara's father was a tall, slender man in his mid-fifties. His olive complexion showed signs of aging. His eyes matched those of Kara's, both as black as coals. Whereas Kara's mom could pass for her older sister, her dad's one defining physical trait that Kara similarly possessed were his eyes. He quickly followed his daughter and knelt beside Lukas, lengthening his arm to touch the top of Lukas's head.

"I believe you will live. The wound is not too deep. However, I will take you the university hospital. Kara will go to tell your parents. Can you walk back home to my car?"

"Yes, sir. Thank you very much for saving me. That dog had quite a grip." He cringed as he spoke, the agony cutting in between the syllables.

Kara's father stood up slowly, leaving the young teenagers on the ground. His eyes darted back and forth between them, taking everything in like the scientist he was. Finally, he spoke to Lukas. "No, young man. I am forever in your debt. My family is. If it were not for you, my daughter would have been seriously injured. The least I can do is take you to the hospital." This was not the man Lukas expected. The great revelation was something he should have known. A creation as special, unique, and wholesome as Kara could only be the product of caring and loving parents.

Lukas nodded in acknowledgment of the kind words. His attention was consumed by Kara, who stared at him without even a blink. He grinned at her. "I suppose we're friends again."

"Friends again?" Her father interjected, puzzled by the

statement.

Kara looked at Lukas and winked at him with her left eye before turning to her father. "He's just kidding, Daddy, to lighten the mood. We've been friends since we moved here." Her father looked at her suspiciously.

"Right, Lukas? I mean we are friends now like always?" Her question sounded far more like a plea than anything else.

"Maybe I've lost too much blood; why wouldn't we be friends?" Enjoying the playful banter in front of her inquisitive dad, he smirked at Kara.

Kara's father put out his hand to help Lukas to his feet. He fashioned a makeshift tourniquet with a handkerchief from his pocket and asked Lukas to hold it tightly against his wound. He began walking ahead, leaving Kara alone with Lukas. Kara whispered to him slowly, "Thank you. I am so grateful that you followed me here today."

"Kara, I am so incredibly happy you are not hurt." He paused, realizing he had her full attention. "Except one thing bothers me."

"What?" she wondered nervously.

"I forgot to bring my sword. That could have helped today."

Kara's father drove slowly to the St. Peter's University Hospital, glancing to the rearview mirror regularly to ensure his young passenger had not gone into shock. Rather, Lukas firmly held the bandage he was given in place over his forearm while staring out the window with a faint grin on his face.

"Young man, Mr. Lukas, are you sure everything is well?"

"Yes, sir. I'm fine."

"Not often to see a grinning young man after a dog has ripped off half of his forearm."

"It's just a flesh wound. Besides . . . it was not a bad night."

"Not a bad night?"

"Kara was not harmed; that's most important." As the words left Lukas's lips, Kara's father could see the intensity in them. His head swung back slightly, registering the weight of Lukas's statement. This boy sincerely only cared for his daughter's safety. For the first time that night, he smiled back at Lukas.

"My family is forever grateful. I mean that."

Lukas absorbed the words while nodding affirmatively. "I think I may be the one forever in your debt."

There was not much more talk between the two men. Finding common ground in the safety of Kara made words unimportant for now.

chapter twenty-three

The torrential rain commenced just as Kara rang the doorbell of the Wunand home. Maggie peered through her bedroom blinds, expecting to see her brother returning. She assumed he had forgotten his keys. When she saw the girl with long silky black hair, her voice exploded in a jumble of words.

"Mom. Dad. Kara. Where's Lukas? It's her. She is here. Oh my God!"

Roman and Grace came racing across the hallway to the front door just ahead of the agitated Maggie.

"Kara is ringing our bell. But I don't see Lukas."

Roman nervously opened the door as his wife gripped his shoulder.

"Hello, can we help you?" Roman's voice trembled as he could sense the young girl looked worried.

"Lukas got hurt. Don't worry, though. He'll be fine. A dog bit him. My father took him to the hospital to get his arm examined."

Grace and Maggie both gasped as Roman moved backward, allowing Kara to enter their home.

"How did this happen?"

"It was entirely my fault. Lukas saved me from the dog, and it bit him."

"Wait to go, bro!" Maggie yelled in the background.

"Shhh! Maggie! Your brother got hurt."

"I'm sure he's back to his old self." She looked at Kara with a wide smile before returning to the background.

"Mr. and Mrs. Wunand, my dad arrived in time to get the dog off him. He says he will likely need stitches."

Roman looked at his wife and then put the young girl at ease with a grin. "We are so thankful you were not hurt. We truly are, and I am sure Lukas feels the same way. That is what would be important to him."

The young girl fidgeted and stared at the ground shyly. "I should be getting home now. My father will bring Lukas home as soon as he can."

Grace moved in front of her husband to get a closer look at the girl. "We appreciate your dad taking care of him, Kara."

Kara nodded, turned, and nearly stumbled on the stairs as she returned to her home.

Grace and Roman turned to find Maggie beaming. "This is great. Great!"

Grace's eyes widened. "A dog attacked your brother. Seriously, Maggie, how can this be great?"

Maggie looked at her mother, almost ready to scold her. "Mom, don't you get it? Kara is talking to Lukas again. Lukas is brilliant."

Roman laughed at his daughter's logic. "Maggie, usually I would disagree with you. However, with Lukas, you never know. Look, Maggie, this is going to be a late night, all we can do is sit and wait to hear about it."

Maggie skipped her way back to her room, excited that Lukas would return with a tall tale to tell. She set up shop by her bedroom window, waiting for the return of her brother. It was well past midnight when Lukas returned home, announced by the sputtering muffler of Kara's father's car, with a heavily bandaged arm and twenty or so stitches.

Roman and Grace barely had time to embrace the young hero when Maggie grabbed Lukas by the hand and whisked him off to hear about his adventures. Kara's father stood in front of Lukas's parents, acknowledging their gratitude for saving Lukas and caring for him. He listened while carefully pondering his words.

"What your son did for my family tonight cannot be thanked enough. I just wish . . ." he suddenly paused as if catching himself.

"You wish what?" Grace asked.

"I . . . well . . . that there are more boys like him on Earth. The world would be a better place." He nodded and quickly did an about face to leave.

Grace looked at Roman. "What was he going to say? He seemed like he had more to say."

"Grace, these university professors are a funny lot. Besides, look at the time. It is late. He must be exhausted."

Grace grabbed her husband's hands and clenched it tightly. "She is a beautiful girl."

Roman sighed. "The kind you would sacrifice more than a chunk of your arm to win over. Our son is more than smitten."

"I hope the belief in karma is enough."

Days of bed rest gave Lukas a perilous look at the bounds of sanity. Ruth and Maggie regularly checked up on him and took turns changing his dressing during the days, with Grace taking over at night. Charcoal circles slowly formed under Lukas's eyes. The Wunand household assumed Lukas had difficulty sleeping because of the lingering pain. Only Lukas knew what kept him up at night. It was the same nightmare, replayed over and over again, one of Kara devoured by a large black dog with glistening white fangs. It was during these nights that Lukas stared at the shadowed ceilings wondering, if, in this world, he had saved Kara. Then a particular Saturday morning arrived, filled with the rising vapors after an early rain.

chapter twenty-four

Apart from the ray of light that flowed through his room before resting on his sleeping cheek, there was no sign of life in the Wunand household. Maggie convinced her parents that new summer clothes were required, so Roman and Grace ventured out with their daughter to hit the shopping malls. No one dared disturb Lukas's lengthy slumber especially after the many restless nights that preceded it.

Such it was that shortly after 10 a.m., the high-pitched twang of the doorbell searched the household for a welcoming ear. Typically, Lukas would ignore the sound. It may have been the sun's hot breath on his cheek or a sense of something else that woke Lukas to the noise on this particular morning. Wearing oversized striped pajama pants with a blue short-sleeved top, bleary-eyed and with a hint of stubble, he made his way to the door. When he opened it, any trace of fatigue or whatever else may have wrapped itself around his brain melted away. It was Kara. She wore a yellow summer dress with her hair pulled back. She seemed genuinely relieved to see him answer; at the same time, her feet betrayed a nervousness about her.

A million words assembled, only to be discarded in Lukas's mind. Even a simple hello seemed imprecise. The intensity of the silence over the fall and winter months coupled with Lukas's heroics smothered any logic he could ever hope to use. When Kara noticed the bandage on his arm, concern overcame the silence.

"Hi, how is your arm?" She looked with sad eyes quickly at his arm before facing down.

"Don't worry about it. I'm going to recover fully. There are no signs of infection, which is good."

Kara could not look at him as she spoke. Trying to communicate, she stammered very softly. "I know we need to talk. I owe you . . ."

Lukas quickly interjected, not willing to bear her distress. The pain was well worth just hearing her voice. "You do not owe me anything, Kara. I'm just so pleased you weren't hurt."

"I would have been here sooner but my parents thought you needed your rest."

"Today or tomorrow. More importantly, you're here now."

"Yes. I am. A bit shook up. If you weren't there, I'm not sure I would be in one piece."

"Don't underestimate yourself. I'm sure you would have charmed the beast in your way."

Kara grinned and shook her head. "You always have the words."

"Kara, how little you understand." Lukas chuckled.

"Well, I want you to know. I did miss you all this time. It's my fault and not yours. You tried so hard to reach me."

"Never apologize to me for who you are. I promise to respect your boundaries. I missed you too much not to."

"You see, that's just it."

"Kara, whatever you're trying to explain, can you please let it blow with the breeze?"

"I suppose." She looked not in his eyes but off into the distance. He noticed yet chose not to interpret her need to tell him something. "There is someone who would like to speak to you right now." Stepping aside, Lukas walked out past her and could see her father sitting on his front steps, waving at him. "My dad asked me to come see if you wouldn't mind talking with him."

"Do I need to be worried?"

Kara was silent for quite some time before shaking her head. The hesitation alone answered the question. He proceeded to shelter her from having to lie to him. "I was only kidding, Kara. I'm sure he just wants to talk physics with me." The smile that flashed back at him was dim. Lukas could all but see the gloom over her head. A year ago, he would have leaped over her head to swat it away. Now he forced himself to ignore it. He refused to believe there was anything more to it than a simple discussion.

Walking back to Kara's house, she whispered to him, causing him to stop in his tracks. "I need to say something to you." Lukas looked over and shrugged with wide eyes. Peripherally, he glimpsed her hands clasping.

"It's just . . . I am sorry for putting you through this." As quickly as the words reached his ear, her head was turned, not waiting for a response.

"Kara, there is never sorry between us. From now on. Nevermore."

She turned back and nodded affirmatively at him. Each phrase from him drowned her further in her torment. A torment that hid from Lukas. A torment to be revealed one day, whether Lukas was ready or not to understand it.

The white cotton Bermuda shorts worn by Kara's dad highlighted the unathletic, scrawny legs of a physics teacher. The striped golf shirt looked straight out of a wrapper, never worn on a golf course. Lukas sat on the porch next to him, following his hand gestures. Promising himself not to stare longingly at this man's daughter, he avoided eye contact with her as she entered the house.

"I see your arm is doing better. Your dad told me you had been catching up on your sleep and regaining your strength."

"Yes, I felt born again today. Must be the summer sun." He wondered if the lie was good enough.

"I asked Kara to request your presence here because I owe you so much. To put your life in danger for anyone is special."

"There never was any way I couldn't. Not for Kara, sir."

"Well, that is why I needed to talk to you."

"I do appreciate your gratitude, sir. I just care for your daughter very much. Kara means a lot to me."

The older man seemed to pause in his train of thought. While not surprised with the young man's sentiment, the sincerity derailed him. "It has not been easy for Kara. Due to my work, we have to relocate often. Do you know what I do?"

"You teach physics at St. Peter's. The search for the theory of everything and all of that."

The man grimaced at the perceived naiveté of Lukas. In some ways, it was a personal affront, as if the pursuit was frivolous. "Physics is much more complex than I think you realize."

"I did not mean for you to think otherwise. It's just not something that interests me."

"I'm surprised. Your father mentioned you do quite well in math. Your mind is obviously quite logical. A future in science may be your calling."

"I'm not sure I would do that well. Math is a language. A way of communicating the pursuit of the laws of the universe, is it not?"

Kara's father scratched his head, not knowing where to start with such an oversimplification. "The pursuit of the laws. Interesting."

"Well, I understand if people are still studying it, there are no rules that are locked in. You know all this quantum stuff."

Kara's father nodded. "Part of what I enjoy about teaching is shedding light on their works."

Seemingly distracted, Lukas looked up at the sky and sun. Kara's father shifted restlessly, wondering if he was wasting his time. Then Lukas turned to him. "For hundreds of years, the most brilliant of people have tried to find laws, rules, and theories to explain what I see."

"We're getting there."

Lukas laughed.

"You do not believe we will succeed?"

"With all due respect, sir, I hope you don't."

The expression on the older man's face changed. He now listened carefully, intrigued. "Go on."

"There's a beauty in mystery. I read about computers. Everything represented in the lowest denominator of an on or off, a one or a zero."

"And you find putting logic to disorder troubling? Some find the pursuit comforting."

"If I do a headstand, the off position looks like the on. What if on and off, one or zero, were the same thing?"

"You are a philosopher, then, young man."

"Maybe, I guess, or I read too much. Ones and zeros are just points. All numbers are just points. If you connect all the points that exist in all possible ways, you could have infinite works of art, infinite lives, infinite everything."

"Enough to make your head spin."

"No, infinite beauty."

"A philosopher and an artist, now."

"Sorry for rambling. I do respect tremendously what you do, sir. I didn't mean for you to think otherwise."

"Not at all, young man. Maybe we just see the world from a

different point."

"Or maybe I am vibrating somewhere between the two points you are trying to connect."

"Well said!"

Though he enjoyed the discussion, Lukas sensed something troubling the older man. It was the way he looked at Lukas and back at his house. "I do not think you wanted to speak to me about the universe, did you?"

"No, Lukas. I know how much you care for my daughter and . . . I am happy my daughter met you." Any second, Lukas expected him to depart. The man clearly had more to say with nothing left to say all at the same time.

Nodding his head as if to confirm some great insight into himself, Kara's dad stretched himself back, reaching for his wallet.

"Lukas, I am told your heritage is Native American. Your ancestors were called Indian like mine. Only different." He laughed at his joke before continuing. "You do know the supposed story of what some natives thought when the white men introduced them to photography. The natives feared photographs thinking they represented a captured soul?"

"Yes, I believe so."

Fumbling through his wallet, he pulled a picture carefully tucked in a compartment. He handed it to him. "It is Kara's school picture from this past year. I want you to keep it."

Lukas's hand trembled as he grasped the photo. Kara's hair was long and flowing down over her shoulders. Her eyes were radiant as was her face with a smile that highlighted her soft inviting lips. Lukas held his breath, hypnotized. "I cannot take this. It's yours."

"I have others. I want you to have this one." The seriousness in his eyes stunted any further debate. "It is important to me that you have a picture of her. You saved her once. Let's say it is good karma from a Hindi physicist!"

"I am humbled." Before Lukas could say any more, Kara's father cleared his voice and coughed, signaling an end to their discussion. He patted Lukas on the shoulder before excusing himself. Alone on the stoop, Lukas knew there were words left buried and it troubled him. Looking far up the street, he was distracted by a mover's delivery of furniture to an older home that had been on the market for a while. A man in his late fifties could be seen directing traffic. A sharp pain from Lukas's wound shot up his arm.

chapter twenty-five

People came and went. Every year one or two families moved out while another moved into the neighborhood. Lukas usually paid no heed. When someone finally purchased the small rundown bungalow at the far outskirts of the street, a short two-minute trek from the park, neighbors assumed the acquirer would raze the house and build a new, more modern one. They reasoned the in-ground pool in the backyard was worth more than the home. But the single man in his fifties who moved in gradually set the neighborhood on its edge as his story, muddied by thick layers of rumor, drifted up from the sewage that incubated him.

On a Sunday morning, a small army of neighbors appeared at the Wunand door. Within minutes, Grace was scrambling looking for a pen before returning to sign papers the neighbors had with them.

Lukas and Maggie were enjoying the summer weather, playing a spirited game of dodgeball with some kids on the street. Lukas's presence at the match resulted from Kara's leaving for the day to visit friends across the city. The return of Kara into Lukas's life had made this a truly special summer for him. His stitches came off weeks earlier. The battle scars were a minuscule price to pay to enjoy Kara's company again. On top of everything else, he now received smiles from both her parents. Subconsciously or not, he was oblivious to the nuances of his interactions with Kara. Her behavior grew different as he sensed a pensive air about her. All his instincts became clouded with her physically maturing before his eyes.

Unbeknownst to his parents, Lukas crept back to his room to retrieve a baseball cap to shield his eyes from the sun. From his room, he could hear the pure panic in his mom's voice as she called Roman in from his backyard chores, not realizing her son's curious ears tuned into her voice.

"Roman, we have to do something. Move, something!"

"Hold on. You're sure about this. About him?"

"Why would they make this up? They showed me the newspaper article from his arrest. It's him." Roman moved into the kitchen, leaving his work shoes on, dragging the garden soil across the kitchen ceramic. Grace's ignorance of his indiscretion emphasized the seriousness of the discussion.

"So a known pedophile with a record is now living in our neighborhood?"

"Yes, he served a couple of years and was released a few years back. He has been chased out of neighborhood after neighborhood once people realized who he was."

"Maybe he's rehabilitated."

"Roman, we have two children. C'mon. The neighbors are very concerned and passed a petition to force him to leave."

"Grace, it bothers me more than you know. You realize a petition won't work. We have no rights. Until the neighbors told us, we would have assumed he was just a strange older man living alone."

"Exactly, a strange old man buying a rundown home with a pool. A home nobody wanted for years."

Roman shifted in his chair and shook his head. "We are not going to move."

"I hate the thought of having someone like that near my kids.

Damn it. He moved in close to the park."

"I'm sure he'll be under the microscope. We'll make sure our kids don't travel alone anywhere."

"I think we should tell them."

"I do not want our kids to live in fear. We know what we're dealing with. How many like him are out there that we are not aware of?"

"Roman, now you're scaring me."

"We cannot live in fear, either. That's not a life." Roman reached for his wife's shaking hand, grasping it tightly. "We will just make sure our kids do not go off alone at night."

Grace looked around the house, following the sun's rays bouncing off the walls, casting shadows everywhere she looked. Never noticing the menacing features of a dining room table when silhouetted by the sun, she shivered, sensing the hint of terror near her home.

After a brief silence, Roman rose to kiss his wife on the cheek with a reassuring pat on her arm. When he returned to the far recesses of the garden, his knees burrowed into the mud. With anger seeping into his skin, he took his small shovel and twisted it roughly into the earth, planting seeds deeper than normal.

From his room, Lukas waited for his mom to wander into the laundry room. Satisfied he could slip back out undetected, he made his way through the home and returned outdoors. Houses and houses away, at the far end of the street, he searched for the enemy that now existed: a stranger bringing with him fear and angst, like some plague in a rodent-infested town. At that moment, Lukas burnt a promise into his being, one which would itch and infect him.

chapter twenty-six

Summer camp drew closer as the calendar switched from July to August. It was a bittersweet time for Lukas. While the friends made during the annual two-week pilgrimage were cherished, not seeing Kara for two weeks proved difficult. Lukas immersed himself in all of the camp's activities, finding solace in writing Kara a long-winded letter at the end of the first week. Knowing it would be his last summer at camp, and he would no longer be far away from Kara, gave Lukas comfort this year.

Silent moments between Lukas and Kara, however, seemed to ferment in the summer heat. Kara, sixteen going on seventeen, had blossomed into an attractive young woman. Her glasses replaced by contacts, her lips more pronounced, and her physique shapelier, all caused great conflict within Lukas. He longed to hold and kiss her again. Knowing he made a solemn vow not to risk their relationship, he committed himself to the self-inflicted torture of suffocating his yearnings. Often, when he held a book in hand, his eyes drifted into space wondering how she felt about him. Summers before, her mere being provided ample comfort. No longer was this case. Patience was his new mantra.

For her part, Kara serenely spent her available time with Lukas. Breathing in his words as though they came from a higher authority, each one etched in her mind. She vowed to be mindful of these moments with him. While Lukas too developed physically, for Kara, there was an allure to him that went beyond his appearance.

The neighborhood kids long ago resigned themselves to the inevitability of Lukas and Kara, instinctively deeming them as one being. Kara even partook in playing street baseball or dodgeball. Jokingly, one girl told Kara that her wedding day with Lukas was in the Farmer's Almanac. Great comfort blanketed the neighborhood, of something bigger than just the setting of the sun or the rising of the moon. Even Maggie no longer snooped on them with obsessiveness. Now near the end of her teens, she settled into her world and routine, whereby Ruth's duties at the Wunand household became solely ceremonial.

In Lukas's stories, the appearance of a dragon to wreak terror on the hearts of the innocent were the significant tests of the knights. Never did Lukas's stories accurately measure the sheer terror in the hearts of the knights as the fiery breaths torched their armor. Nor could he appreciate the insidiousness of evil and its manifestations. The sun had begun to draw down its curtain as Lukas and Kara were embarking on a walk through the park. A stray poodle ventured upon their path, with white curls and a silver collar attached to a leash but without a master.

"Poor thing must have gotten away from its owner. He's getting close to the woods!"

Lukas knew the fear Kara had immediately. It was these woods, now thick, from where Lukas's previous attacker emerged. Without hesitation, he yelled, "Kara, stay right here on the path. I'll get him before he gets into the woods. His owner must be looking for him."

"I'm not moving from here. Be careful, Lukas."

"Don't worry; I'm a professional dog whisperer now."

"Twenty stitches later," Kara said, grinning.

Lukas raced through the grass, approaching the dog as it sniffed some flowers by the edge of the woods. Following along like a skilled trails man, Lukas positioned himself within leaping distance, and in one outstretched motion jumped toward the leash. The sudden noise caused the dog to bolt forward only to find all the slack of the leash now in the control of Lukas. Satisfied with his effort, Lukas pulled the dog toward him before picking him up. The playful dog slathered Lukas's face with zeal as his fingers fumbled around the collar, looking for identification. Footsteps, growing louder and more frantic, came from farther in the woods. A young man and woman appeared before him. The woman spoke breathlessly.

"You found him. Thank you so much. He got away from us, and we were all over the woods looking for him."

The young man looked at Lukas sheepishly. He appeared disheveled and, like the young woman, took an exaggerated breath. With the safety of the dog ensured, Lukas realized Kara was alone, so he quickly excused himself. Racing his way through the woods and back where he entered, Kara appeared to him at a distance. She was not alone.

As his eyes magnified the being next to her, Lukas's heart raced. It was the new neighbor. *The man* his parents feared. The man was slight at no more than 5 feet 5 or so. He was almost entirely bald, with gray hair. As Lukas approached, the man's retreat from Kara became hastier until he sped-walk out of sight and onto the nearby street.

"Kara, is everything all right?"

Shaking her head, Kara looked at him, any hint of a smile erased from her expression. She appeared angry, almost stammering. "Yes, I am fine. Did you find the dog?"

"Yes. Found his owners, too."

"Good." Burdened with thought, Kara looked down at her shoes. "The man was strange. Very bizarre." She began walking toward the park exit, forcing Lukas to keep up.

"What do you mean by strange?"

"He told me he was new here. Um . . . then he said something weird. He said he had seen me around. He told me he had a pool in his backyard even though he couldn't swim, but neighborhood kids are always welcome. He said I can come by anytime, even after sundown, and the gate's always open." By now she stopped walking to observe Lukas's reaction.

Closing his eyes to paint over the anger he felt rising within him, he smiled at Kara. "Yes, that is weird." He paused. "Did your parents ever tell you about him?"

"Only that he was new and had moved to one of the older homes near the other side of the park."

"Anything else?"

"Just to stay away from him. Then again, they say that about everyone, except maybe you." A smile rose to her face.

Lukas returned the smile. A smile much different than any other ever to grace his face. His teeth gritted together, propelled by an intense burning within him. The overheard conversation about the man repeated itself over and over in his mind. The place where the dog had dug its teeth into his arm stung with excruciating pain. Looking into Kara's trusting eyes, he reached out and instinctively grabbed her hand—squeezing it tightly with his scarred arm visible to her.

She did not run from him this time.

chapter twenty-seven

The steady Sunday morning drizzle did not deter a flurry of activity in the neighborhood. The phone rang constantly. Either Grace or Roman would answer or precipitate the calls. Maggie hovered around her parents, ever hopeful to put the pieces together. All she could decipher was a sense of relief exhibited by her parents. At 10 a.m., a distinct absence in all the buzz was Lukas. Just days away from going to summer camp, there was much to do. Lukas often was the first up, especially in the summer. Maggie grew restless, knowing her brother could perhaps help her find out what was going on.

No light peeked through the slit at the bottom of the door to Lukas's room. Despite the overcast sky, his room was normally the brightest in the house as it faced the morning sun. The lack of color suggested his blinds were completely drawn. The door creaked slightly as she entered. Lukas's running shoes were scattered haphazardly on the floor. His socks lay about, also strewn in no particular order. Still unable to see Lukas's head as the thin blanket covered most of him, she moved closer. Playfully, she pulled the blanket back, only to shudder at the sight of her brother. His face appeared aged. It was the large circles visible under his eyes which got her attention the most. His legs twitched spasmodically further, suggesting a poor night's sleep.

"Lukas. Lukas. Wake up." Maggie aggressively tugged at his

shoulder. With a slow moan, he awoke.

"Maggie, what time is it?" He was clearly surprised to see her. On top of it, she was more excitable than usual.

"It's already 10 a.m., brother. You look so tired."

Lukas did not answer right away. One of his forearms lifted, only to rest heavily over both eyes, covering them from any light. Maggie could tell he was entangled in his thoughts—almost confused. "Maggie. I had such a weird nightmare. I mean, I think it was a bad dream. Maybe more than one."

"Tell me about it."

"I can't remember. I just know it was something creepy."

"Well, there is something strange going on."

Startled, Lukas looked at his sister. His eyes moved beyond her to his shoes and socks sitting in the distance. Closing his eyes, he let out a sigh and shook his head. Whatever image or thought had lodged itself in his head was most unwelcome. "Tell me."

"I don't know. Mom and Dad have been on the phone all morning. They seem pretty happy with whatever it is."

Lukas sat up. The world of his nightmare and the world he awoke to had slowly integrated together in the last few minutes. He grew pensive and his eyes fluttered off in a million directions around his room. "Maggie, I'll see what I can find out. Just give me a second and let me change."

Within seconds of Maggie leaving his room, he regretted her departure. Alone with his thoughts, he found neither escape nor distraction from them. Everything around his room looked different. Shadows formed in the backdrop of each object. Shivering slightly from a cold sweat, he felt as though he had run a thousand miles through a desert. His legs ached. His heart pounded mightily like some great ape announcing its dominance. Every breath was dipped in butter. He knew it would not be long before

Maggie returned wondering where he was, anxious for him to go into the world and investigate the commotion that beat a rhythm against the walls of their house.

With his hands covering his face, he sat up in his bed, desperately trying to collect his thoughts. Fatigue and confusion pulled him in a thousand directions. Looking across his room to a nightstand, he could see the picture of Kara, given to him by her father. He smiled at the image and the reassurance it provided. His need to see her energized him. Finding her safe focused him, however irrational that fear appeared to be.

Lukas burst through the doors of his home and looked up the street to Kara's house. Neighbors dotted the sidewalk, more than usual, and spoke in murmurs. He had barely stepped off the curb in front of his home when a welcome voice filled his ear. Before he could even look up, Kara's footsteps, now in a run, could be heard approaching him.

"Lukas, did you hear? Did you hear the news?" Kara asked, almost gasping for air.

"No. Maggie told me something was up. She requested that I come find out."

"Well, that old man. You know the one who spoke to me the other day."

"Yes. Of course, I do. The creepy one." Lukas's voice glided through the air without inflection or tone, landing cold against Kara's ear.

"He's dead. He drowned in his pool."

"Holy cow. When did this happen?" Lukas's hand rubbed his scarred arm as he spoke.

"Someone said last night. The neighbors behind his house saw something floating in his pool. They called the police. He is dead. *Drowned.*"

Lukas studied Kara's reaction carefully. Almost stuttering as she spoke, he also sensed the relief in her voice. It reassured him. An awkward silence hung between them until he finally spoke.

"I suppose things like that happen for a reason."

Kara could sense Lukas's uneasiness discussing the news. Death is not a subject which people handle similarly. The calm of Lukas's demeanor surprised her very little. Whatever situation confronted her, this constant port was a sweet shelter. Her breathing relaxed as she stood in front of him, completely in tune with him. The events of the morning were a far greater diversion for Kara than Lukas could have known. Time was ticking more loudly with each passing day. Each interaction with Lukas propelled her higher and closer to the sun. The top of the rollercoaster was nearing. The death of the old man merely took their eye off the approaching peak.

"I need to head back home as my mom has some errands that I need to do."

"Sure, no problem. I'm around for a couple more days before my summer camp starts."

"You're leaving to camp on Thursday night, right?" she asked with her voice trembling slightly, enough for Lukas to notice.

"Yes, why?"

"No reason. Just I wanted to wish you a safe trip before you go."

"That is sweet of you. Besides we still will have a week or so to spend together before school starts when I return."

"Yes. As always, you're right." Her eyes shifted quickly to the ground as she spoke. Before Lukas could react, Kara was up the street and entering her house. Kara rarely asked about when Lukas would leave for camp and return. Usually, Lukas, who bathed himself in every word Kara uttered and recorded in his mind every expression on her face, would question Kara's strange behavior further. However, her reporting of the death of the creepy old man, although many houses away, preoccupied him. He stared up the street toward the park and where the dead man's house was located. *Drowned.*

During supper that evening, Roman and Grace spoke of the man's death in a matter of fact tone. Maggie grew intrigued by how an adult could drown in his pool.

"Like maybe he drowned himself. Eh, Dad?"

Roman looked at his daughter. "It could be. Sometimes things happen to people for a reason." He looked over at his wife, smirking. The table shook as Grace kicked her husband before casting him an icy stare. With that, the subject was changed.

Lukas made his way through the nightly meal with barely any words spoken by him. He grew pensive and sullen. A million thoughts raced through his mind, each holding an image like luggage. It did not occur to him while speaking to Kara, however, upon returning to his home, he noticed something horribly wrong with his running shoes. Racing to his room he witnessed his socks scattered on the floor. The reality pierced his armor—his socks were damp, as were the shoes he wore. The fear of why devoured him at supper.

chapter twenty-eight

Kirsten remained comfortably ignorant of the changes Rosemary and Ram had seen in Lukas. His coffee cup took a greater hint of vodka with each passing day. His writing took a more pointed and satirical tone. When she could, she would sit all afternoon in his company at the edge of the cafeteria table. Often she would do her work while he and whoever joined him read aloud and laughed. For Lukas, there was always a smile, a kiss on the cheek, and when she could, on the base of his neck.

Rosemary had mixed emotions about Kirsten's flirtations. On the one hand, she wished a wave of lust would sweep over Lukas, and he could succumb to the charms of this young admirer. Instinctively, she sensed something seriously amiss. Ram believed it would all work out fine. Lukas was going through the normal phase of coming to terms with his graduation and moving on to the work world.

It was late March now in the faculty. There was no mention of any assaults around the campus. Students wondered if it was because they had stopped or perhaps the assailant was finally captured. Others suspected, with the departure of Ally, such information now was suppressed by Tobin. In any event, the vast majority appreciated the lack of news over issues as heavy as that. No news was good news in the school of business. The last classes for the semester ground down to their usual barren climaxes. The last faculty party of the school year, the infamous March 29 date, was days away. The last party for the graduating students. The end of an era.

Lukas flung his backpack across the cafeteria table. Skilled at balancing his Styrofoam cup and its now potent payload, Lukas settled in without even looking to see who was at the table today. It no longer mattered. Someone would be there. The company was welcome in this new game he learned. Being alone with his thoughts worried him. His role was about to end—the idea of the next act troubled him.

A welcoming smile greeted him today. The gentle giant known as Ram sat across from him this morning, grinning from ear to ear. Unlike Rosemary, Ram paid little heed to the contents of Lukas's cup. He was not the worrying kind. A former jock, getting through school and finding the next party was a priority. He genuinely admired the ease with which Lukas confronted life, not knowing the internal battle lurking behind the flesh.

"Rammy, someone is seriously sporting a smile. Shit, looks like it will jump off your face."

"Yeah. I'm in a good mood today. Last class today and last party on Thursday."

"I'm sure it is more than that, my friend." Lukas raised his eyebrows and winked at his friend.

"Well, there is more. I got an offer to work at a marketing agency in New York in the fall. I got a fricken job, man. In New York!"

The enthusiasm in Lukas's expression testified to his true feelings of happiness for his friend. However, the words were a reminder to the forthcoming finality of this chapter of their relationship. So many words rolled across Lukas's mind, he settled on the one emotion that gave him comfort. He was proud of his

friend. He had been there when Ram limped back into the cafeteria after football tryouts, his knee ballooned like a baby beluga.
Knowing his athletic career was over, Ram sat alone in the farthest
corner of the cafeteria, until Lukas, a fellow first-year, spotted
him. The friendship formed in an instant. Both boys, with their
hopes for their future, deviated from their chosen path, finding
themselves together in a new world.

"Proud of you, Little John." Lukas laughed, reminding Ram of
his nickname when they first met. Ram understood the reference
to *Robin Hood,* but Lukas quickly corrected him. It came from
Rocket Robin Hood, the cartoon TV show from ancient times.

"You will visit me?"

"Of course, I will."

"How about yourself? I assume you are no longer working for
Tobin's dad's firm next year."

"That is for sure. No, I think I'll take some time. Working on a
few things." Lukas's voice grew more baritone as he spoke. There
was nothing on the horizon anymore. "And let's not forget the
big party on Thursday. Time to blow the doors off this place once
and for all."

"So maybe you and Kirsten will finally do the deed?" Ram
punched Lukas in the arm, beaming. "The calendar hath proph-
esied it."

"She's a good kid, Ram. An honorable kid. She's still a kid."

"Look at you. You are not some old man. Enjoy, brother. Enjoy.
You got some cute first year who worships the ground you walk
on, and you act like the celibate priest on top of some mountain
in India."

Lukas fidgeted in his chair. He brought the cup to his lips
and emptied the contents with purpose before tossing the cup
into the nearby wastebasket. "Maybe you're right. Um . . . I just

don't think I'm all she expects me to be." All humor cast aside, he looked at Ram. "Next year, I won't be here. I don't want to hurt her or take advantage of her."

"For fuck's sake. Kirsten is an adult. Let her decide. Stop thinking so much. She likes you. Accept it."

"You're right. I know you are."

On cue, Rosemary and Kirsten approached the table with a bunch of students. To make room for them, Lukas pushed his backpack to the floor. Without missing a beat, he winked at Kirsten. "You will be at the party? Not studying for finals that night or washing the curls out of your pretty hair?"

"You know I would not miss your last party for the world, Lukas. Besides, there is a prophecy that night. Isn't there?"

As the students laughed at his awkwardness at the joke he, himself, created, Lukas's face blinked in shades of red. Just as quickly, Lukas leaped from his chair, excusing himself to get himself a muffin. He gave Kirsten a welcoming kiss on the cheek as she, too, rushed off to her class. Rosemary settled in across from Ram.

"So, Ram, you aren't concerned at all about this?" Rosemary whispered to Ram as she settled in across from him.

"The whole Lukas-Kirsten thing? It's all good. I had a little father-son talk with the boy before you arrived." Ram leaned back in his chair almost flopping backward on the ground.

"No. It's everything about Lukas. I know him. This Lukas is not the same guy we knew months ago, let alone a year ago. He's running on fumes. I can smell it. He does not talk about his career. He avoids talking about anything past graduation. I'm worried about him."

Refusing to let Ram in on the complete source of her anxiety, she replayed in her mind that night when Lukas walked her home. How he chased some ghost from his past and how easily he let go of that pursuit to return to the old Lukas. The transformation was too easy. As she sat in Lukas's seat, she felt strange. A seat which would be forever empty in the days and weeks to come as they all moved on in their lives. She wondered now what lay ahead for him. For the past few years, so much of their lives were spent basking in the light he made for them, they may have forgotten about what happens to him. Long after the zoo closes for the night, the animals remain in their cages.

"Rosemary, Lukas is the most in control person I have ever known. Kirsten will do wonders for him. It's just what the doctor ordered."

Rosemary smiled meekly, thinking back to the image of Lukas under the street lamp staring at something from his back pocket. Soon enough, Lukas had returned. Rosemary was about to return the throne to its rightful king when Lukas motioned for her to remain seated.

"Don't move, Rose. I have to go upstairs to the administration offices."

Rosemary grew immediately suspicious. Students, especially graduating ones, avoided the administrative offices. "What's going on?"

Lukas sensed her uneasiness so quickly offered an explanation. "They had the wrong mailing address for my transcript. Just going to correct them." Avoiding any further queries, he turned and briskly made his way out of the cafeteria. Walking past the Student Society offices, the scene of his exile, he returned to the boys' bathroom and sought the farthest stall. Closing his eyes while leaning back against the wall, his hand fumbled into his back pocket. He opened his eyes and stared at the wrinkled photograph partially faded by time and light. He thought of Ally leaving suddenly, Ram graduating and moving to New

York, and his sister, Maggie, older and more independent with a boyfriend now. He remembered Ruth passing away a couple of years ago. Mostly, though, his mind lingered over the image of Kara, wondering if she ever did exist or was she a mere apparition, appearing before his desperate eyes that day in September. The alcohol coursing through his blood did little to numb him let alone calm his spasmodic mind. His head thumped against the hard plastic gray wall of the stall. He returned the picture to his pocket. What he truly longed for was forgiveness. The only key to unlock this cell was the absolution he so longed. Even then, he doubted it would be sufficient. Only a few more days or weeks until his friends' graduation. His future was as confining as the stall surround him.

. . .

The cafeteria drained itself of the morning student crowd as the classroom bells range but for a few stragglers. Rosemary sat alone now in Lukas's chair. How many students wandered into his kingdom over the years? All preferring comedic relief over academic advice. A powerful feeling came over her, sugaring over all thoughts. *Her friend had done so much for them. What had she ever done for him?* Feeling empowered by an unseen force, she bolted out of her seat and entered the elevator, pressing the button that would bring her to the administration floor. Bouncing out of the elevator before the door completely closed, she sought a bespectacled, gray-haired lady named Wendy who manned the front desk.

"Hi, Rosemary. It's been awhile since you've been up here."

"Too long, Wendy. I came up here hoping to catch up with Lukas Wunand."

"Lukas? He hasn't been up here in awhile or at least ever since he had a chat with the Dean back in January."

"Chat with the Dean, what for?" Rosemary grew angry more than worried that perhaps Tobin had actually complained to the Dean.

"About leaving the faculty."

"What? He's leaving with us when he graduates in June, right?"

Wendy could see the bewilderment on Rosemary's face and sense the motherly concern. "I should not tell you this. I assumed everyone knew. Lukas is not graduating."

"What do you mean?"

"He hasn't been attending classes since October and wrote none of his December finals."

"Oh shit!"

"Dean Wallis likes him so he wanted to talk with him. Lukas told the Dean he had no intention of graduating, though he asked one favor."

"I'm listening." Rosemary could barely find the words as she gasped.

"He asked to be allowed to hang around the faculty to be with his friends for their last semester until he figures out what he wants to do. I'm sorry you heard it from me."

"No, I appreciate you telling me. We care for Lukas a lot. At least, I do."

Wendy smiled. "We all do. The Dean does not generally go out of his way. Why just the other day, he mentioned he would try to get Lukas into the arts faculty."

"Arts faculty?"

"Yes. My friend over there told me she sees Lukas there all the time. He asked her about some student he was seeking. An old friend."

"Did he say the name of the friend?"

"It is on the tip of my tongue. Short name. "Sara . . . no, Kara,

I think. It is short for a longer name. Let me write it out for you from what I recall."

"So is she is a student?"

"No, my friend couldn't find any record of her. Lukas asked her to check the registrar records for him. No sign of her, although her dad did teach here years ago."

"You said Lukas is there all the time."

"Yeah, my friend told me she would see him many times just hanging around the atrium or in the halls. She assumed he would eventually transfer to the faculty."

Rosemary shook her head while processing the information. She bit her lip, knowing what she needed to do. "Look, Wendy, I took up too much time already."

"Sorry, Lukas didn't say anything. If you see him, please tell him the Dean would be more than willing to recommend his transfer.

"Thank you very much. I'll make sure to let Lukas know. So there's no such Kara registered as a student? Not even an employee, like teaching aid or assistant?"

"There is no one at the school with her name."

Rosemary proceeded back down elevators, confused. She was on a mission, now unsure of where it would lead or how much time she had to complete it.

chapter twenty-nine

Faculty parties took over the upper floor of the Student Recreational Center on Thursday, Friday, and Saturday nights. The Center was situated next to the Faculty of Arts within the central complex of the university. The Faculty of Business parties normally were the last Thursday of each month. Being the end of the semester and the school year, the March 29 party took on special significance. In the large hall on the upper floor, a student DJ pumped out the latest tunes. Some partiers overindulged in the cheap alcohol served at the make-shift bar; others overindulged on the dance floor. Cafeteria tables lined up on the peripheries for those with a more voyeuristic bent. The dimly lit corners of the hall were lined with chairs for those couples seeking privacy.

For the Student Society, the final party was the curtain call for the graduating students and a heavily promoted event. The funds raised from the alcohol sales helped fill the coffers for future activities.

Rosemary arrived early that morning, brushing past the throng of students assembled in the hallways of the faculty. Her target was the Student Society offices. Kyle rolled his eyes as she entered. Ignoring his glare, she took a seat at a nearby desk and quickly manned the phones. Finally, curiosity got the better of him.

"Everything good? You seem frazzled."

"Just trying to locate someone here at the university, a student."

"Who are you calling?"

"Different student societies. To see if they've heard of her."

Kyle smirked, leaned over to his desktop, and started typing away. Within seconds, he found what he was looking for and motioned Rosemary to come over. She sped across the room, positioning herself over his shoulder.

"What is this you have access to?"

"University student database. All the Student Society execs have access to it. Just need to know where to look."

"You mind?" She motioned to the search feature.

"No problem." Kyle left his chair and gave her access to the computer. "Promise me you won't tell Tobin I showed you this."

"Scout's honor. I'm doing this for Lukas."

"Even more reason not to tell Tobin." Kyle winked.

Rosemary typed the name over and over again. Nothing. She shook her head in defeat. "Maybe she doesn't exist after all."

Kyle looked at her, reached over, and logged her out of the computer before shutting it down. "Sorry you couldn't find her. It looked like you were doing some heavy duty forensic work."

"I just do not get it. Thanks anyways, Kyle." She lifted herself off the chair before sitting back down heavy in thought. Out of the corner of her eye, she saw the signup sheet for the Walk Safe Program. Closing her eyes, she bit her lip hard, hoping to remember her conversation with Lukas word for word about where he saw Kara that morning. Walking toward the arts building. That's where he saw her. With her head bobbing up and down in determination, she left the office and made her way out of the building.

Following the path Lukas had taken, the low probability of success smothered her need to help her friend. She only had a name, never saw the girl, and could only imagine her appearance. Most of all, her hope was for inspiration. For months, Lukas combed not only the faculty but the university for her. Registrar records searched. Hell, the people in the arts building even thought of Lukas as one of their own. Paying no heed to reason or statistics, Rosemary surmised that Lukas's search could never be in vain. She willed it not to be.

The vastness of the main lobby of the arts building dizzied her. Marble statues, high ceilings. *Freaking awesome*, she thought. Deciding she needed time to think, she took a spot at one of the large oak benches along the walls of the lobby. Her eyes darted around the room, going from gargoyle to gargoyle perched high atop the door frames. Her breath grew more uneven as she realized she didn't have a clue as to how to proceed. *How does one search for a ghost?* She sunk back against the brick façade, closing her eyes briefly. Upon opening them, she stared at a work of art directly across. It was a replica of Michelangelo's "Creation of Adam." Drawn to its majesty, she got up and moved across the lobby toward it. Her eyes caressed every inch of the work. She took a step back, noticing a bulletin board hanging discreetly a few feet away. "Arts Faculty Classifieds."

The bulletin board was littered with posters and various pinups from used books for sale, to service offerings to advertisements for local shows. Hidden beneath the various postings, Rosemary could make out the words, "Children's Literacy Mission." The title was all that protruded from the many other postings now pinned over it. Clearly, this had been on the board for quite some time. One by one, she removed every pin and announcement until she found the one that caught her attention.

Children's Literacy Mission
The Children's Literacy Foundation is looking for volunteers to spend 10-12 months helping to teach local children to read

in impoverished communities in Central and South America. The deadline for applying is December 31. Volunteers will be leaving in spring on their respective missions. Volunteers will be staying with local families. If interested or would like more information, please contact the number below.

At the bottom of the page were cut-outs of a phone number so students could tear off the contact number. One number was left. Next to the phone number was a name: Kara.

Rosemary's hand trembled as she reached to tear off the contact number. Once nestled between her fingertips, she stared at it. Terrified about smudging the ink with her now sweaty hands, she committed the number to memory, repeating it over and over again. Seven digits danced pirouettes around her skull. *Kara.* A smile rose to her cheeks. Lukas had indeed seen Kara. She did indeed exist. Her jubilation crested quickly upon rereading the posting. *Leaving in spring.* Crap! Snapping herself out of her elation, she searched her pockets for change or even a pay phone. Realizing none was readily visible, she tore through the lobby and up the stairs to the Arts Administration offices.

Her breathless arrival through the administrative office's doors caused the receptionist to spill her coffee across her desk. "Hold on, young lady. What is so urgent?"

"I'm sorry." Rosemary quickly realized pure panic would get her nowhere with this woman. "Wendy from the business school said if I needed anything, you would help."

"Say hello to her. By all means, what can I do for her?"

"I just need to make a phone call."

"A phone call! Nothing else?"

"Yes. I need some privacy, though."

"Fine. You can use the empty office over there. As long as it isn't long distance."

Rosemary looked back down at the slip she had taken. "No, it isn't long distance."

"Well then. Make yourself at home."

Closing the empty office's door behind her, Rosemary settled into the edge of the chair. Before dialing, she paused, trying desperately to calm herself down. The clock was ticking. Despite her excitement moments earlier, the fear of failure began choking her. The posting was months ago. The phone number could be disconnected by now. Certainty rested with the digits on the page and the name attached. If anything at all, she could apologize to Lukas for doubting him.

Her fingers slowly and methodically pressed the buttons for each number. Every moment of silence between rings seemed to last forever. By the fourth unanswered ring, her heart pounded recklessly. Suddenly, a click followed by a voice with a distinctive young British accent. "Hello."

"Hello." Rosemary, so pleased to utter a single audible word, left a trail of silence.

"Hello, can I help you?"

Rosemary was almost crushed by the weight of the next question. "Is this Kara?" She closed her eyes, committing all energy to listening. Every word, syllable, and intonation needed to be remembered.

"Yes, it is."

"Great. I was calling about the Children's Literacy . . . um . . ." Rosemary's mind went blank. She memorized the phone number although not much else.

"The Children's Literacy Mission."

"That is it." *Darn great!* Rosemary thought. *Now I sound like a total idiot. Of course, Kara knows the name of it.* "I mean. When are you leaving?"

"Next week. I'm leaving then, and another group is expected to join us after final exams. Why, may I ask? It is a bit late if you want to join."

"No, it's not for me. I was calling on behalf of a dear friend of mine."

"Well, it is a fantastic cause. Children's literacy is something near and dear to my heart."

Rosemary smiled. There could be little doubt who she was: the Kara of Lukas's quest. "It is quite unique. I mean, you are quite extraordinary for organizing this."

"I'm just one of many. Or I hope many. It's important to me."

"Yes. I can tell."

"The deadline was December 31, but there is always room for one more. Is your friend with you? Maybe I can speak to them."

"He's not here now. He's a classmate of mine. His name is Lukas."

"Oh." There was a distinct pause. Subtle though very distinct.

"His full name is Lukas Wunand."

Rosemary heard the gasp and the knock of the phone against something plush as if dropped. Rosemary constructed sentence after sentence in her head with computer-like precision. She needed to get this conversation right. She needed to reel this one in and not lose it to the seas.

"Lukas Wunand? Are you sure? Sorry, it sounds strange. Certainly, you are sure." She giggled nervously.

"Lukas Wunand is indeed his name." Rosemary thought carefully before adding, "Why? Do you know a Lukas Wunand?"

"Yes. I do. Umm . . . Are you related to him? Maggie, is that you?"

Rosemary exploded in delirium inside the second she heard Maggie's name mentioned. She realized Kara might be wondering if Rosemary were a girlfriend of Lukas's.

"No, I'm not Maggie. I'm just a school friend of his. But he does have a sister named Maggie." Rosemary paused to listen to the breath grow unsteady on the other end of the line. The raw emotion being stifled sifted through miles of copper wire. A faint shriek or hint of a sob could be heard. No longer did reeling in this young woman remain as her foremost objective, instead empathy for this stranger overpowered her. The connection to Lukas went beyond what she expected, almost soulful.

"Kara, I'll be honest with you. I was hoping to find you. Lukas is a close friend of mine."

"Are you and he . . . you know?"

"No, we're not dating or anything of that nature. We go to school together. I'm doing this for him. He is special to me."

"Special. Yes. Forgive me. It has been so long."

"I only know Lukas has some affinity for you. He won't tell me what happened between you. All I know is that there is some connection."

"He never told you. I'm not sure what I can say then." There was another period of silence before the voice on the other end grew quieter. "Is Lukas all right? Is that why you're calling? Did something happen to him?"

"No, he is alive and well, sort of . . ."

"I am truly thankful for that. If Lukas didn't say anything, why are you calling?"

"I need to ask you a question instead. Would you like to see him again?"

"Oh dear! You're sure he didn't say anything to you about the last time we spoke? About what happened?"

"I promise you, he didn't say anything."

"I'm just not sure he would want to see me or speak to me."

"You didn't answer my question. Would you want to see him again?"

"Certainly. I'm not so sure it would be a good idea."

Rosemary stopped to play back the conversation to see what she was missing. "Is it because you're married or seeing someone?"

"No. It's too hard to explain, especially if he didn't tell you."

"I don't know what Lukas was like years ago. All I know is the person I know now. Speaking from the heart, you know, woman to woman, please see him again." She shuddered as she said the words, unsure how they would settle in.

"It's a lot for me to process. Where is Lukas studying now?"

"He is at St. Peter's. Faculty of Business."

"Really? He's studying business! Not philosophy or literature?"

There were more puzzle pieces than Rosemary ever could have dreamed of resting on the edges of her mind. "Yes, he's in the school of business. You seem surprised."

"I shouldn't judge. It's just not where I envisaged him."

Rosemary laughed. "Sweetie, I am now convinced you do know Lukas better than anyone."

A faint sound of a smothered laugh emerged through the receiver. "I never once thought that."

"Please consider seeing him."

"I'm leaving next week. I wouldn't even know where to find him."

"I know where you can see him. He'll be at our year-end party at the Student Recreation Center. Party starts tonight at 9 p.m."

"I do know where that is. I promise to think about it. Please do not say anything to him. Please don't. I don't want to make any promises."

"I see. I pray you seriously consider it before you leave. Not for me. For Lukas."

"Yes. I will. Don't get me wrong. I do appreciate you calling me. I'm glad and appreciate knowing he is fine."

A thought penetrated Rosemary's mind. "Kara, have you

always been living here?”

“I only lived here for a few years. I returned late last summer.”

“I presume there is a reason you didn’t look for Lukas.”

“I didn’t think he wanted me to find him.”

“When he sees you, you’ll know the answer to that. I’m sure about it.”

“I am afraid of that in so many ways.”

Rosemary could sense fear, a feeling of loss. It was the same feeling she had when Lukas walked her home that night. Two people, both carrying some burden, keeping them inexplicably apart. Even as she pushed all the pieces into place, she saw the puzzle enlarging with more pieces remaining lost.

“Try to be there tonight. I won’t say anything to Lukas.”

“I beg of you not to.” Just before she hung up, she added, “Thank you.”

“You need not thank me. Showing up will be more than enough.”

“No, I meant to thank you for being a good friend to Lukas. I am grateful someone is watching over him.”

The other end of the line went hush as the voice dropped off. Rosemary held the receiver to her ear as if to vacuum out every particle of data she possibly could. Finally, she put down the phone and reclined back in the chair, closing her eyes in the process. That was Kara on the line. She found the mysterious Kara. Would this girl show at the party? Should she betray Kara and warn Lukas? All of the combinations played out before her. Something had kept Lukas and Kara apart through the years. Were they even ever together? The one thought that pervaded all else was telling Lukas about Kara only to have Kara not show up. It would devastate him, she surmised. The small ripped out paper with the phone number sat on the desk in front of her. Placing it carefully in a neat fold deep inside her jean pocket, it would act as a backup plan if Kara did not show. Satisfied that she had covered all the bases and reached the proper conclusion, she emerged from the office to make her way back to her faculty.

In the corner of the cafeteria sat Lukas with a throng of students assembled, two to three deep around him. He was reciting a poem.

> *A glimpse through an interstice caught,*
> *Of a crowd of workmen and drivers in a bar-room,*
> *around the stove late on a winter night—And I unremark'd*
> *seated in a corner;*
> *Of a youth who loves me, and whom I love, silently*
> *approaching, and seating himself near, that he may hold me*
> *by the hand;*
> *A long while, amid the noises of coming and going—*
> *of drinking and oath and smutty jest,*
> *There we two, content, happy in being together, speaking little,*
> *perhaps not a word.*

When he finished, he sat back down and smiled across the cafeteria at Rosemary, who flashed him a big thumbs-up sign. As the students slowly moved away once the finality of the reading became evident, Rosemary saw the curly-haired presence of the young, doomed Kirsten in the front row, applauding feverishly. Lukas bowed down before her in comical exaggeration.

With the ease of a soldier marching into a landmine-infested field, Rosemary walked toward Lukas. The permutations and combinations she scuttled about her brain minutes earlier broke apart in chaos before her eyes. The one independent variable she had conveniently forgotten was Kirsten. The ever-present Kirsten.

Rosemary recalled why she hated statistics so much.

"Hey, Rosemary!" Kirsten bellowed enthusiastically. "You're going to be at the party tonight?"

"I certainly plan to."

"You better. It is, after all, Lukas's big day." Kirsten rose up, walked toward Lukas, and elbowed him gently on the shoulder.

Rosemary took a step back before composing herself. "What big day?"

"Remember, the joke on the calendar. The Student Society calendar."

It suddenly dawned on her. "Sure, yes, now I remember."

While Rosemary seated herself and put her hands on her face, shaking her head, Kirsten departed, leaving Lukas alone with Rosemary.

"You seem a little out of sorts there, Rosie. Enjoy. Tonight is the big party. Our last hurrah."

Rosemary looked up at Lukas and smiled. "Whatever you do, Lukas, just do the right thing. I mean follow your heart."

"Have I not always?"

chapter thirty

The loud beat of the DJ started sharply at 9 p.m. By 10 p.m., the ballroom was alive with the hysteria of drunken youth. The last party or beer bash of a school year took on special significance. Rosemary arrived early, her anxiety palpable from the way her beer cup jiggled precariously. Too nervous to enjoy herself, she surveyed the surroundings. Lukas stood near the bar, large plastic cup in hand, likely his vodka-cranberry concoction. Assembled around him were a contingent of fellow students. From the gesticulations and laughter, they were telling tall tales of the exploits of their university years. All was good, so far. Kirsten was nowhere around. She would show for sure. Would Kara show? How the hell would she ever know it was her?

The tap on her shoulder caused her to jostle her beer, catching it precipitously close to her blouse with slight spillage. "Geez, Ram, you scared me."

"You forgot? They're looking for you behind the bar."

"Christ. So sorry. I was just . . . oh never mind." She dared not tell Ram anything as he had the biggest mouth in the faculty. Besides, how could she ever explain what was supposed to happen? In all the excitement of the day and night, she forgot her responsibilities. She had committed to working at the bar behind the scenes, tracking inventory and managing the cash. She slowly wandered behind the tables past the counters to the far back of the bar area. She yelled over to Ram.

"Keep me posted."

"Posted about what?"

"Just keep an eye on Lukas. Promise me!"

"Yeah, yeah. Sure." Ram chuckled. Lukas always had a way of being just fine. Besides, Ram had loftier ambitions. At around midnight, the graduating students were taking on the rest of the faculty in "boat races." Ten racers on each side lined up on their knees across adjoining tables. Each with two beers. Starting at the front of the line, a racer chugged his or her beer, and when the cup hit the table empty, the next racer proceeded. The anchor had to down two beers back to back for the order to shift back down the line. The first team to finish all twenty beers won. It was a badge of honor for the graduating students to win. Ram looked at his boy and anchor, Lukas, giving him the thumbs-up sign and pointing at the clock. Concern stretched across his face as he watched the vigor with which Lukas was drinking. *Too early*, he thought, *you are peaking too early.*

It was not unusual to see Lukas on the dance floor, especially when the DJ went through a "grunge" set, turning the dance floor into a mosh pit. In his black jean shirt and well-worn jeans, the yellow laces of Lukas's shoes darted to and fro to the beat of Sonic Youth's "Dirty Boots." A hand surgically reached into the masses and pulled Lukas by the bottom of the shirt, yanking it out of his pants. He dutifully followed Kirsten as she dragged him, staggering and all, across the room to the far reaches of the ballroom.

"I scoped out this place and found a quiet spot." She pointed to the darkest corner, behind rolled back curtains that, when extended, separated the ballroom in two. Lukas did not say a word of protest. For the observers around them, it looked of total submission. Ram laughed at the sight and gave an all-clear sign to Rosemary far away.

Kirsten wore a white, almost see-through, lacy blouse, tucked into her jeans. Her hair smelled of cinnamon and her lips bore a touch of lipstick. She leaned into Lukas as she pushed him against the wall with a strength that surprised him.

"It'll be midnight soon. You know what that means."

Lukas smiled. "The boat races?"

Kirsten laughed but was visibly annoyed. "Tonight is your night. Remember?"

"You know it was all just a joke and . . ."

"You need not say another word. Think of it as my graduation gift to you."

Before he could respond, the room suddenly and then slowly began blurring in front of him. While not outwardly shivering, he could feel his body tremble from within. Something was not right. He assumed it was the vodka cranberry. Kirsten pressed her knee in between his legs, pinning him to the wall. Her head leaned forward, her tongue softly caressing his ear before entering it gently. Lukas closed his eyes as her mouth moved toward his trembling lips, a hint of her tongue and then her enthusiastic kisses on his neck. Her hands moved skillfully to his waist, slowly unbuckling his belt. Her delicate fingers pulled his zipper down, bit by bit, with every kiss on his neck.

Her head suddenly pulled back and she smiled at him. "Now we are talking."

Lukas's eyes grew blurry, entering into a trance-like state, and images dashed before his eyes, fighting off each sensation he felt. In so many ways, he wanted to give in. Something profoundly ingrained within him tortured him with a guilt he could not understand. Kirsten tugged tighter at his hips, her hands stretching to the back of his jeans, pushing him closer to her. Her hands slithered down the back of his pants and slowly tunneled into his back pockets. "Hmm." She hissed. "What have you got hidden back here. Protection? Perfect." Lukas's eyes opened wide with terror to see her face look perplexed before she continued. "A picture?"

Like lightning launched down to beat back mere mortals from the gods, Lukas's eyes erupted in fire. "No, Kirsten. I can't."

"Let me see." He could feel her hand grabbing at the photo, trying to pry it out.

Lukas's hands wrapped her wrists, squeezing tightly enough to cause Kirsten to grimace. "Please let go."

"Ouch." Frightened, Kirsten pulled back with tears streaming down. "What the fuck is wrong with you?"

Words failing him, Lukas let go as she inched away from him. His hand went back to his pocket, tucking the picture back in. "Kirsten. I am sorry."

"No, I'm sorry ever to think you were not weird. I can't waste my time anymore." She bit her lip as she wiped the last trickle of tears from her cheek. A cheek red with anger.

Standing alone, Lukas watched her depart. Tears rolled down as well but not the ones visible. He leaned back against the wall and crouched down. Far away from the view of everyone, safely behind the curtain. His head nestled between his hands, which pressed tightly against it. He now wondered if he could ever escape the torment. All that he had done was for her. All this pain, sorrow, he suffered and now caused. Only to be alone.

chapter thirty-one

His eyes noticed the curtain next to him. A devious smile broke away from his face. The clock neared midnight, the music strangely stopped. Lukas remembered the boat race and how Ram would surely be beside himself with worry. Fear of losing without him as an anchor, he pulled himself up with the help of the curtain. The show needed him, and for now, it was all he had. He staggered across the room, sliding into his anchor position at the end of the table. Ram smiled at him. From behind the bar, Rosemary was not sure what was happening. Standing puzzled, she had seen Kirsten wander by and disappear with maroon cheeks. There stood Lukas, where one expected him to be. Something remained horribly missing from Rosemary's world. There was no Kara.

Beer cup after beer cup toppled along the table. The delirious cries of "spillage" filled the air as the assembly line efficiency of the boat race reached the anchor position. With whatever capacity he had left for alcohol intake, Lukas guzzled back one beer, bouncing the cup off the table as he hoisted the second. Before the first could even bounce more than once, the second cup fell next to it amidst the roar of the crowd. The ensuing victory celebration with Ram at its center created a diversion. The music roared back to life for those now bored with the festivities. Nobody noticed a disoriented and confused Lukas wandering to the far reaches of the room. The world around him spun at a dizzying pace beyond his current capacity to bear.

A solitary figure appeared before him. How long had she been standing there? He could not guess. Whatever the case, the figure stood silently, observing the spectacle before her. Lukas stopped dead in his tracks. The slumped shoulders stood upright with military perfection. While the vision before him started as a shadow in the distance, the form slowly gained color as he approached. A primordial instinct whispered with certainty the name to him, *Kara*. Each step grew slower as he neared her. Fearful and uncertain, he finally stood before her.

Kara's endlessly dusky eyes grew wide as she heaved a heavy breath that rumbled like an earthquake. From the tears basking in the glow of sadness, sheer joy formed on her face. Finally, her lips parted. "Lukas."

He stood before her, hearing his name. The alcohol absorbed it through his skin. Believing himself about to be tortured one final time, he stood expressionlessly. Again, she spoke, "Lukas, it's me, Kara."

He looked at her and tilted his head. "Yes, Kara. I'm Lukas."

She could smell the heavy burden of alcohol on his tongue and could see the gaps where his shirt remained unbuttoned. His belt was open, haphazardly fluttering against his hip. His half open zipper was partially concealed by the wild wanderings of his shirt. "Lukas, are you okay?"

"Okay, yes, I'm quite satisfied. I guess. Actually, maybe a little unsatisfied."

"I don't understand. I was told. I mean, I thought you would be happy to see me."

"Yes, I would be glad to see you. But you're just my imagination playing tricks on me. It isn't possible. You left all those years ago. You left."

She looked at him with all smile gone from his face. "I know I should have told you I was moving in person. I couldn't summon the courage to face you."

"You left me."

"Lukas, I meant what I said. My grandfather was dying. My father had no choice but to go back to be with him. His contract at the university was over."

"Only ghosts disappear."

"I am here now."

Lukas's eyes blurred. "What I did. I did for you, because of you. Then you were no longer there."

"I told you why; I explained why. All the letters I sent . . . not one reply."

Lukas looked at the ground.

"Lukas, what did you do with all those letters? Why did you not answer me?"

He looked back at her defiantly, shaking his head.

"You never read my letters, did you? You refused to answer my calls, too. The phone would ring and ring."

Lukas looked at the sky and finally to her. "I ripped up the letters. I asked no one answer the phone when it rang long distance. I begged them all not to answer. Mom, Dad, and Maggie. I forbade them to answer."

"Lukas, all this anger." Before she could say more, he grabbed her wrists.

"Will you kiss me now, as you did then?" There was no smile on his face. She pulled her arms free in horror. Shaking her head, she stared into his eyes and cried before turning to run to the exit. Within seconds, she was making her way down the stairs.

His hands remained extended with his palms open, having

released her. The one vibrant image he had of her branded into his tired eyes. He caused those tears. The beautiful though sad and now scared face. A face now fearful of him or the monster he believed he had become. As the music played loudly from within the far recesses of the room, buried within the bowels of his soul, something rose from within.

"Kara, wait!" he screamed, summoning his drunken feet to join in the chase. Speeding across the floor, he reached the stairwell just in time to see her reach the bottom and move toward the exit. Leaping, two sometimes three stairs at a time, he vowed to win this race. Reaching the last twist of the stairwell, his dangling clothing and drunken feet betrayed him. Missing a step and skidding off the edge of the next, he lurched forward, his cheek crashing against a bottom stair, his body crashing down behind him.

The noise he heard was that of the door closing. It was the last sound he heard before falling. Whether he lost consciousness or not was anyone's guess. Stumbling to his feet to escape before being seen, he bolted for the door. He ran aimlessly amongst the buildings, blood seeping from his cut cheek. He didn't search for Kara, he only sought a refuge. The massive stone façade of a building appeared before him. He looked at the gold plated plaque: "St. Peter's Faculty of Music and Drama." Next to it was a smaller poster: "St. Peter's Drama School Presents Frankenstein." He rounded the corner to the side of the building, finding a side entrance. The door was unlocked. An actor, at last, found an inviting home.

The late hour gave him the impression he would be alone in his self-pity. The blood trickled down from his cheek. His nose throbbed in pain. His vision blurred from the blood and sweat. His thoughts smoldered in flames, suffocating and choking.

Fortunately, Lukas was not the only night owl to breathe the air circulating through the drama school building and theater this evening.

chapter thirty-two

The phone rang with intent and purpose. Ram tossed and turned, pinning the pillow to his head. The ringing finally stopped. Seconds later it continued, more violent in tone, at least from the perspective of hungover ears. Succumbing to its persistence, Ram answered. "Hello."

"Ram, it's Rosemary." The voice on the other end bordered on hysteria.

"Geez, Rosie, it's like 6 a.m. I only got in a couple of hours ago."

"Where is Lukas? What the fuck happened last night?"

"I haven't seen Lukas since the boat race."

"What do you mean? Don't you know where he is?

"How should I know? It was one helluva a party. Wasn't it his night with Kirsten?"

"With Kirsten! Ram, have you not heard what happened?"

"Obviously not."

"Kirsten was attacked last night. Someone tried to rape her."

"What? When? Holy shit. Is she . . .?"

"Yes, she was attacked near our faculty building around 3 a.m. She got away from her attacker. He jumped her from behind. He was wearing a mask."

"Thank goodness she got away. She wasn't with Lukas?"

"No! That is the problem. She is certain it was Lukas who attacked her."

"What! No fucken way. Not Lukas. You said the attacker had a mask."

"Yeah. She's convinced it was him."

"Why would she ever think that?"

"She refuses to tell me why she thinks it's him other than he freaked on her at the party."

"Where is she now? Did she go to the police?"

"She's at my place. Right now she's taking a shower."

"A shower. Shouldn't she go straight to the police?"

"She refuses. Besides, she got away before it went too far."

"And she thinks it's Lukas! It can't be."

"Do you know where is? We have to find him."

"I'll try his folks."

"I called there already. Lukas never came home. I told them he was probably with you."

"What can I do, Rose?"

"There's more. Kirsten wants to see Lukas. She needs to confront him. To make sure."

There was no voice coming back from the other end of the line. It was unlike Ram to be at a loss for words. "Ram, snap out of it. Whatever happened, Lukas is missing!"

"I'll meet you back at the offices. I'll call you when I'm heading there. Let me freshen up a bit."

Rosemary was about to say bye when her curiosity overcame her. "Did you ever see Lukas at the party with a girl. I mean, a girl you didn't know."

"No. Why?"

"Never mind. Just thinking aloud. See you later." She hung up quickly before Ram could ask more questions. The girl never showed. She never showed. Suddenly, a hoarse voice filled the room.

"Who was that?"

"If you don't mind, I told Ram what happened."

"You said I think it was Lukas, didn't you?"

"Yes, I did. I hope you don't mind."

"You think I'm crazy, right? To believe it was him." Kirsten's tired eyes could not hold back the tears.

"Kirsten, I'm so elated you escaped. If it was him, he deserves to be punished."

"He's your friend. You know how much that bothers me?"

"No, Kirsten, you should never feel guilty. But you're not sure?"

"Rosemary, I cannot say anything. I want to see him. When I see him, I'll know." Kirsten moved across the room to the chair she draped her jeans over. Sliding her hand into a pocket, she felt for something before pulling her hand out.

"Kirsten, what's in your jeans? Is it why you think it was Lukas?

"Yes, Rosemary. It's something that belongs to him."

Rosemary took a step toward her and put her arms around her shoulders. "We will find him, I promise."

Kirsten rested her head on Rosemary's shoulder. If she had the power to end nightmares, she would.

chapter thirty-three

Professor Solterre was accustomed to many all-nighters over the years, editing scripts, drafting his department's budget, or just reading for the sake of reading. Tonight, he listened to a tale woven by young Lukas Wunand. The young man skimmed over the night a body was found in the pool. The professor returned to that night as he would return over and over again to a line his actor struggled with.

"Lukas, what happened the night the man drowned?"

"Professor, you are not a clergyman. I cannot ask for your forgiveness."

"You told me you caused a man to die. Now, you talked about the day you were told of his body dead in the pool. You mentioned your socks and shoes were damp the next day. No need for a science degree to solve the puzzle."

Lukas finished the last of the milk and walked over to the cold coffee, filling his cup with its blackness. The professor did not intervene, studying him carefully as he walked, wondering if the truth would finally come out. Lukas returned to his seat and drowned the words upon his tongue with the cold coffee. He sat back in the chair and bit his lip before speaking.

"When I saw a convicted pedophile talking to Kara that evening, I felt her fear. I felt it when I held her hand." Lukas rolled up his sleeve to show the scars left by the dog that attacked him.

"The day Kara was cornered by the dog; I didn't see the same fear in her eyes. This man drew fear from her beyond anything I could imagine."

"It angered you."

"I vowed to protect her. Kara did not need to live with the danger so close to her."

"What did you do?"

"I snuck out of my house around 2 a.m. and made my way to his backyard."

"Right, he told her he liked to leave the gate open."

"I had a flashlight with me. It was pitch black. There were no lights in his yard just an in-ground pool. I meant just to talk to him. To maybe scare him but . . ."

"You could not scare him, could you?"

"I flashed the light against his window to get his attention. Soon enough, he came out wearing a robe. I went down the pool stairs into the water. I told him I heard I could use the pool any-time. He said he could not swim, so he likes to watch children swim. He said many kids had been in his pool."

Professor Solterre shivered as he listened. "Dear Lord," he mut-tered. "You put yourself in grave danger."

"I didn't think of any danger. I didn't fear him until . . ."

"Until . . ."

"He followed me into the water and sat on the steps. He asked me to swim just for a bit. He said once I got tired, I could come into his house to change into something dry."

"This is crazy, Lukas. You could have been . . . The man was sick."

"I didn't care. I said I would swim with him if he promised never to bother Kara again. To never even look at her, let alone speak to her."

Removing his glasses and rubbing his eyes, the professor looked at Lukas solemnly. "I take it that is when something happened."

"He told me he could never make that promise, and he looked forward to her one day swimming for him. He said it was inevitable."

"My God, Lukas, what happened?"

"I saw the look in his eyes. I could never describe it. I can never forget. I imagine it's what evil aspires to be in physical form. In all my life, nothing ever scared me. That look terrified me. I shut my eyes not to see that look while I dove underwater and swam to him. I grabbed him by the ankles and dragged the bastard under the water pulling him to the deep end. No one could hear him scream; I was so quick."

"He must have put up a fight."

"Maybe. But I was the best swimmer in my summer camp. Could hold my breath forever. When I got him in the deep end, it was so easy. He was old and no match for my fury. I got him to the bottom and put my full weight and hate on him. It didn't take long for the twitching to stop. I don't recall the walk back home. Only the nightmares. The next voice I heard was my sister, Maggie, waking me."

By now Lukas's head was bowed down before the professor. Not wanting to face him, Lukas pointed to the phone in the corner of the room before speaking. "You can call the police; I would not respect you less if you did, sir." Lukas could see the lowered head before the wrinkled, aged hand of Professor Solterre reached over and lifted his chin.

"Lukas, listen to me. Nobody else on Earth can ever forgive you for what you did. Not even a priest."

"I see you understand, sir."

"I am not finished. You are the only one who can forgive you. The forgiveness you are seeking alludes you because you alone can forgive. It is not found outside here." He reached with his finger and tapped Lukas's chest.

Lukas looked at Professor Solterre. "Justice requires I pay for my sins. I killed someone, you must . . ."

"Lukas, my memory has failed me more and more as the years turn the pages of my life. Perhaps it is the late hour, but I am finding it more and more difficult to focus. What were we just discussing?"

"You know perfectly well, sir."

Professor Solterre took the picture of his wife and two daughters in his hand as his back nestled against the chair. Turning the image to Lukas, his brows narrowed together, his voice resonated from between his lips, carving through Lukas's mere flesh, aiming at his soul. "These are all I have ever loved on this Earth. Judging you would betray them. I would do anything to protect them, too."

Lukas rubbed his scarred arm. The bloody cloth lay on the desk in front of him. In a night, years passed. Lukas's eyes slowly closed as he drifted off to sleep in his chair. Professor Solterre adjusted the chair to recline back so Lukas could be more comfortable. Lukas barely moved. Just as the professor finished properly calibrating the chair, a soft whisper emerged from Lukas's mouth. The melodic tone of the whisper hypnotized the professor, his ears moving closer and closer to Lukas's lips.

One name rippled like a leak from Lukas's subconscious. Over and over again, the name "Kara" flowed from Lukas's lips as he slept. Professor Solterre brought the glass frame to his mouth, kissing it before gently placing it down on his desk facing the sleeping young man.

chapter thirty-four

Maggie pulled back the curtains in Lukas's room. The sun's rays exploded into color, waking Lukas. "C'mon, sleepy head. Camp day today. It's 5 a.m. Dad told me to wake you."

Lukas rubbed his eyes. A two-hour car ride, followed by Lukas's last two weeks of summer camp, awaited. Making his way robotically through the house, he grabbed two pieces of toast, munching on them as he brought out his gear and began storing them in the trunk of the family car. The street was eerily calm with the chirp of birds the only sign of life. Once his task was finished, he decided to enjoy the warmth of the sunrise and waited outside for the rest of his family to finish breakfast. No one talked about the death of the strange old man anymore. The ugly ashen cloud lifted. Miracles were something best enjoyed than proven of mortal intervention.

While fiddling with his shoelaces, he heard the faint sound of footsteps approaching. A slight morning breeze preceded the appearance of Kara before him.

"Hi, Kara, why are you up so early?"

Kara looked at him strangely. Her face seemed suddenly aged. Her eyes were silhouetted with tell-tale signs of a sleepless night. "I came to wish you a safe and happy camp." Lukas's eyes raised ever so slightly as he stood to face her. Kara never came to see him off to camp before, let alone at such an ungodly hour.

"Well, it is a pleasant surprise. Thank you so much. It made my day."

"You are welcome." Her feet shifted from side to side. "Uh, there is something I have meant to say. I just haven't been able to."

Lukas smiled. "Don't worry; we'll have plenty of time to talk before school starts. We'll have a whole weekend. Besides, it's not like last year. You'll talk to me in the winter, right?" His eyes were beaming, flashing different shades of brown to her.

Kara looked into his eyes, losing all rationality and any semblance of order. Her heart, having waited long and patiently, grew restless. For a moment, Kara danced to the music playing inside her. Taking a step toward Lukas, she raised her two hands and stretched them across the side of Lukas's head, meeting at the back. With all her strength, she pulled his lips to hers. Her mouth opened slightly in tune with the closing of her eyes, and she kissed him for an eternity of memories if not time. When she pulled her head back, she gazed intensely into his eyes, making sure he saw the words parading from her lips.

"Lukas, always remember how much I love you. It is a love beyond mere words." Her eyes were watering slightly; she stepped back.

Lukas brought his fingers to his lips, caressing the remnants of her touch. The eruptions of pure joy within him sunk any form of reason. He refused to allow any cloud pass before the sunlight currently shining on him.

"Kara, I love you, too. Please take care of yourself while I'm away." He smiled, bravely returning her words.

"Take care of yourself." She turned to begin the short trek home, her pace quickening with each step. Lukas was unaware or chose not to notice the faint symbols of the emotion erupting exponentially within her. By the time she reached her home, she had cried to the point of siphoning off all air, almost collapsing at her door. The courage to tell him the secret she kept from him for months shredded her.

For the next two weeks, Lukas basked in the warm glow of Kara's words. Replaying them over and over, the sun now rose and fell to his beat. He even believed he could taste its sweet sugary center hidden beneath its protective incendiary pulp.

chapter thirty-five

Unnerving. The only word to properly describe the silence in the automobile the day his parents picked him up from camp. Cold water splashed his anticipation of seeing Kara, his confessed love again. From the back seat, he could see their pensive looks.

Immediately not seeing any sign of life at Kara's house as they passed, his heart raced. His hands clenched and unclenched. He knew something was horribly muddled. The details of how and exactly what they told him evaporated with his labored breaths. Kara's family needed to return to India and a dying grandfather. Her father's contract at the university was up, and the family would be following him to wherever there was work. They had known for months, including Lukas's parents. They were all sworn to secrecy so Kara could tell him. She never could find the proper words or muster the courage to witness his hurt. Maggie watched her brother return to his room and go into mourning. Before doing so, his parents handed him an unopened letter. Kara had left. Nothing else could stop the darkness. The universe drained of its light.

Lukas stared at the letter. By the time he allowed his sister passage into his room, the letter was drenched in his tears, still unopened. Maggie's heart sunk as he ripped the letter for what seemed like an eternity before asking her to dispose of the remnants. She refused. Just as he rejected the letters that continued to come for months and even the next year. Soon there were long distance calls that he vehemently declined to take. Despite Maggie's pleadings, Lukas dug a bottomless trench around him. Roman and Grace valiantly tried to console him. Disarmed by his reassurance that he would survive, his words kept them at bay. "I need to move on for my peace of mind."

The truth floated like a body in a pool, ugly and bloated. A sin required a sacrifice, a punishment. Kara's leaving would be his purgatory. The sentence handed down, as two plus two equals four.

Time drifted in Lukas's world like a tumbleweed in a forgotten town in the old West. Lukas's decision to enter business school elicited surprise. The logic and reason of his maturing, moving toward the practical, soothed his parents' concern. Only Maggie was not fooled. Each Christmas and birthday that passed, she searched the city's used bookstores and bought him books, nothing except books.

Placing the picture of Kara in his back pocket, it reminded him of the penance he need serve. He vowed to keep it with him for eternity. As the world around him lost its meaning, serving his friends gave him purpose. The role he chose, he sincerely enjoyed, that of trusted friend and confidante. He vowed to set himself aflame to be their light.

Now, with a scarred arm, wounded cheek, and bleary-eyed, it appeared there was nothing left to burn, and all that was left would be ash. His arrogance lay in his belief that this was solely his stage and his play to interpret. Mercifully, the play itself is infinite, holding many mysteries and debuting many heroes and heroines.

chapter thirty-six

A new dawn had indeed begun as the sun's rays streaked across the one window of Professor Solterre's office. The warmth of the light upon his skin elicited his mouth to twitch. A sliver of drool trickled down his chin. The night's excitement made sleep, even in a chair, welcome. His watch revealed he had drifted off to sleep for at least an hour. Surprise was something he abhorred. No doubt about it. However, a rub of his eyes did not ease his disorientation. What was he doing in this uncomfortable chair? Usually, he enjoyed watching annoying visitors fidget in it, trying to find a comfort that did not exist. No, his unease came from a greater discomfort. The chair before him was deserted. The walk-on actor had vanished. The professor's eyes zipped wildly about without pattern. Logically he had not just vanished. Words from their conversation hijacked his thoughts. Then the thunderbolt struck. The young man bore a terrible burden and now was missing. Then out of the corner of his eye, across the table, and just beneath the picture of his family, was an identity card. "Lukas Wunand, Student, Faculty of Business." No time for further napping. He'd never stepped into the Faculty of Business building before. Another first.

chapter thirty-seven

When she finally arrived home from the party at about 3 a.m., Rosemary welcomed the emptiness of her temporary home. One of her roommates was spending the night at her boyfriend's. The other left earlier in the week to visit family. The emptiness of the house was most welcome until the frantic knock on the door. Rosemary immediately knew whatever happened to Kirsten was horrific. When Lukas's name became the focal point, she froze. Not wanting to question Kirsten further, her disbelief was tucked away in sympathy for the young girl.

The two now sat hours later, coffee in hand, both quivering with each sip. Things would never be the same at the faculty. The joy and tribulation of graduation were forever marred. Ironically, it was Lukas himself who foresaw this. Rosemary could not fathom any scenario where Lukas could harm anyone, let alone Kirsten.

Kirsten began sobbing again, placing her cup down to spare staining the beanbag chair. "Damn, Rosemary; this is where I met him the first time." Now, what seemed like a lifetime ago, the happier night of the infamous drinking game rolled through their memories. Rosemary shook her head, mindful how once her only worry was that of damaged furniture and her parents' disappointment.

Pacing helped. For a second, it allowed Rosemary to walk away from Kirsten to hide her expressions from her. The gentle knock on the door called her name. She knew without opening who stood on the other side. No one tapped a door quite that way. She escaped to the front of the home, leaving Kirsten behind, hopeful her hearing was not nearly as acute.

Behind the door stood a tired, broken man. Barely a man. Looking like the loser of a schoolyard fight, Lukas stood before her not saying a word, not wearing an expression, not even a smile. Whether her gasp was audible or not became irrelevant. The mark on the face and bruising around it broke her heart. She searched his eyes, her stare snapping him out of his stupor.

"Rosemary, I don't mean to bother you. It's been a rough night."

"I can see. Um . . . Lukas, you need to know something." Before she could warn him, his eyes drifted past her.

"Kirsten, I wasn't expecting you here." Ignoring Rosemary's pensive façade, he smiled at her.

Rosemary tried to dismantle the live bomb before it exploded. "Lukas, something happened."

"I know."

Kirsten slid past Rosemary, staring intently at Lukas, her eyes locked in on his face. Before Rosemary could intervene, Kirsten's hand opened and swung wildly at Lukas, catching the side of his face. "How dare you! You need help! How could you?" She broke out in tears before disappearing back into the house behind Rosemary.

Horror ate Lukas's face whole. Both sides of his cheeks now throbbing in pain, he brought both hands to his face, his eyes pure death. "I never meant to hurt her."

"Hurt her?! Lukas, what are you saying!"

"I hurt her feelings at the party. It's my fault. The night was not a good one for me or the women who crossed my path."

"Her feelings?" Confusion curled itself around her waist, cutting off all air and rational thought. "I don't understand."

Lukas shifted from side to side, completely bewildered but fully attentive. "Rosemary, what is going on?"

Rosemary bit hard on her bottom lip. "Kirsten was attacked last night. Don't worry. She fought off the attacker."

"Attacked? By who?"

"After the party, behind our faculty. Kirsten was heading downtown to grab a cab and took a shortcut."

"Rosemary, who did it? Why don't you answer my question?"

"Christ, Lukas, she says it was *you*." She stepped back, her hand gesturing to his face.

"Me? I would never hurt her. Why? Because of the party?"

"She won't say why she thinks it was you. The attacker had a mask and jumped her from behind."

Lukas brought his hand to his face, feeling his cheek. "Crap. Now she sees me with this."

"Well, it looks bad, Lukas. Looks really bad."

"Long story. I need to see Kirsten, then. Please let me in."

"Of course, you can come in. I just don't know you should . . ."

"No, it's all right." Kirsten stood at the entrance to the kitchen, motioning for Lukas to enter. "I need to face him."

Rosemary grabbed Lukas's shirt by the lapel and pulled him close. "I believe you, Lukas. You know that." He nodded and moved past her. She chose not to follow him, instead retreating to a chair on the side, wondering how Kirsten could be so sure it was and how she could be so sure it was not Lukas. From a distance, she studied the two, summoning all energy to her ears. Despite her straining every muscle in her ear, she could not hear a word.

Kirsten waited for Lukas to approach her and come within a

foot of her before speaking. "Why? Why did you do it? Do you hate me? Or do you just hate girls?"

"Kirsten, why do you think it was me? I mean, at the party. No one ever . . . got that close to me. I freaked."

"I put up a good fight, Lukas. Did I surprise you?"

"Please, Kirsten, listen to me."

"Look at your face. I did that to you."

"No, you did not."

"C'mon, Lukas. You need help. I won't go to the police if you get help."

"But you did not hurt my face. I tumbled the stairs chasing her."

"Stop it. I'm trying to help you. I hit you in the face through your wool toque pulled over your eyes. A pointy key can do a lot of damage."

Lukas nodded from side to side, analyzing her words. Now fully cognizant of the harrowing ordeal she had faced, his rage simmered. "Kirsten, what key did you use?"

"Your key."

Lukas's eyes opened wide. "My key, I have no key. Just my house key." He reached into his pocket, pulling out a single key.

Kirsten reached into her pocket and pulled out a different key. Lukas's face exploded in expression upon seeing it. His eyebrows rose. "When you were trying to get on top of me, I pulled it out of your pocket and began stabbing your face with it until you took off in bloody pain."

"Kirsten, show me the key. I need to be sure."

"Sure of what, it's your key. I know it is. You showed it to me once. It has the "K" on it." Extending her hand with an open palm, the white "K" appeared before his eyes.

Staring at the key, Lukas's face grew red. "The bastard. The son of a bitch." The room emptied around him, leaving only the key. Ignoring Kirsten, he suddenly turned, his pace growing livelier with each step. Rosemary arose, wondering what had happened. Lukas bulldozed past her, not even acknowledging her. What she saw on his face was an expression that frightened her. It was pure madness. Before Kirsten or Rosemary could react, the door opened and closed in front of them. By the time they could reopen it, the figure of Lukas in his black shirt was running down the street, his yellow laces flashing in the morning light like spokes on a bike. The direction he was heading clear enough, their faculty.

"See, Rosemary; it was him. He freaked when I showed him. He freaked."

"Kirsten, if it is him, you need to call the police. But I know in my heart it isn't him. That I could tell you for sure."

"Why are you so certain?"

"Because I know him and that look. That look. He knows who it is. He knows."

"Rosemary, it was him. You should have seen his face when I showed him the key I stole from him."

"The key? Show me. Show me, now."

"Look." She opened her palm before Rosemary.

"Lord help us, Kirsten, if what I think is happening is correct, Lukas is going to get your assailant."

"No, it's Lukas. I'm sure."

"Kirsten, get your sneakers on and come with me . . . Maybe we can stop him."

She paused, bewildered. "Stop him? What do you mean?"

"Before Lukas commits a real crime. I don't have any time to explain." Rosemary raced to the phone. She fidgeted, waiting for an answer. "Ram, meet me at the faculty. Now. Like right now. No questions." She hung up before he could answer.

Rosemary had a similar key. A key to the Student Society office. At this hour of the morning, the Student Society usually had one early bird. Lukas knew full well he would be there today.

. . .

With each stride he took, the adrenaline flowed in Lukas. Primordial and primitive with each muscle longing for vengeance, the thought of Kirsten fighting in fear fueled him. That she suspected and accused him tore him to pieces inside. Disgust replaced the face she used to show just to him: the gentle, innocent, and naïve look. Someone had desecrated that face.

Reaching the back door of the faculty, he opened it slowly in the manner of Carter opening Tut's crypt.

. . .

At the same moment, for whatever reason, Professor Solterre recalled a passage from "Frankenstein" as he made his way slowly down the stairs. An image of Lukas Wunand delivering them on stage drifted in his thoughts:

> *"I have love in me the likes of which you can scarcely imagine and rage the likes of which you would not believe. If I cannot satisfy the one, I will indulge the other."*

The professor's gait quickened to a sprint.

chapter thirty-eight

The day after a party, the faculty usually was abuzz only with the sounds of chairs shifting and brooms sweeping. Fridays were the off day for the business school. A time for batteries to be recharged and hangovers nursed. Tobin arrived early on his final day of the semester and his tenure as president. His absence at the final party of his term was conspicuous. He opened the office, relieved to find no hint of graffiti. The bathroom beckoned soon enough, so down the quiet corridors he marched. The custodian worked methodically on an upper floor. The cafeteria closed. Signs of life were minimal. One character, however, was unaccounted for and unexpected. Lukas eased his way in through the back door and waited patiently for Tobin in the bathroom. Hidden within a closed stall, his anger was shackled briefly.

Tobin approached the bathroom mirror, cleaning his hands thoroughly. He wet his fingertips slightly, bringing them to his short blonde hair. Carefully tucking a stray hair to the side, he noticed the stall swinging open behind him and a figure emerging.

"Lukas, what the . . ." Before air could escape fueling words, his arms were clasped behind him. Lukas's hands locked firmly behind his neck, controlling Tobin's head as he dragged Tobin to the stall and forced his head into the bowl. Leaning forward, he plunged Tobin's head into the water. Gurgles churned, offset by the sound of thrashing. Just as abruptly as the attack started,

Lukas pulled Tobin violently back to face the mirror. Gasping for air, Tobin came face to face with the vengeful rage behind him. He could see Lukas's distorted face and the colorless abyss of his eyes. Without any hint of emotion, Lukas glared back at Tobin. Moving his head behind Tobin's ears, he finally spoke. "I need to know why."

"Why!" choked Tobin. "Let me go, please."

"Why did you attack her? Why have you been attacking them?"

"Who? What? You think I'm the one. A rapist! Me?"

"Damn it, Tobin. I know now. I know it was you. I need to understand why. Why do you do it? I never understood."

"Oh my God! It is not me. I promise, so help me. Please, let me go."

"Why Kirsten? Why her?"

"Kirsten! She was attacked? It was not me." Tobin began screaming, "Is she okay? Tell me she is okay!"

"She had the goddam key you took from me. Took it from him. The bastard had the key you took from me! "K" and all. The fucking key!"

"Oh fuck." His expression went from terror to shock. "Please, Lukas. Stop. It was not me. But I know. I know. Shit. Please stop, I am sorry."

The cries sounded like shattered glass against Lukas's ears. In one motion, he threw Tobin back into the stall and pushed his head down into the bowl. To his terror, Tobin could feel Lukas's grip tighten, and he knew he had no hope to survive much longer. Lukas's eyes closed shut, siphoning off all light as he held Tobin. The image of Tobin in the mirror appeared before him. He could see Tobin's soaked and dripping hair. He could see Tobin's eyes searching him, pleading and confused. He could see his clear pale skin spotted by water droplets. Eyes wide, Lukas released Tobin.

Lukas staggered away and fell to his hands and knees. His tired, throbbing head buried itself in his hands. Tobin slumped to the side of the bowl, gulping the air from the room to fill his empty lungs. He looked over at Lukas, crying off to the side. Tobin clumsily arose, standing over Lukas. Awaiting his fate and preparing for his eventual arrest, Lukas planned to stay prone and compliant when they came for him. It was over.

Seconds passed. The footsteps he expected to hear escaping the washroom were not heard. Thinking his ears deceived him, he raised his head. Tobin stood over him watching, Lukas presumed to judge him. Beads of water dripped upon him, some more accurate than others. Wiping away the last tears in his eyes, he felt a nudge on his shoulders. Keeping his head focused on the ground below him, he wondered if his imagination had taken control. The second nudge was more forceful. On the third, he could feel the fingertips penetrating into the crevice between his shoulder and neck. He glanced over to see a hand extend toward him. With an ever-blinking eye, he thought the sight would disappear. It did not. Tobin stood with a worried look on his face and a welcoming arm.

"It's over, Lukas. Please, take my hand, before you hurt yourself."

"Tobin, I don't know what to say," Lukas said, fighting fatigue, his legs wobbling.

"Follow me." Tobin turned and departed the washroom quickly leaving behind a stunned Lukas. Within seconds, the door reopened. "Are you coming with me or you want another game of hide and seek, you freak?"

Tobin entered the Student Society office and took his customary spot behind his desk, waiting for Lukas, who entered slovenly. He took one step inside and stood solemnly awaiting the punishment that was sure to come. Tobin reached for the office phone and dialed. Lukas could tell it was campus police since he heard only a couple of buttons pressed.

"Hello, this is the Student Society President for the Faculty of Business, Tobin Preston. Yes, I believe I have a lead on the rapist. Yes, sir. I have a name for you. Um. I can explain why I think it is him. I can come by and explain."

Lukas's eyes closed partially; he held his breath. Suddenly, Tobin mentioned a name Lukas knew as one of Tobin's fraternity brothers who was in law school. "Yes, I am now convinced it is him. Please look into it. " Tobin put down the phone and stared at Lukas.

"Tobin, what are you doing? You should be calling them on me. I attacked you. I almost killed you."

Tobin looked up at the ceiling before settling in on the calendar. "How is Kirsten? Tell me what happened."

"She was attacked last night. Luckily, she got away. She's pretty shaken up."

"You thought it was me. That's why you came to me. The key."

"Yes. The attacker had that stupid bloody key. Kirsten must have gotten a hold of it and used it to fight him off."

"So, she's fine?"

"Yes, but the name you gave. It's a frat brother of yours."

"I gave him the key I confiscated from you." Tobin motioned for Lukas to sit. "He would help me around here late at night. I trusted him. Trusted him more than I did you."

"Look, Tobin, I don't need your mercy. You have every right to press charges or have me expelled."

"Expelled! I already know you're not graduating." He smiled at Lukas. "Toss me that roll of paper towels."

"Who told you?"

"The Dean. He asked me if I minded if you hung around as a favor to him."

"I see." Lukas unwrapped the towels and walked over to Tobin.

"You don't see. I told him I would do it because you're my friend."

"Friend. After all the stunts I pulled. Seriously, Tobin."

"No, seriously. It's because of all the stunts, I suppose. You do things I can't. I admire that in you. I admire it. Being serious, the voice of reason and correctness, is not easy."

"Tobin, you like the power. That's the price you pay."

"Yes, but it doesn't mean I'm proud of myself. Order and control. Managing every outcome. It doesn't mean I'm happy."

"I tried to drown you, Tobin. Kill you. I would have, too."

"I'm sure I don't know what you're talking about. Other than you did it for Kirsten, right?"

"Of course. I was so pissed that someone would harm a friend of mine."

"And you risked everything."

"I'm not proud of what I did. There's more to it. Why I wanted to . . . well, you know."

Tobin leaned forward in his chair to listen. His hands sloped down over his knees as Lukas spoke. "Tobin, she accused me. She believed it was me. When she saw me with this face, I must have looked like a monster to her."

"Hmm . . . I thought it was an improvement." He winked at Lukas. "And what happened to you?"

"A long story. A fall. Seems like ages ago."

"All these attacks. It hurt me more than anyone would ever know. I could not have people panic. There had to be order. Without order, it, well, it's just how I was raised."

"Tobin, let us just hope this comes to an end, all of this, once and for all."

Lukas started to pivot, about to leave, when Tobin said, "Why didn't you kill me? Why did you believe me? You know I am a pretty good liar, after all. But what made you stop."

"I saw your face from the mirror. Your eyes, they didn't have that look."

"That look?"

"The look of evil, of hate. I didn't see that in you. Plus, Kirsten said she stabbed her assailant with the key pretty hard. Look at your face. Not a mark."

"Thanks for not killing me, then. By the way, where are you heading this early in the morning?"

"Home. My parents must be freaking."

"Close the door, and please tell me the tall tale of your facial wound. I doubt you were in the bathroom all night." He glanced at the calendar. "And if I recall, was it not to be your night last night?"

Lukas closed the door.

chapter thirty-nine

Rosemary and Kirsten arrived at the back door of the Faculty of Business just an older man emerged behind them at a frantic pace. Smiling, he stepped in front of them, and in true gentlemanly fashion opened the door for them.

"After you," he said.

"Thank you, sir."

"Ladies, perhaps you can help me."

"We're kind of in a rush."

"It will be a second; I need to return something to one of your students. He forgot it in my office last night."

Rosemary stopped and looked at the professor quizzically while Kirsten looked on, annoyed by the distraction. "I pretty much know everyone here. Maybe I can help, sir. What is it?"

"It is a student ID." He peered into his wallet, carefully going through all the cards neatly tucked in their appointed slots. "Ah, here it is. Do you know him?"

Rosemary looked at the name and shrieked, "What? You are kidding."

"You know him, then?"

Rosemary grabbed the card and handed it to Kirsten, who looked at it in shock.

"Yes, I know him. When was he in your office? You're not a professor at this faculty."

"I am a drama teacher as you would say. I came upon Mr. Lukas doing an impromptu performance on my stage just after midnight."

"After midnight?" Kirsten interjected, visibly excited. "What exactly was he doing?"

"I would call it 'improv.' More importantly, he was injured, amongst other things, so he rested in my office until he got his legs back."

"Injured." Kirsten trembled. "He was already injured?"

"Bad scrape on his cheek. A bit of a bloody mess. He lived."

"What time was this, exactly?" Rosemary moved closer.

"Right before 1 a.m."

"He was with you until when?" Kirsten now continued the interrogation.

"Until I dozed off. He ran out on me around 5 a.m."

"What! Then it couldn't have been him. Oh my God, I accused him." Kirsten began mumbling to herself in confusion. "I mean, the key and all."

"Wait a minute." Rosemary now realized a happy end was not so close at hand. "Ran out, why?"

"Not sure. All I know is, I would like to find him. We had quite a substantial discussion. I wanted to continue and make sure he was all right."

Kirsten put her hands on the professor's arm. "We're friends of his. I promise we'll take care of him. I swear."

Rosemary smiled. "Yes, thank you. It looks like you've had a rough night yourself."

"I am content, ladies, that your friend is in good hands." He handed the card to Kirsten, and as he departed back in the direction he came, Rosemary ran to catch him, tapping him on the shoulder.

"What exactly did he tell you?"

"The usual stuff between a director and actor. It was about love, in the final critique of it. The rest is probably not too important. My memory is fading." He put his head down and left from whence he entered. "I will make sure to see him again once I get some rest of my own."

Kirsten shook her head as Rosemary approached. "Rosie, I accused him of something horrible. How will I ever make it up to him?"

"How will *we* ever make it up to him? Let's find him first and hope I was wrong about where he was heading."

The two raced down the stairs, finding nary a sign of life. Looking down the corridor to the basement, Rosemary noticed the streaks of water leading from the washroom to the Student Society office. Motioning for Kirsten to follow, she made her way to the door. She could not hear even muffled voices inside, unsure of who was there or not. Kirsten reached into her jeans and handed Rosemary the key. Rosemary stared at the key and the "K" on it. Turning the handle, they witnessed Tobin legs up on his table and hair matted down with water. His fingers were pressed to his lips, signaling his request for silence. With his other hand, he pointed to a seat in front of him. There slumped in a chair and fast asleep was Lukas.

Tobin left his seat, motioning for the girls to leave and let him sleep while they spoke in the corridor. He closed the door behind him.

"Is he all right?" asked Kirsten.

"He'll survive, and so will I. How about you?"

"He told you?"

"Yeah, come, girls, we need to talk. I'll explain everything. Kirsten, it wasn't him, but I do know who attacked you."

Within minutes, they were joined by Ram. Tobin had called Lukas's parents to help him explain the night and injury away to university indulgence. Each littered the table with puzzle pieces, trying to understand what had transpired. Each grew more confused as they spoke about their role that night. No one saw Lukas fall. No one saw him from the boat race on. He disappeared.

Rosemary grew impatient, upset she could not solve it. Growing more agitated, she began twirling the key in her hand, the "K" twisting before her eyes. Then she pounded her fist on the table. "Kirsten, at my place this morning, when Lukas showed, he mentioned women, right?"

Kirsten sat back thoughtfully. "Yeah, he said he had a terrible night with women, so?"

"Plural. What other girl did something happen with?"

"No idea, Rosemary. You seem to know." Kirsten could sense Rosemary approaching a "eureka" moment.

"She was there. She showed."

"Who showed?" asked Ram. Rosemary smiled back at him. "Kara was there."

"You think *the* Kara showed?"

Rosemary smiled. "Who else could turn Lukas's world upside down like that?"

"I think you need to fill me in," Kirsten announced.

"I would have told you yesterday. I didn't know if she would be there." Rosemary grabbed Kirsten's wrist, explaining to her how she called Kara.

Kirsten's shoulders sagged slightly before she sat upright. "Guys, I am not a child. I get it. Shit, I basically called him a monster."

Tobin brought them to the task at hand. "Well, if it didn't work out last night, what can we do now?"

"Man, our boy was not at his best last night. The boat race and all that. He was doomed to fail," Ram stated.

"Let's just get the boy home," Rosemary concluded. She didn't tell them Kara would be leaving in a few days.

Later that night, Rosemary circled and circled Ram's earlier words. Kara saw a drunken Lukas, and not the boy she knew. How would she ever convince Kara, especially since she had to beg her the first time? She went out onto her front porch to get some fresh air. The distant streetlight flickered on and off sporadically. It dawned on her. There was a person on Earth who knew the Lukas whom Kara once knew. The one person who had seen Lukas at his best. Her hand frantically searched her pockets, then her purse. Throwing her purse across her bedroom in frustration, she finally found it, the sliver of paper with a phone number on it, sitting mockingly on her dresser.

She dialed Lukas's home, hoping it would not be him answering.

"Hello, Wunand residence, this is Grace."

"Mrs. Wunand. This is Rosemary, Lukas's friend. How is Lukas?"

"He's been sleeping most of the day. Must have been some party. That was quite a fall apparently. I have warned him about drinking too much in the past. I can check if he is awake if you want to speak with him."

"It's not him I need to speak with. It's Maggie. Is she there?"

"Why, yes. Just give me a second." Grace went into Maggie's room. "Maggie! Rosemary needs to speak to you." She handed her the phone.

"Hi, Rosemary! How are you?" Maggie declared excitedly. "I have a boyfriend now. Finally."

"That's great, Maggie. You'll have to introduce me to him one day. I called because I need a big favor from you. Like the greatest I could ever ask."

"For sure, Rosemary. Anything. Just ask."

"Lukas can't know. I'm going to give you a phone number. I'm sure you'll know what to do when I tell you whose number it is," Rosemary said slyly.

"Now I'm curious. Go ahead, I'm ready to write it down." Maggie scribbled down the number given her. Repeating it three times, Rosemary ensured she had it correct. "Now tell me, who am I calling, Rosemary?"

"You have to promise to keep calling until you speak to her."

"Sure, who is it? The queen?" Maggie laughed.

"Kara."

"You said 'Kara'?"

"Yes. Why, is there something wrong?"

"Not at all. I won't let Lukas down."

"Thanks. I knew I could count on you."

Rosemary began working the phones. In her heart, while she hoped Maggie would get somewhere, she also tapered any hope with the realities. However, Maggie grinned from ear to ear upon putting down the phone. She ventured down the hall and peeked into the room of her little brother. Slowly, she secured it shut, soundproofing it to the best of her abilities. Roman and Grace looked on from the kitchen in fascination.

Roman could not stifle his curiosity. "What are you up to, young lady?"

"Sorry, Dad, no time to talk." With that, she wandered off into her room, phone in hand, and closed the door.

"Roman, you think it has to do with Lukas?"

"Of course, it does. See how excited she got?"

"Was Lukas all right when you picked him up? His face looked awful."

"University parties. How many times I fell down some stairs! I would hate to tell you some of the stunts I pulled. He'll sleep it off."

"Well, I'm glad it is all over. All this university life," Grace said, shaking her head.

Roman looked over at his wife and smiled meekly at her. A young university student once, he knew the lie he told his wife would have to suffice for now.

chapter forty

Lukas was unsure how many hours he slept. It took him minutes to calibrate that it was now Saturday morning. His alarm clock showed 10 a.m. For the first time in a long time, he strained to remember the chronology of events leading up to this morning. He had an image in his head of a woman in a picture frame. He didn't even know her name. Love was either a master illusionist or had the most wicked sense of humor, Lukas decided. A look into his dresser mirror revealed a massive blue contusion on one side of his face, a faint smear of blood, and a semi-swollen eye. For some reason, a smile snuck up on him. Imperfection had its personal beauty.

A smile can be many things; in this case, it was the balloon at the end of the string attached to his heart. It existed, as did Kara. An epiphany caressed his thoughts. He searched the floor to find his discarded jeans, discovering with great delight the photograph they carried. The Kara he met looked older, wiser, and prettier than he ever imagined. There was no defeat that night; she came to find him. Whatever brought her back into his world, she came back. Pressing the picture to his lips, he made himself a solemn vow. Whether Kara's appearance and his fall were the last act or not mattered less now. There always would be a play.

The ringing of the phone brought Lukas back to reality. The silence of the house forced Lukas into action. He presumed his parents and sister had hit the mall early this Saturday or even that his sister ventured off with her boyfriend. Lukas answered, "Hello."

"Lukas. Hi, it's Tobin."

"Hey, good morning, Mr. President."

"Yeah, about that. Um . . . How are you feeling?"

"Much better. Thanks. And you?"

"Feeling a little woozy. Toilet water on an empty stomach, you know."

"Yeah, I can't ever . . ."

"No, not another word. This should never have happened to Kirsten. Her well-being is all that counts."

"Right. So, why . . ."

"I called on behalf of someone."

"Who?"

"Dean Wallis was wondering if you could come in today. It's important."

"I don't know, Tobin. I kind of wanted to do something."

"I think he wants to offer you a chance to stay for another year. Another chance."

"Well, I appreciate the gesture, but you and I both know I don't belong."

"Lukas, just hear him out. For me. You owe me. I won't ask any more from you."

Lukas sighed. "Yeah sure. When?"

"First thing this afternoon. Is that okay?"

"Sure."

"Before you see him, please come see me in the office. I need your help." The phone clicked.

Lukas hung up the phone. The Dean wanted to meet him. Another year in the faculty treading water was not his intent, but he owed the Dean the time of day. More importantly, Tobin needed him. A friendship reclaimed meant a lot to him that morning. He showered and dressed before heading for the bus stop just after noon.

The bus driver wondered why Lukas stared at him as he boarded. Most passengers paid and headed for the back. The driver glared at him. "You want something?"

"No, I just thought you looked familiar, a friend maybe."

"There are lots of drivers and passengers on this route, we all look alike." He laughed.

From the bus stop, the walk to the front doors would take seconds. Today, every step proved torturous for Lukas. He expected to return to clean up his locker. There were no exams to write or graduation ceremony to attend. He would need to tell his friends the truth. He cherished the times with his friends. Why he lingered had much to do with practicing the words to tell the Dean. "*Thanks for allowing me to come back. It would not be right. I cannot accept.*" A handshake, a goodbye, and it would finally end. The lines repeated over and over again. However, he could not quite nail them.

Kara's appearance grew as willow's roots would in search of water, taking hold and expanding with each step. His mind would not stop. Kara's return represented something he could not understand. All along he had been right to search for her those many months ago. Years ago, he would have done anything for her, sacrificing his soul. Now, he had become selfish; a love turned into a desire to possess her. How wrong it was, how anger had corrupted so much. Luckily, he escaped with only a contusion. Somewhere in this city was Kara. However comforting the thought, the grim honesty he faced was the fact she fled from him. The two large oak front doors focused his mind again on the task at hand. The lines forgotten, he pulled one of them open.

The lobby of the faculty opened up stark and naked. An expected scene for a Saturday. Far off in the distance, a buzz drifted toward him. He imagined hearing voices in the distance. No one could be here today, he convinced himself, except the Dean, himself, and Tobin. He made his way down the staircase to the basement. When he arrived at the bottom of the stairs, there was a flurry of quickly muffled shouts followed by silence. All of this coming from the cafeteria. It drew him there. For an instant, he hesitated, plotting a final prank on the faculty would be a fitting end. A final one on Tobin, perhaps. He smiled at the thought before shaking it away, recalling how this was how it all started. Kings and Queens ultimately lopped off the head of a court jester who became too popular. The cafeteria doors were open, awaiting him.

Astonishing would be an understated description as to what he witnessed. Surreal. Lukas was greeted with a sprawling banner, hung at against the far wall, which read, "Faculty of Arts." The cafeteria was not empty. The silence, however, mimicked a library. Every now and then, a page turned, or a chair scraped along the floor. The sound seemed accidental. Some muffled voices seeped toward Lukas. The cafeteria tables and chairs were scattered haphazardly with no shape. Not one row was aligned properly. That was a hint of utopia. A student occupied each seat with each one's head buried in a book and reading. None looked up at Lukas. All ignored his presence. His feet dragged with every step, scared to make a noise, scared to break the silence. He wasn't sure if he was fearful of waking from a crazy dream or realizing it was not one. Carefully, he studied each face as he entered. One by one, the faces shook memories and names loose. These were the seniors, his graduating class. Just as he was about to shout out to breach the silence, a voice called from the far familiar recess of the room. Sitting in Lukas's sacred spot was Tobin waving at him.

"Lukas, it's about time. Come over here." He gestured wildly to an empty spot across from him. "I was just about to start."

His mind was confused. His heart recognized the tribute. While he would never admit it to anyone, a solitary tear formed, which he frantically wiped away. His eyes darted left and right as the giggles and chuckles exploded like firecrackers around him. Holding his emotions in check meant deafening his ears for now. He pulled back the chair in front of Tobin and shook his head at him, partially smiling. "Tobin, what is going on? It's Saturday. Umm . . . Faculty of Arts? I get it, well I think I do."

"Lukas, this is what you always wanted, right? Look around; everyone is reading. Not textbooks about finance, marketing, or strategy. Books about dragons, medieval knights, body snatchers, anything goes."

"Geez, Tobin. What am I missing?"

"This is all for you, buddy. My grad gift to you."

Lukas leaned and whispered, "You recall I tried to drown you, and I basically got kicked out of this faculty. Besides, you're in my seat." Lukas smirked.

"Lukas, I should have come here with you guys more often. Let me have my moment. Besides, I am no longer president."

"What?"

"True leaders protect those who trust them. They don't stay in their ivory towers. I let everyone down. Damn it. It was someone I trusted. Shit. I let Kirsten down."

"The seat does suit you."

"You are welcome to join us. I was just about to start."

"Oh, I would not miss this." Lukas slid into the seat, acknowledging the familiar faces around him. Kyle, at the far end of the table, put a finger to his lips, acknowledging his friend with a frown aimed at Lukas, demanding mock silence. He followed with a wink and a smile. Lukas took a deep breath to take it all in.

Tobin leaned back in his chair, reaching for a tattered old book before rising to his feet upon the orange plastic chair.

"To all, please may I have your attention. My reading is about to begin." He paused and sternly circled the room with his eyes. He looked back at the book, finding his spot.

> *"Once upon a midnight dreary, while I pondered, weak and weary,*
> *Over many a quaint and curious volume of forgotten lore—*
> *While I nodded, nearly napping, suddenly there came a tapping,*
> *As of some one gently rapping, rapping at my chamber door.*
> *"'Tis some visitor," I muttered, "tapping at my chamber door—*
> *Only this and nothing more."*

He paused after the first stanza and continued culminating in the immortal words "nevermore." He closed the book and continued. "This reading of 'The Raven' by Edgar Allen Poe is dedicated to my good friend, Lukas, who taught me the true meaning of being a student." Tobin stepped down from his pulpit and nodded to Lukas. The applause grew louder and louder. Lukas could no longer contain wave after wave of pure joy and emotion. The tears streaked down his cheek, stinging his wound and cleansing it.

Tobin reached across and tapped him on the shoulder. "Dean Wallis does want to see you." He pointed to the far side of the cafeteria where the food counter was. There stood Dean Wallis waiting patiently. "I suggest you do not keep him waiting."

Two steps into his walk, books could be heard falling upon

table after table as Lukas's graduating class rose in a cheer to him. "Nevermore. Nevermore" they repeated over and over again. Dean Wallis greeted him with an envelope. Behind the counter stood Willie beaming.

"Willie and I were just debating who was older." Dean Wallis chuckled. "He let me in on a secret. It's the coffee." Willie winced at the joke.

"Tobin told me you wanted to see me. Said something about you allowing me back. I need to be truthful; I just do not believe . . ."

Dean Wallis placed his large bear-like paws on Lukas's shoulders, shaking his head. "I already know what you're going say. Someone else wants to admit you as a student." He pointed to the banner and handed him a letter of acceptance. "It is signed by the Dean of Admissions. You are accepted by the Faculty of Arts. So that you are aware, the acceptance is any time you wish. Just in case you want to take some, or rather more, time off."

"Honestly, I'm overwhelmed. Thank you. Why me? There are so many deserving students."

"I hear you spend a lot of time over there. What pushed it over the top was a personal reference someone sent on your behalf. A Professor Solterre, I believe. He got them going on the paperwork yesterday."

Lukas smiled and shook his hand. "I'm not saying yes. I need to let it all sink in."

"Sure, I understand."

Willie extended his right hand for Lukas to shake and in his left had a Styrofoam cup. "You better visit me. The arts building is only ten minutes away. Here's a drink, on the house for old time's sake."

"Thanks." Lukas took the cup. Turning away from the two men, he faced the cafeteria one more time and raised his cup in salute, racing to the exit before the emotions cemented him in place. In the middle of the long corridor, he realized Ram and Rosemary were conspicuously absent. Then, a loud booming voice hollered from down the hall by the Student Society office. "C'mon down, dude. We got you good."

Rosemary and Ram waited in the Student Society office. Her voice trembling, Rosemary said, "I'm going to miss you, my friend." She hugged him tightly. Her tears moistened his hair as she tucked his head close to hers.

Lukas pulled himself away, holding the cup at a distance. "I know where you live. I plan to visit you a lot." He turned to Ram. "Same for you, big guy. New York is a train ride or even a bus away." Ram turned away awkwardly before swinging around and grabbing Lukas around the waist, lifting him up.

"Guys, I need to tell you something. The night I got hurt. Kara was at the party. I don't know how she got there. She was there."

Rosemary threw a harsh glance at Ram, who chewed on his lip, holding back whatever he wanted to disclose. Before anyone could speak, Rosemary plotted the course of the discussion. "Lukas, what are you going to do?"

"Find her. I cannot have her last vision of me be this wretched drunken fool."

Rosemary smiled and grabbed his hand firmly. "Show her the kid I met. Show her the one everyone came in to pay tribute to today."

"I will do my best. I need to find her, though."

Rosemary grabbed Ram by the arm, tugging him. "Ram and I have to go. We do have finals to study for."

"Sure. I'll pop by for a visit as soon as you're done with exams."

Rosemary and Ram streaked off down the hall. Ram finally got a chance to speak. "Why didn't you tell him you found Kara?"

"I want him to think it was pure fate."

"Well, it sort of was flukey."

"Trust me. Not like it was a big success."

"You think his sister got anywhere?"

"I can only pray. No one answered the phone when I tried calling to see if Maggie made any progress."

Lukas stood now alone at the entrance of the offices. Papers were neatly stacked on tables. Tobin's desk looked stark naked, his nameplate gone. Lukas slowly began to close the door when he took a last look. The calendar hung teasingly on the wall. It taunted him to approach. His eyes danced from entry to entry before settling on March 29. "Lukas finally gets laid." now had an added caption, "Postponed." Lukas laughed. Stepping back, he noticed an entry for today's date. "Tobin Gets Even With An Old Friend." His hand stretched out to the entry, touching it. Yes, something good had come out of that night.

When he closed the door, he could only think of the one last stop he needed to make, to retrieve his backpack from his locker. The last task before he could focus himself entirely on finding Kara. However, one person remained, patiently sitting by his locker, Kirsten.

Kirsten rose to her feet as he approached, a slight fluttered look on her face. He grinned. "Kirsten, I am so happy to see you."

"You are?"

"More than you can imagine."

"Well, the surprise was from your graduating class, so I didn't want to intrude. I figured I could wait here for you."

"About the other night. I want you to understand how desirable you are. A man would be lucky to have someone like you."

"Lukas, you have nothing to explain to me. I appreciate the effort. It just was not meant to be. I realize that what I wanted from you was to possess you. I didn't think about what you wanted. It was about what I wanted. I was selfish and arrogant. You were a perfect gentleman, sort of, and I lost it because I couldn't get my way."

"You need not explain. I just am not ready, however wonderful I'm sure it would be."

"I need to explain. I accused you of the most horrific thing imaginable. You did not deserve that."

Lukas placed his hands behind her head and kissed her on the cheek. "A man will be very fortunate one day."

"Thank you, Lukas. I only ask one thing."

"Anything, Kirsten."

"The picture. Show me the picture, please. I want to see her."

Lukas smiled and dug anxiously into his back pocket, producing a now wrinkled picture.

She held the picture delicately, studying it. "She's lovely, Lukas." As she gave him back the picture, her eyes exploded open wide. Lukas's eyes no longer were blanketed in black, no longer swallowed the light. She could see color reflected in them. She smiled, touching his cheek gently. "I think it's time for you to go home."

Nodding, he tucked the picture into his pants before slinging the backpack over his shoulder.

Instead of sitting at the back of the bus with his headphones on, he sat close to the driver, enjoying the view. He sipped on the cup he was carrying. Milk.

chapter forty-one

Since beginning his university studies, the Wunand household consisted of Grace, Roman, and Maggie. Even with a boyfriend, Maggie remained a fixture at home, filling in the gaps for the prolonged absences of her brother. Lukas's home became a stopover, especially during the school year. Roman grew accustomed to late-night phone calls from his son, announcing he was crashing at a friend's house. Lukas's parents did not mind since the bus ride to the suburbs was lengthy, whereas the proximity of Rosemary and Ram's residences allayed their fears. Independence represented part of growing up, as did trust.

Today, however, truly marked a return home. Lukas's tenure in the school of business ended mercifully for him in a tribute he, himself, would be hard-pressed to top. Ahead of him were mounds and mounds of stark white blank pages. Whether any ink remained in his pen or not would be up to him. When he arrived at his front steps, he placed the backpack in front of him, staring at the door. Once opened, he would need to face his parents and explain his demise as a business school student. The mark on his face he already passed off as young adult foolishness. He was not sure about dropping out. Would he return to St. Peter's as an arts student? He need not decide now. He laughed to himself. For so long, he craved to find mystery, reveling in spontaneity. Now with no linear path before him, a well-constructed joke was on him.

"What are you smiling about, silly boy?" shouted a voice at the top of the stairs. Having immersed himself in his thoughts, Lukas had not heard the door open or noticed Maggie patiently watching from above.

"Silly boy. Seriously! You have not called me that in ages."

Maggie laughed, fussing with her feet as she did. Years ago, she would wait for him to return or watch him from afar like a good soap opera. His sister remained full of surprises and today was no different, he mused.

"Come on in. I want to hear about school. How did it all go? I just came back from shopping with Mom and Dad, and I . . ." She grew silent, bringing her hand to mouth. Her face turned slightly to avoid eye contact with her brother.

"So, you knew?"

Maggie turned red; her fiddling got more pronounced. "Um . . . knew what?"

"What they planned for me at school. You knew. Didn't you?"

Her foot stopped tapping, calmness returned. "Yes. Rosemary told me to make sure you went in no matter what. Come in and give me details."

Lukas now understood why Tobin called. Maggie never could keep a secret for long. Satisfied he had deciphered his sister's behavior, he walked up the stairs. With the appearance of someone anxious to show off her home to a new guest, Maggie grabbed her brother's hand and dragged him through the house. Stumbling as he went, Lukas's ride came to an end in his sister's room, the door slamming behind him. Bank vaults had less security and less demanding guards. There was no way out, other than the bedroom window.

"Lukas, take a seat." She pointed to a wood chair by her desk in the corner.

"Sister, you certainly have my attention!" He placed his backpack on the side of the bureau. "Something tells me you have an announcement to make." A slight smile poked its way through his semi-serious frown. The excitement, the secrecy—his eyes shifted to her hand. In her mid-twenties and with a boyfriend for the last couple of years, the timing was right. Relaxed and bracing himself to rise and move forward with a congratulatory hug, he waited, completely not expecting what was to come.

Moving to the desk, she reached for a loose-leaf sheet resting near the edge. She returned to her spot in front of the door and began reciting.

> *"Dear Lukas. Please know that for the longest time I have wanted to speak to you and tell you face to face. Sadly, my courage is lacking. Looking into your eyes, I could not. I hoped you would not find out like this. I beg you to forgive me."*

Maggie took a deep breath. Wisely, she did not look at Lukas. Terror spread like a virus through his body. Bitten by the toxin within the words, he was paralyzed by the emotion bubbling in his chest. He, too, took an elongated breath.

> *"My grandfather has been ill for some time. The end is near, and my parents have decided to return to be with him. My father's university tenure at St. Peter's ended in the spring. He has not been able to find any position here in North America and will be seeking a position overseas once my grandfather passes. I will be going with my family. I am everything to them. My heart breaks at the thought of leaving you. Maybe there is a choice I have. I am not so brave as to find it."*

Lukas rose, shaking his head. "Please stop, Maggie. Where did you get this? I destroyed the letter. I burnt them. How did you get this?"

Maggie returned his look sternly. "Be seated, young man. I vowed one day I would read to you like you did all those years. Let me finish. These words are long overdue, you stubborn, silly child." Studying the conviction in her eyes, Lukas could not take his eyes off his sister's face as he slid back into the chair.

Her voice went from stern and terse to soft and angel-like as she returned to the loose-leaf.

"I love you, Lukas, I always did, long before the first time you kissed me. I always will. This love drives me to be stronger. You have always been my strength. I vow to return to you, one day, whatever it takes, to come back to you strong and be your strength. Please, never lose faith in my feelings, however far we are apart. I pray to return to you. Love, Kara."

Maggie put the paper down and looked upon Lukas, whose head was now burrowed in his hands. "Brother?"

His face dripping with tears, he sniffled, trying to compose himself. All thoughts were blurred by tears that bathed the weeds that long ago took root within him. "Where did you get this? Did you make it up?"

"Like you think I'm so clever?"

"Maggie, I saw her. She stood as close as you right now. I f'd up, again. She ran away from me. This time completely on her own. Why did you not show me this letter?"

"Would you have read it or destroyed it like all the others? Besides, it's not exactly correct."

"Maggie, this is not a very good time to play games." Lukas

reached out quickly and snatched the paper from her hands. He recognized her handwriting immediately. "Geez, Maggie, you wrote this. It is your writing, spelling errors and all."

"It is my writing. Of course, it is. You got rid of everything else."

Lukas's head tilted, perplexed. His sister stood, smiling at him. "Why did you write for me? Why now?" His thoughts began to form, the shapes coming together. "You knew I saw Kara, didn't you?"

"Too many questions, my dear brother. Yes, I wrote this down, I could not memorize it all."

"Memorize it!"

"Yes. You needed to hear it. I knew you would listen to me."

"What game are you playing?"

"Lukas, remember as children we used to play hide and seek?'"

"It was your favorite game."

"Where was my favorite hiding spot?"

"My room, under the bed. I always knew you were there. I chose not to look until the end to keep the game going."

"Close your eyes. Count to ten and see if you can find me."

"Seriously, you want to play a kid's game now?"

"For me, I beg you."

"Well, all right. You promise to explain everything to me if I play?"

"Of course. That is the prize for finding me. Now start counting to ten."

Lukas dutifully closed his eyes and counted to ten. He pretended not to know where she was, wandering around the house aimlessly and without effort. Finally, he settled in front of the door to his room. "Gee, Mags, I have *no idea* where you are."

The door was closed, and he could hear activity inside. Drawers opened and closed loudly with footsteps in between. He barged through the door announcing, "Okay, Maggie, one last place to look."

Swinging the door open wide, he saw her bent over, taking clothes from his drawers and placing them neatly on his bed. Only it wasn't Maggie. There stood Kara smiling at him. From behind him, a hand reached out and squeezed his shoulder. "I guess you won, brother." She ruffled his hair and backed away, closing the door behind her.

"Hello, Lukas," she said. "I'm just organizing things for you. I trust you'll understand."

"My goodness, Kara, I am so happy to see you, I truly am."

She moved toward him, noticeably examining his face. "Quite a story to go with the bruise, I hope. Were you again saving a damsel?"

"No, chasing a ghost, a beautiful ghost. Hoping to catch up to her to beg for forgiveness. To tell her how ecstatic I was to see her again. How she meant everything to me."

"That's not what you said that night."

"Anger is ugly, Kara. It was anger at myself for not trying hard enough. You deserved so much more than that."

"Lukas, I reacted poorly, too. It was the jealousy of seeing you having fun. I thought you had moved on. It killed me inside. The thought that the boy I once knew and loved so much was gone."

"What Maggie just read to me. Was that what you wrote to me?"

"Yes, I dictated it to her from my memory. Every word I mean now and I did then. I truly do. I understand why you never wrote me or read my letters. I should have been brave enough to tell you the truth."

"You came back today. Why? You ran from me."

"Remember when you kissed me, the first time, and I exiled you. You never were upset at me. You waited calmly and so patiently for me to come to my senses. I enjoyed the attention, being chased by you. I had power over you. It was so wrong of me to behave that way. Like being mad at you for not reading my letters or answer my calls. I wanted to control you. Forgive me."

"Kara, there is so much that requires your forgiveness. So much I did that I knew I no longer deserved your love. It's why I couldn't face that you left. I did something horrible."

Kara moved quickly across the room and grabbed Lukas's hand. "I know what happened that night. I know what you did. We kind of all did. I forgive you. It belongs in the past."

Lukas's hand shook with hers. Her palm squeezed tight, choking his fear of the truth. "Why did you come here today? Why did you show at the party?"

"Rosemary called me, Lukas. She cares for you a lot. And Maggie called me yesterday. I could never refuse Maggie. She told me what you had gone through. She told me what you did to protect me."

"I could not find you at St. Peter's except that one morning."

"I don't go to St. Peter's yet. I plan to. I've been working to raise the money to go to school. I put off my studies to work here. I never thought I would see you again. I only came back here because this was where I truly found bliss."

Lukas noticed behind Kara his traveling luggage was open with clothes placed in neat piles next to it, waiting to be packed. "I cannot believe you're back."

"Lukas, I leave in a few days. I'll be gone for ten months or so."

Dejection spread across Lukas's face. Avoiding his stare, Kara proceeded speedily to the task she was performing. "Well, now that you know, please help me pack your things."

"I don't get it. Why are you . . ."

"Because you're coming with me. We leave on Wednesday." She reached into her pocket and unfolded a paper. It was a copy of the announcement Rosemary had seen on the arts bulletin board.

"You're going to teach children to read?"

"We are. You're coming with me. We leave in a few days. We'll come back in time to start in arts faculty together the following fall. I'm applying before we leave."

Lukas stared in total disbelief. "You're serious, right? I had a prank pulled on me already today. I learned that being the joker is more fun."

"That is funny. Of course, I' m serious."

"I need to talk to my parents. They don't know about me not graduating this year."

"Lukas, I spoke to your parents. I explained everything. You are not the only one who can charm parents. Your parents said it would be their graduation gift to you."

"I'm not graduating anything."

"Lukas, maybe you are." She smirked. "Maybe we both are."

"And your parents? Like they're on board with all this."

"Your sister can read you what I wrote again. I promised not to return to you unless I can be strong and confident. My parents had one stipulation."

"Just one?"

"An important one. They made me promise to have the wedding in the summer. You know, when the school year is over so my dad won't have to take time off from teaching."

"For sure." The words then caressed Lukas's heart, playfully tickling it. "Wedding?"

"Well, the whole point of you coming with me is for us to get to know each other before the wedding. There will be a wedding at some point when we get back. When the time is right."

"Kara, are you asking me?" Suddenly, the door swung open. Maggie's head popped in. "Geez, Lukas, of course, she is. Don't mess it up again."

Lukas looked at his big sister and grinned. He walked to the door and closed it as she protested. "Some things don't change. Thankfully."

He and Kara laughed. "Well, are you?" Lukas said.

Kara stepped toward him. "You and I have played the game of words for what seems like a million years. Our hearts know. They have always known, mine and yours. Shall we just let them speak?" Putting both her hands upon his, she pressed her lips forward to meet his. Words no longer mattered. They probably never did. When tongues are burnt from the taste of the sun, only the soul can speak without a voice. Nothing is louder or more melodic.

Outside in the hallway, Roman and Grace Wunand entered the house to find their daughter posted outside Lukas's bedroom door. They quietly moved next to her. Grace whispered to her, "Is it going well?"

Maggie smiled and bowed to her parents.